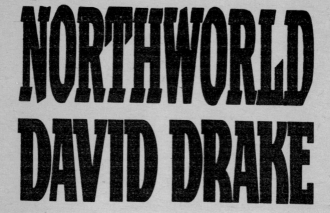

NORTHWORLD
DAVID DRAKE

ACE BOOKS, NEW YORK

This book is an Ace original edition,
and has never been previously published.

NORTHWORLD

An Ace Book/published by arrangement with
the author

PRINTING HISTORY
Ace edition / April 1990

ISBN: 0-441-84830-3

Ace Books are published by The Berkley Publishing Group,
200 Madison Avenue, New York, New York 10016.
The name "ACE" and "A" logo are trademarks
belonging to Charter Communications, Inc.

PRINTED IN THE UNITED STATES OF AMERICA

10 9 8 7 6 5 4 3

Fortin stared at them coldly. "This isn't for you," he said, jutting his hips forward to emphasize his words.

The girls' bright, scrubbed faces changed. One of them quickly closed the door.

Fortin entered the white angora room that was Penny's particular favorite. He paused when he heard laughter, but the balcony door was open and the sounds came through it.

The necklace was on a dresser. Fortin fingered the stone for a moment. It was warm, blood hot, even though it must have been several minutes since Penny tossed it aside to get on with a variation of the one matter that interested her more than her own appearance.

Fortin slipped the transparent strap over his head and let the jewel bounce against his own chest. For a moment he looked at himself in the dresser's triple mirror and saw the form of Rolls, complete with the first hint of a paunch rolling over the cord of his orange jockstrap.

And again, a muscular stud with sullen, swarthy features, not Fortin but any one of a thousand men who'd gained Penny's attention in an existence where duration no longer had meaning. The jewel concealed itself.

Fortin looked toward the balcony door. It stood open at an angle. Reflected in its crystal surface, ghostly against the cloud-streaked sky beyond, he saw Rolls and Penny.

The palace's mistress was leaning her whole torso out over the top rail. Her chubby calves intertwined with the railing's vertical supports, and Rolls' great hands gripped her breasts.

Penny cried in delight as Rolls stroked into her again from behind, and again, and again.

A risky position, even with Rolls' strength and Penny's own undoubted athleticism. But what was even godhead without risk?

There was no expression on Fortin's face as he stepped into the lift shaft. He would leave the palace as a faceless member of Rolls' entourage and hand over the necklace as soon as they were clear.

When Rolls was done with it, Fortin would slip the necklace back here.

And Fortin would revisit Ruby.

≡ 16 ≡

IN ORDER TO accommodate the influx of recruits drawn by rumors of war, the tables were butted end to end. They were clear of food now, and the night's serious drinking had begun.

Hansen squeezed the shoulders of the men to either side of him, Malcolm and Maharg; muttered, "Wish me luck"; and ducked under the trestles to reach the service walkway between tables and hearth.

"Hey!" called one of his fellows. A husky woman with pitchers in either hand stopped so abruptly that some of her beer sloshed, but Hansen strode directly toward Golsingh at the cross-table.

He'd learned by now that Taddeusz wasn't going to permit an underling—particularly Hansen—to approach the king if he could help it. With the table between them, the warchief *couldn't* prevent the contact, unless he was willing to lower himself and his dignity by crawling under the trestles the way Hansen had done.

Malcolm sat less than a third of the way down the left bench now. Most of the recruits were gutter-sweepings, not respectable warriors. Good warriors were going elsewhere. That was one of the things Hansen had learned in talking with Malcolm and his fellows.

Servants fluttered out of Hansen's way. At the head table, Unn and Krita stared at him. The face of Taddeusz' daughter was flushed from the hearth, but Unn's pale skin was perfect except for a smudge of ash on her forehead.

Krita smiled, filled a square-bottomed cup of mammoth ivory, and handed it to Hansen without a word. He took it, startled out of his focus on what he was about to say to the king.

"Ah, Your Highness," he blurted.

"That's the servants' side of the table!" Taddeusz snarled. He'd started to rise when his daughter offered the cup to Hansen, but his chair and the table trammeled the abrupt action. He fell back. "Get out of there—and *away* from here!"

"I am His Highness' servant," Hansen said, thinking of what he'd told Walker and smiling inside at his own duplicity.

But—he didn't *trust* the squirrel/titmouse/crow, and he didn't understand enough about what Walker was trying to do to protect himself. Hansen thought he understood Golsingh—and the other factors in *this* equation—well enough, certainly better than the actors did themselves.

Which didn't mean that Hansen was safe. Just that he knew the name of the lion into whose jaws he was sticking his head.

"Sir," he said, looking at the king and ignoring the way Taddeusz twisted his chair sideways so that he could get up, "if you'll let me talk with you, I can serve you better. Maybe—"

He bobbed his beard-stubbled chin toward the warchief with "—better than anybody else. Which may be why they're afraid of letting me talk."

"You—" Taddeusz bellowed, lifting his goblet of silver-mounted rock crystal. He might have thrown it, except that Krita stepped between her father and Hansen.

"Sit down, foster father," Golsingh said. Taddeusz remained frozen in a posture of agonized fury.

"Sit down!" cracked the king's voice.

"Yes, milord," Taddeusz muttered. He sank down as if in a state of exhaustion.

"Milord," said Hansen, wondering what the other warriors in the hall were making of this, "your father and your father's father were kings, but they didn't rule farther than their armies could march in three days—and that only when their armies *were* marching. Is that correct?"

"We have the submission of a hundred lords!" Taddeusz snapped. "You're talking nonsense!"

"And those hundred lords fight each other, one pair or another of them every day, every year. They'll send you tribute, and they'll send a message of congratulation when you win a victory, but they won't send troops to join yours when you march—"

"Some—" said Golsingh with a frown.

"—unless you're marching by their keep on the way, with enough force to burn the place around their ears," Hansen continued, speaking with the same brutal frankness that had gathered him enemies regularly during his decade in Consensus bureaucracy.

That had its advantages too. His enemies had made sure Hansen was sent where it was hot; and, since he'd survived, he'd been promoted rapidly into the shoes of officers who hadn't.

"Do you want tribute and the name?" Hansen said. "Or do you really want peace—Golsingh the Peacegiver?"

The warchief shook his head in frustration. "The business of a king is war," he said. "And power. Milord, it's unlucky—unmanly, I'd almost say—to talk of imposing peace. The gods don't approve."

Golsingh's youthful features hardened. "I'm king here," he said sharply to his foster father. "The gods can rule in their heavens, but—"

He turned toward Hansen. His face was suffused with a hot passion not so very different from what roiled unseen in Hansen's mind.

"Yes," Golsingh said, "it's peace I want. A peace in which a man—a woman!—can walk from one end of my kingdom to the other and never be molested. A peace in which a purse can lie in the center of the road for a year and no one will steal it. *That's* what I want!"

Taddeusz got up. "My son," he said, "you're tempting the gods. I hope you think better of your words before it's too late."

The warchief's voice was firm with sadness and anger, but he was no longer trying to shout down the discussion. Taddeusz stalked out of the hall, his felt boots cushioning the beat of his heels on the puncheon floor.

Krita turned to watch him go. Hansen had been aware of the warmth of her body ever since she'd interposed between him and her father, although she'd moved a step away afterward.

Hansen swallowed the beer in his cup with a surge of thirst and reaction.

"Milord," he said, "then the way isn't to fight each lordling who defies you. You've got to take Frekka, make it your capital, and use the trading wealth to build an army that—''

"Frekka?" said Golsingh. "Frekka? Don't be silly. My ancestors have lived at Peace Rock for generations, and—"

"Sir, your—"

"—and besides," Golsingh continued in his royal voice, "Frekka is already a part of the kingdom."

"Then why is the shipment of armor you're expecting— you *need*—for your expedition delayed?" Hansen retorted sharply. "And why are the merchants of Frekka paying subsidies under the table to whichever of your barons looks least trustworthy?"

"You don't know that!" Golsingh snapped.

"Everybody knows that," Hansen said with flat brutality. "We have the choice of pretending not to believe the report of every traveler who's come from Thrasey or Frekka in the past month. But we don't have the option of not *knowing* it."

"Why would they *do* that?" the king said in a suddenly gentler voice.

He set down the cup he'd been playing with and kneaded his cheeks with the fingers of both hands. "I'll give them safe roads for their commerce. That's one of the main things that I want for the kingdom, for everyone."

"You'll give them a king they have to obey," Hansen said simply. "The caravans from Frekka are safe enough on the roads now."

"But they have to hire guards to—" Golsingh protested. He caught himself. "Oh."

"Yeah," said Hansen. "That's what I've heard, too. That the Syndics of Frekka have more warriors in their hire now than you do."

He started to drink, remembered that he'd finished the beer in his mug—and found it full again. Unn smiled coldly and bobbed the silver pitcher in her hand.

"The Frekka merchants want the same sort of kingdom as you do, Lord Golsingh," Hansen said. "The only thing is, they want to be the rulers of it."

"Did you come here from Frekka, then?" Unn asked unexpectedly.

Hansen looked at her. "No, milady," he said. "I came from much farther away than that. And—"

He swigged beer in order to settle his thoughts before he finished the statement. "And I think it helps to come from a distance, sometimes, when you look at a problem."

Unn leaned forward to fill her husband's agate cup. There was nothing in her expression to suggest that she'd heard or spoken in the past moments.

"Lord Golsingh," Hansen said earnestly. "Give me five men of my choosing for the battle against Thrasey. Tell them to do exactly what I say for the next two days of training, and the same in the battle. And I'll *win* the battle for you."

"Don't be absurd!" Golsingh snapped with more anger than the request itself involved. "I'll do nothing of the sort. A nothing like you, with no pedigree and no war honors anybody's heard of!"

I asked him to do something that even he can't order these stiff-necked warriors to do and be obeyed, Hansen realized.

"And anyway . . . ," Golsingh added in a very different voice. "Even if I were to—do what you suggest. You'd never . . ."

The king looked down at his hands, then up so that he faced Krita but watched Hansen out of the corner of his eye. "You'd never be able to do what you say. Would you?"

Hansen smiled his dragon smile at Golsingh. "One of these days, milord," he said, "you and I are going to find a way for you to give me what *I* want . . . and then I'll give you the kingdom you want."

He turned to go back to his seat, then turned again. "That's if we both live long enough, milord," he added.

Golsingh's face was expressionless. But Krita was smiling ferally . . . and so was Unn.

≡ 17 ≡

THE COLD OF Ruby's winter was shocking. The wind drove ice crystals like miniature scalpels through the close weave of the Inspector General's dress uniform.

The company of infantry drawn up at attention wore coveralls the color of dirty snow. The faces of the troops were as impassive as the armored bows of the tanks among the stunted fir trees, aiming their guns at Fortin.

An officer wearing a patch over her right eye stepped forward and saluted. "Sir!" she said. "I'm Major Fernandez, in charge of your escort. The High Council has already been briefed. They're proceeding to a rendezvous point."

Warts and knobs studded the tanks: weapons and sensors and defenses of various sorts. Snow collected on the angles and aided the camouflage of the huge vehicles, instead of melting from warm metal as Fortin would have expected. The shielding which hid the tanks from thermal imagers was obviously of exceptional quality.

As was every other facet of weaponry and mayhem in Ruby.

"Very good, Major Fernandez," Fortin replied without bothering to salute at all. He strode toward the nearest armored personnel carrier. "Let's get started then, shall we?"

The troops broke for their vehicles with a shout at Fernandez' order. Their noise didn't completely mask the whine of the hydraulic motors rotating the tank turrets so that their guns tracked the Inspector General to the millimeter as he walked.

A visitor to Ruby was a potential threat. North the War God was sacrosanct in Ruby, but security was greater even than North.

Though there was no wind to bite within the vehicle, the

metal frame of Fortin's seat was cold. The APC made a lumbering take-off and turned hard to starboard.

Fortin smiled. If he'd really cared to know where he was being taken, the artificial intelligence woven into the metal braid of his uniform would have told him.

Neither where nor how they were going mattered. Nonetheless, Fortin was amused to know that his hosts would follow a unique course to a unique location; a location that shared with previous meeting places only the fact that it was a barren wasteland as far as possible from anything of significance to the security of Ruby.

"Brace yourself, please, sir," said Fernandez, locking the Inspector General onto his jumpseat with a powerful arm as the APC descended abruptly. She was missing two fingers as well as the eye.

Fortin's stomach squirmed with a feeling of queasy pleasure, like that he felt when he realized the tanks' big guns were tracking him and might at any instant blast him to vapor. It wasn't danger which provided that almost sexual thrill, but rather the thought that there might suddenly be a universe in which he didn't exist.

The drive engines howled to full power, buffeting the vehicle with echoes reflected from narrow walls to either side. Motion stopped except for engine vibration; then the APC dropped the last centimeter to the ground.

Fernandez slammed open the vehicle's hatch with the same motion in which her other arm released the Inspector General. He stepped out.

The sidewalls of the APC hadn't dropped because there wasn't room for them to do so within the narrow gorge in which the vehicle had landed. Two infantrymen were facing Fortin with automatic rifles leveled. Twenty meters above on the rim of the canyon were a pair of tripod-mounted plasma weapons whose bolts could devour the armored personnel carrier itself if circumstances required.

A colonel behind the infantrymen said, "All right, port arms." As the men obeyed, the colonel went on, "This way, sir. The Council is awaiting you."

The Council's command vehicle was fifty meters away, out of sight behind a kink in the gorge. Snow had drifted over the rim to knee height. High boots were part of the colonel's camouflage uniform, but Fortin wore polished shoes. Snow seeped over the tops of them, and he smiled at the discomfort.

Marshal Czerny leaned out of the side door. "Come aboard, sir," he said. His voice rasped as though he'd drunk lye, but it was probably just age. "Glad to have you with us again."

Of the five marshals around the table this time, Moro and Stein looked old, and Czerny looked as old as life itself. Tadley and Kerchuk were gone, replaced with a pair of men whose nametags read Breitkopf and Lienau—both of them middle-aged, wolf-lean, and with features that would have looked unusually cruel on sharks.

Fortin was a god to whom duration meant nothing, but duration meant decay and death for the tools he used. Despite the arrogance of the folk of Ruby, they would all die—and they didn't even care about that, so long as the system they served survived.

"Sit down, comrades," the Inspector General ordered. "I've come to see how you've succeeded with the task I posed you."

Fortin knew the answer already. The grins that not even discipline could hide, the wolfish joy in the faces above the gleaming gorgets—those were the signs of success.

The other four marshals looked at Moro. He spread his plump fingers as if to examine his nails and said, "We believe we may have a—theoretical—solution to your problem, yes. We first used the Main Battle Computer to locate the target—"

"Locate the position it would occupy if it actually existed," Breitkopf interjected in a surprisingly smooth voice. "The target is of course beyond even the possibility of actual observation."

"By us," added Stein.

"And quite a pretty problem it was then," Lienau continued, "since we still couldn't hit a point of separate spacetime with which we were in perfect balance."

"That balance was the key," said Marshal Czerny in his cadaverous voice. "Marshal Moro calculated—"

"The Main Battle Computer calculated," said Moro, fluttering his fingers in protest but unable to keep a note of pride out of his voice. "I merely suggested certain parameters."

"Marshal Moro calculated," Breitkopf said, "that the statistical identity of Ruby and the target point could be converted to *physical* identity."

"That if we bring Ruby into phase with the target," Moro amplified, "then we become the target—"

"And displace whatever's there now. Displace it out of the universe," Czerny concluded.

He coughed, lightly at first but growing into a racking series during which his fellows looked studiously at their displays and pretended not to hear.

"You say, 'out of the universe,'" Fortin said. "Where, then?"

Lienau smirked. "Somewhere incomprehensible, sir," he said. "Certainly out of play."

"Ruby has been in a dynamic balance with the target—assuming the target exists," Marshal Stein said. "If we displace the target, then *our* segment of phased spacetime remains in static balance within the greater universe."

"Which is perfectly safe, of course," Moro said.

Czerny cleared his throat. No one except Fortin looked at Czerny until the old field marshal managed to say, "The security of Ruby must be our chief goal, of course, sir."

"As it is yours," Breitkopf added, in certainty as complete as his error.

"You say, 'bring into phase,'" the Inspector General said, examining his own perfect fingernails as he spoke. "How would you propose to go about that—if I were to give you the order to proceed?"

"Quite simple, really," Stein explained. "Just a matter of reversing the magnetic pole, Moro thinks."

"The Main Battle Computer indicates that would be the preferred course, yes," Moro agreed absently as his eyes focused on a hologram aligned so that only he could see it. "And the computer would, of course, control the power fed into a planet-wide network which would achieve the switch."

"It would have to take place when our phase was positive," Breitkopf said.

"Otherwise—" He drew his finger across his chrome gorget. There was a smile on his hard face, but madness winked behind his eyes at the thought of taking the action that would destroy Ruby rather than the target.

"So," said Fortin. "Physical preparations have to be made before your plan could be executed?"

Czerny began to laugh, a terrible sound that doubled him over in obvious pain. No one spoke.

Czerny straightened slowly and said, "Extensive preparations are required, sir. And they are already complete."

"We could not be sure when you would visit us again, Inspector General," Moro said. "So we decided to—improve our time while waiting."

"Nothing remains," said Lienau, "but for you to order us to execute the plan."

Fortin felt time stop—for him, for Ruby . . . for all the planes of the Matrix. Paths branched here, and ends approached with absolute finality.

"Very good, comrades," he said. "Execute your plan."

His face twisted. He began to laugh, louder and louder, until his eyes no longer focused for the quivering anticipation in his belly.

≡ 18 ≡

GOLSINGH'S ARMY CAMPED in the forest on the first night of the expedition against Thrasey. Hansen saw his breath when he awakened. Snow had drifted onto the furs that covered him, and there was the threat of further snow in the sullen sky.

Slaves were building up the long fires and clattering with food preparation; ponies whickered. Hansen swore, scratched, and got up. He hadn't gotten chilled in his cocoon of heavy furs, but the irregularities of the ground left him stiff and sore.

They were camped in a valley of pine trees shattered two meters in the air. During a grim winter several years before, the trees had been buried in snow to that height. An avalanche blasting down from the crags to the right had sheared off the trunks above the level of the protective snow.

Hansen glanced up uneasily, but the high rocks were mostly bare and seemingly too distant to spawn such a catastrophe anyway.

Which was a reminder to be wary at all times, here no less than when he headed Special Units on Annunciation.

Shill sat on a log by a fire and stared into the mug he held before him. Hansen snapped his fingers at a slave, called, "Something hot to drink!" and seated himself beside the older warrior.

Shill gave him a nervous smile, as though he expected to be kicked. There was a bruise on the older man's forehead from one of the work-outs Hansen had put him through.

"I was wondering," Hansen said as he took the cup a slave brought him, "who was on guard last night?"

"Guard?" repeated Shill. "Guard against what?"

That was exactly the reply Hansen had expected, but he'd been too tired the night before to go into the matter then. When you ache all over, from training and from the unfamiliar exercise of riding a pony, it was easy to tell yourself that everything would be taken care of by the people whose business it was. And anyway, there wasn't anything he could do to change accepted practice.

The second part of the proposition still looked accurate in the grim light of day.

"What if the Lord of Thrasey attacked us at night?" Hansen asked, simply to get a reaction which would represent the attitude of everydamnbody in this sorry excuse for an army.

The older man was honestly puzzled. "Huh?" he said. "Nobody fights at night. And anyway, the battlefield's still a mile ahead. Though I guess we'll have to suit up and walk it," he added glumly, "just in case Thrasey jumps the gun."

Hansen sucked at the contents of his cup. It was fresh mead or perhaps honeyed wine, sweet enough to qualify as food and warm from being mulled in a water-jacketed boiler—which was the most sophisticated device he'd seen on Northworld, apart from the battlesuits.

"So," he said as his mind digested the information. "The time and place of the battle are arranged already? And that's always the case?"

"Sure," the older man agreed with a nod. "How else would you do it?"

He gestured. Trees of considerable size grew on the valley's distant southern slope. A mist hung among their branches, indistinguishable from the bitter smoke hovering over the pine-log fires of the encampment.

"Blazes," Shill said. "We could stumble around for weeks and never find Thrasey—nor the other way either."

A group of freemen were mounting their ponies. When the riders were safely in their saddles, slaves handed them weapons—lever-cocked crossbows or three-meter lances.

Some of the freemen had already ridden off. Scouting appeared to be as disorganized as every other aspect of battle management.

Hansen abruptly slugged back the rest of his drink. "I'm going out with them," he muttered.

"Why d'ye wanna do that?" Shill asked.

"Because I think *somebody* in this army ought to know what's going on," Hansen snapped.

He looked around. "I gave my pony to a couple slaves to off-saddle and feed," he said. "Where would they be now?"

"If you're really going to do that," Shill said, "take one of those." He pointed to the gaggle of freemen, mounting and equipping. "They're saddled already, after all."

"Right, thanks," said Hansen, striding toward the freemen.

The older warrior shook his head in wonderment. "Sometimes I wonder what sorta place you come from," he called.

Hansen turned his head. "That's fair," he retorted. "Because I sure-hell wonder what sort of place I've come!"

The leader of the half-dozen freemen whom Hansen accompanied was named Brian. He was about Hansen's age; a husky, steady man whom Hansen would've been glad to have as a unit leader back on Annunciation.

The remainder of the troop were fire-eaters averaging about nineteen years old, jerking their ponies with heavy hands and boasting about what they were going to do to Thrasey's scouts and warriors. Since freemen were less than cannon-fodder if matched against warriors in battlesuits, Hansen expected their enthusiasm to wane as they approached the enemy, but it made him uneasy to listen to their nonsense.

They rode through the trees, listening to the calls of scouts who'd left before them and sometimes crossing pony tracks in the snow. Half a mile from the encampment, the shallow valley Golsingh's men had followed most of the way from Peace Rock opened onto a broad plain.

The snow was deeper than it had been among the trees. It crushed flat the yellowed grass that would have been several meters high if erect. Sight distances were deceptively short. The open country seemed to stretch for kilometers in every direction, but swells too gentle to be noticed cut visibility to a reality of a few hundred meters.

They crossed a frozen stream. The banks were straight and little more than a meter high, but willows and coarse reeds grew so thickly along the margins that the ponies had to force their way through.

Hansen's mount didn't want to chance wetting its feet. He

kicked it repeatedly in the ribs and had just regretted his lack of spurs when the pony decided to cross the narrow stream in a rush that almost unseated him.

Fur hats showed above the hillock beyond the creek. The younger freemen kicked their ponies into a wild gallop, yipping and cheering. Brian followed, calling to his men not to get carried away.

Hansen gripped his saddle with both hands to stay aboard and allowed his pony to gallop along with her fellows. It was unlikely that a rider as unskilled as he was could have controlled the animal anyway.

When the troop reached the top of the hill, they could see two Thrasey riders galloping back toward their encampment, less than a mile away on another rolling peak. One of the Thrasey freemen turned in his saddle and fired his crossbow in the direction of his pursuers. Two of Brian's men responded.

The snap of bowstrings was flat in the open air. None of the missiles came anywhere near a target.

Hansen reined up his pony to take stock. Brian shouted some warnings that showed he understood the danger of the position. Despite that, he and the remainder of the troop of freemen continued to pursue the Thrasey riders.

Other horsemen were coming from the encampment and along the plain to the right.

The Lord of Thrasey's encampment was a straggling thing with no more sign of a berm or other protection than Golsingh's own. The huge black forms of mammoths wandered in small groups, sweeping snow from the prairie with their trunks and lifting bushels of grass into their mouths.

Golsingh's force had carried fodder for their draft animals. The Thrasey army must have packed firewood over the treeless prairie, for a pall of smoke hung above their encampment.

Wan sunlight shone from battlesuits being polished by slaves. There seemed to be a surprising number of the suits.

Probably more than the hundred or so warriors in Golsingh's force this time.

Two riders from the camp joined the pair whom Brian's men were pursuing. The four turned to face their opponents.

The ground between the Thrasey encampment and the rel-

ative height from which Hansen watched was flat and almost
as perfect for battle as the center of an amphitheatre. The
stream closed the left margin, while the right curved out of
sight within the slightly higher ground. Hansen had a box
seat for the skirmish.

One of the Thrasey freemen raised his crossbow and shot.
The black speck of the bolt snapped toward Brian—and on,
vanishing in the snowy grass. Hansen thought it was parallax
which had made him think the missile had struck, but then
Brian swayed in his saddle and flung his lance aside.

The two crossbowmen accompanying Brian were desperately trying to reload their weapons. Their leader must have
given an order Hansen couldn't hear for the distance, because
he and his whole troop began to trot back the way they'd
come.

The Thrasey freemen started to follow. One of Brian's men
turned and shook his lance in threat. Another band of horsemen burst through the willows at the creekbed a kilometer
away.

Hansen doubted that either side could be sure which party
the newcomers supported. The Thrasey patrol began walking
its mounts up the gentle slope toward their camp.

Hansen's pony had settled to crop the long grass. It looked
up without particular interest as its fellows rejoined.

The younger freemen were flushed and panting. Brian
looked sallow. His left sleeve had been torn off, and he
clutched his biceps with his right hand.

"Let's see it," Hansen directed, clucking his pony nearer
to the wounded man.

"Bastards," Brian muttered.

The clouds had thickened. It was beginning to snow sparse,
tiny flakes. The temperature had dropped a degree or two
since dawn.

Hansen pried the freeman's fingers from around the deep,
ragged tear. The wound was bleeding badly, but the square-
headed quarrel hadn't smashed bone or nicked an artery.

With only direct pressure on the arm, Brian would've bled
out if an artery were severed.

"Right," said Hansen, squeezing Brian's hand back over
the damage. "Is there a—medic, whatever, back in camp?"

"Old Jepson, he sets bones sometimes," one of the free-men said.

"Does he stitch wounds?" Hansen demanded, and the blank expressions he received were the expected answer.

The wounds warriors took on Northworld were usually fatal and certainly self-cauterized. There was little that even the finest medical facilities of, say, Annunciation could have done for injured warriors except perform limb-grafts. And it wasn't the business of *this* society to worry about wounded freemen and slaves.

"Right. You—" Hansen pointed to the freeman on the strongest pony "—ride back for the camp as fast as you can, and stick your shirt in boiling water. *Fast!*"

"Huh?"

"It'll be the bandage. Now ride, damn you!"

The freeman didn't understand the purpose of the orders, but he heard the death threat in Hansen's voice. He dug the jangling rowels of his spurs into his pony and began to canter back toward the camp.

"I'm all right," Brian said. He kneed his mount into careful motion. "Bastards."

"Sure," agreed Hansen, walking his pony alongside. "One of you," he snapped to the younger freemen, "make sure we're headed straight back."

If he could have trusted his own riding skills, he would have tried to support Brian . . . though the wounded man seemed to be doing pretty well.

Brian's waxy complexion was the main concern. The wound wouldn't be directly fatal, but shock might very well finish the job.

Brian urged his pony into a trot. His reins hung loosely in his left hand.

"Tooley's there," he said loudly, instinctively aware that if he let himself slip into shock and somnolence, he wouldn't come back. "I saw his suit, red and white."

"Naw," objected one of his fellows. Hansen, his knuckles white on the reins, marveled at the way the other men could ride and talk. "He's with Count Rolfe, ain't he?"

"Frekka," said Brian. "He quarreled with Rolfe this summer and went to Frekka. Holroyd and Finch, they hired on with Frekka too. And they're up there."

It was snowing harder, but they were back among the trees now and the needles caught some of the flakes. The trees blocked much of the wan sunlight as well. Hansen looked forward to boosting the light amplitude on his battlesuit's display.

"Finch ain't nothin'," said another man. "An' Holroyd ain't much."

"Tooley's shit hot, though," Brian rejoined. He must be in considerable pain, but he was looking better for the hard ride. "And there's a lot of the buggers. I'd figured sixty, maybe eighty tops at Thrasey if the Lord'd been hiring his ass off."

"There's more 'n that," said one of his men. Despite their youth and indiscipline, these freemen had enough experience—and intelligence, Hansen was realizing—to make them good scouts.

"There's a hundred 'n twenty easy," Brian agreed grimly.

The camp was in sight. Warriors were getting into their armor near each of the fires.

"Course," Brian added, "the king 'n Lord Taddeusz they'll clean 'em up anyhow."

The freeman might have sounded more confident if it weren't for the wound sapping his vitality.

Hansen would have had doubts in any case.

Hansen saw Malcolm's brilliant suit on the left edge of the encampment, closely accompanied by Shill and Maharg.

Low-status warriors could be identified as a class—as cannon-fodder—by the amateurish detailing of their armor. That would be easy to cure: buff all the suits down to bare metal and let the artificial intelligence separate friends from foes.

Hansen should've thought of that sooner. It was too late to change for this battle. And it was beginning to look as though that made it simply too late. . . .

He slid from his pony and left the animal to wander as it chose while he opened his armor. He tossed his fur cloak onto the bundle a slave had made of his bedding, then stripped off his fur breeches.

The wind was cold, but the interior of Hansen's battlesuit would be colder than hell until it came up to operating temperature in ten minutes or so. Delaying wasn't going to help matters. Hansen clambered inside and latched the suit over him.

The technological ambiance calmed and reassured him more than he'd expected. Hansen didn't belong in the feudal museum that was Northworld society, but he'd lived the most important parts of his adult life in a battlesuit of one sort or another.

And maybe he was kidding himself about the society as well. He belonged here a lot more clearly than he had on Diamond.

"Remote, quarter, Malcolm," he said, putting his suit through its paces before he needed to use them for real. The upper right-hand quadrant of his display showed Hansen, on a reduced scale, what the veteran warrior was seeing.

Malcolm faced Lamullo, the commander of Golsingh's left wing. Lamullo's father had left him an excellent battlesuit, painted in candystripes of bronze and black; but the son had inherited little of his father's aggressive drive. Hansen suspected that Lamullo's lack of ambition was as much the reason Taddeusz supported him as the suit itself was.

It was snowing harder. Hansen pursed his lips and glanced around him—then said, "Mark Golsingh," and let his AI do the work.

A caret pulsing on Hansen's display indicated where the king was hidden at the center of a group of twenty-odd warriors, most of them well equipped.

"Remote quarter Golsingh," Hansen said as he started in that direction. Golsingh and his warchief were listening to Brian say, ". . . and a lot of 'em been at Frekka, Thrasey must've hired 'em away in the last week or two."

The freeman's left arm was in a sling. One of his fellows was standing nearby, ready to support him if needed. Hansen hoped they'd used the—hopefully—sterilized cloth for a bandage, but there was only so much one could do. . . .

The error in the scout's report had no tactical significance, but it made all the strategic difference in this world. The Lord of Thrasey hadn't hired mercenaries from Frekka; they'd been sent as a gift. Hansen was willing to bet his life on that.

Of course, he wouldn't have a life to gamble with unless things worked out better today than they were likely to.

"That doesn't matter," said Taddeusz contemptuously. "Nobody who'd take service with merchants is of any concern."

Hansen reached the back of the circle of high-ranking warriors. He put a gauntlet on the shoulder of a man, hoping the fellow would make room. The man turned slightly and shoved Hansen away.

"I remember Tooley," Golsingh replied, sounding thoughtful. "He was here a few years ago. Terrible temper, but . . . Not a warrior I would dismiss lightly."

"Command channel," Hansen directed his artificial intelligence.

He shouldn't have access to a commo frequency intended for top-ranking personnel, but there was nobody except Hansen in the whole army who knew how to activate the push, much less lock out middle-rankers like himself.

"Don't worry about—" Taddeusz was saying when Hansen's voice broke in on his earphones with: "Lord Golsingh, I'm sorry to interrupt—"

"Who!" Taddeusz shouted. They all used amplified voice communications instead of the excellent radios built into their suits. "Hansen? Is that—"

"—but I've viewed the battlefield and there's a way we can win this, I think pretty easily, especially with the low light conditions."

An arc blazed up from the center of the group of warriors.

"Taddeusz?" the king said doubtfully.

The circle broke outward like a ripple spreading.

Hansen also began backing away. "Lord Taddeusz, please," he said. "The terrain—"

The warchief's weapon slammed down.

Hansen jumped back. The arc, though attenuated by three meters' distance when it struck him, screeched in Hansen's ears and blurred his display into hash. He fell over.

Taddeusz shut his arc down instead of stepping closer. "If I hear your voice again this day," he said in a distinct tone more threatening than a bellow, "I will kill you. Begone!"

The circle of warriors closed about the leaders again.

Hansen got to his feet. His suit wasn't functionally damaged, but the paint had blistered off most of his breastplate.

He'd been this angry before.

He began walking toward Malcolm and the left wing.

He'd been this angry before. He always felt better when he'd killed something. As he would very soon.

Trumpets across the camp blew. A freeman near Lamullo took his own horn out from under his cloak and responded with a two-note call.

Cold and distant as the wind, other trumpets answered from the Thrasey encampment.

The sky was sullen. The upper left arm of Hansen's suit had been repaired, but he hadn't thought to replace the suede liner. Each time his skin touched the casing, the steel felt like a burn.

Warriors were moving out in clumps, forming a line of sorts.

"Maharg," Hansen said. "Shill. Come with me. We've got a battle to win."

Sometimes when Hansen felt the way he did now he slammed the heel of his hand into a wall. His battlesuit would knock over the stump of any of the nearby trees.

He clashed his palms together. The shock of power-driven steel against steel rang through the nearest warriors, turning a dozen faceless helmets toward him.

"For people who don't deserve it any damn way," Hansen added bitterly; though the good lord knew he should've been used to it by now.

Shill and Maharg swayed in their tracks. Hansen looked at Malcolm and said, "Malcolm. Come with us. You go out there like the rest—"

He nodded, uncertain whether the gesture was distinguishable while he wore armor. "—and you'll just get yourself chopped up. There's too many of them."

"Come along, you lot," Lamullo called over his shoulder. The gaggle of armored men was drifting into the woods. Freemen on ponies were intermixed with the warriors for the moment.

"No," said Malcolm. Then, sharply, "No!"

But instead of moving immediately to join the rest of the left wing, he pointed to Shill and Maharg and said, "You two. You can go with him if you want to. You—do what he says, all right? Do what the laddie says. But I can't."

Malcolm turned and followed Lamullo with long, clashing strides.

"Remote, quarter, Malcolm," Hansen ordered his AI. "Local unit, secure communications."

He grinned invisibly at Shill and Maharg who quivered between frightening alternatives. "Come on then, guys," Hansen said. "We've got a battle to win."

≡ 19 ≡

HANSEN LED HIS little unit into the bed of the stream. Here, the watercourse was barely more than washed stones, ice, and the brown, hollow stems of frozen reeds.

Trumpets called frequently, but Hansen now realized the cries were more generally for the amusement of the freemen with the horns than they were signals or commands. Warriors argued with what their king told them directly—or ignored him, if they had Taddeusz' stature, at any rate. They weren't going to take directions passed by members of the lower orders.

One of the hobbled draft mammoths joined in with a series of piercing shrieks, as meaningful and perhaps as musical as the human notes.

"This isn't taking us toward the battlefield," Maharg said. They were all stumbling and patting their hands on the bank to keep from falling down. "They'll . . . Taddeusz, he'll give us the chop for deserting like this."

"We're going to get to the battle," Hansen said. "The streambed curves around, no problem."

He hoped it did. If this wasn't the same creek, he was going to have some explaining to do.

Though not, he suspected, to Golsingh.

"We're gonna get there late, though," Shill said with an undertone of . . . 'satisfaction' might be too strong a word. Might be.

Hansen crashed on. So long as the others' suits didn't have to power their arcs or electronic defenses, they could match his more efficient unit stride for stride. It can't have been a pleasant march, but it wasn't for their leader either.

They were getting out into the prairie, where herds of

mammoths had kept the grassland open with their destructive feeding. The stream banks were a little deeper.

Hansen could see nothing directly beyond the reeds and alders. His quadrant of Malcolm's display showed the main line of Golsingh's army straggling up the hill which overlooked the chosen battlefield. Their footing had been much better, and they were, as Shill had said, well in advance of Hansen's unit.

They didn't look like an army, though. The warriors were in blobs and clumps, with potentially dangerous gaps all along the line. They had no more organization than bits of popcorn strung into a necklace by a kindergartner.

Taddeusz, with a dozen or so followers, was far in the lead on the right flank. Just as he had been during the battle against Count Lopez.

Taddeusz hadn't learned a damned thing. Which figured.

Hansen used his artificial intelligence to identify the players. Even without the compression of the remote display, he would have found it difficult to tell one set of painted armor from the next.

The sky hadn't brightened since dawn, and the snow was falling thicker.

"Mark friendlies blue," Hansen muttered, watching tags flicker across the quadrant. If he looked behind him, he'd see the same markers of blue light on the helmets of Shill and Maharg.

"You two," he ordered. "Say 'Mark friendlies blue' the way I told you in training."

"We did that," Shill grumbled. "Back to the camp."

Good lord, they were learning!

"Any chance we could siddown and rest?" Shill asked abruptly. The microphone in his helmet picked up his panting breath. "I won't be good fer shit if I don't get a breather."

"When were you ever good fer shit, Shill?" Maharg gibed.

"If we rest now, there won't be anything to do but count the corpses by the time we get where we're going," Hansen said. His body felt as though he'd spent the morning as a tackling dummy.

"Suits me," the older man muttered; but he kept up, and they all kept going despite the fact that the water was now knee deep. Occasionally they broke through the ice, then tripped on hidden rocks.

The banks were waist high and slightly undercut. Willow roots provided solid handholds for Hansen and his men when their feet slipped.

Malcolm had reached the top of the hillock. Through the veteran's eyes, Hansen saw freemen shout thinly and charge in the center of the plain. The Thrasey riders were badly outnumbered. They fell back immediately behind the oncoming row of warriors.

Crossbowmen banged bolts toward the freemen and occasionally at the warriors as well. Hits sparkled vainly on the battlesuits.

The forces of the Lord of Thrasey outnumbered Golsingh's by at least twenty warriors.

On the far right flank, a knot of men under Taddeusz charged the Thrasey line at a lumbering run. They were a good hundred meters ahead of the king's more regular array in the center, while Lamullo's left wing was echeloned back about the same distance behind Golsingh's division.

And, thanks to the rough going and the way the creek meandered, Hansen's pitiful unit was just about that far behind the left wing. It made good geometry but bad war.

"Come on," Hansen snarled. He started running. If that stupid bastard of a warchief could do it, so could he.

Shill fell headlong. Hansen turned, but Maharg was already helping the older warrior to his feet. They pounded down the creek like enraged hippos, striking sparks from the rocks and cursing monotonously into their microphones.

The Thrasey right wing was thrown forward also, so the forces engaged along their full lengths more or less simultaneously. Rippling arc weapons reflected between the ground and the low clouds.

Hansen noticed a phenomenon which had escaped him during the forest battle of the previous week: at the moment of contact, each battleline spread into two lines. The well-armored champions engaged one another in the front ranks, while lesser folk in scruffy, cobbled-together armor hung back a pace or two.

Malcolm snapped his arc at a warrior in black and white from four meters out. His opponent blocked the stroke and replied with a cut of his own. Armor of the quality of either suit was impervious at that distance, but neither man seemed inclined to close for the moment. Three other warriors flanked the Thrasey champion—from a step back.

Malcolm was missing the support of Shill and Maharg. Not that his juniors did anything, not really; but they were there.

Hansen fell down. Shill put out a hand, but Hansen grabbed a tree root and jerked himself upright by it.

At the edge of Malcolm's display, Hansen saw Lamullo being pressed hard by a warrior in red and white. *Tooley, the one with a terrible temper but nobody you'd wish to see on the other side.*

Lamullo was blocking his opponent's strokes adequately, but he seemed unable to counterattack. After each parry he stepped backward.

Malcolm rushed his man with a shout. The Thrasey champion dodged back and collided with one of his own supporters. Malcolm's arc crackled the length of his opponent's outflung left arm, glancing but shearing also in a fountain of sparks.

The Thrasey warrior staggered in the opposite direction and fell. One of his retinue stepped over the champion to guard him. Malcolm cut vertically. The other warrior caught the arc on his own weapon, but he didn't have the power to stop it from sizzling into and halfway through his helmet.

Malcolm slashed to his right, taking the second member of the retinue on the hip joint and crumpling him like a sheet of heated polyethylene.

The third low-status warrior turned to run. Malcolm's arc sliced off his feet at the ankles.

Hansen swore. He'd seen in the swirling action what Malcolm didn't have the time or inclination to notice.

"Hold up!" Hansen snarled to his men. He thrust his arm into the reeds to clear a sight line. The growth was too thick. His arc scythed down the reeds in a cloud of steam.

They hadn't come as far as he'd intended, but the battle itself had moved toward them. Hansen was slightly behind the right flank of the Thrasey line. The nearest warrior was twenty meters away, watching his front, and the nearest actual fighting was ten meters beyond that.

Tooley jumped over Lamullo's body and bore down on Malcolm with a roar.

"All right," said Hansen, cool again. "Let's go."

He gripped a willow trunk and started to drag himself up. The roots pulled out in a shower of dirt.

"Here," said Maharg, making a stirrup of his hands. Hansen stepped into it and felt the other warrior's battlesuit lift him. Shill followed by the same route, then bent and with Hansen jerked Maharg to the top of the bank.

A pair of Thrasey freemen watched with amazement as the three warriors appeared from the dense growth. They rode into the battleline, shouting a warning.

A warrior—it looked like one of the Thrasey side—cut them both down with as little hesitation as Hansen had shown when he cleared his sight line.

"Remember . . . ," said Hansen. He didn't feel the aches and battering he'd just given his body, but his forearms were quivering with adrenaline. "When the marker goes red, everybody hits 'im together."

But Hansen took the nearest Thrasey warrior himself, cutting the man so deeply through the shoulderblades that the arc crackled out through the flimsy plastron before Hansen shut it off.

They dropped three of their opponents before the fourth man even turned around. The warriors hanging back behind the real engagement weren't well equipped anyway.

Maharg's arc froze the fourth man. Hansen swatted away the fellow's life with something near contempt, as though he were scraping cow manure from his glove.

They struck the front rank, unaware and from behind; three of the Thrasey champions went down under the multiple attacks as easily as the hirelings had.

The air stank of ozone and burned flesh. The snow softened the outlines of the bodies, but it couldn't hide the smells of death.

Golsingh's collapsing line stiffened. Several of the more formidable surviving warriors on the left wing fell in with Hansen and his crew. They were turning the Thrasey flank.

Tooley screamed an amplified challenge as he lunged toward Hansen. His arc was a dense blue-white, even though it was extended more than a meter.

Malcolm must be dead.

"Strike!" Hansen shouted with his arc hovering just above his right gauntlet. He stepped close, the opposite of what he wanted to do and—with luck—not what Tooley expected.

Shill and Maharg had jumped back from Tooley's furious rush. Hansen was alone.

Hansen knew he couldn't block Tooley's weapon, even with his own flux as dense as his suit could produce. He caught Tooley's downward slash and held it momentarily while his body twisted out of the way.

Their armor clanged together. Tooley's arc carved into the sod explosively, covering both men in a veil of steam.

Hansen's right arm was numb. His chest shuddered as he tried desperately to hold his opponent's weapon aside.

Something crackled at the lower edge of Hansen's vision—an arc, Maharg stepping in to cut at Tooley's hip joint. Red and white paint blistered in the dancing arc, but the electronic armor held—

Until Shill squeezed between Hansen and Maharg. The old man thrust home at the core of the younger warrior's attack, and Tooley's battlesuit failed with a *crack!* that blew a doughnut of soot and steam across the field.

Tooley fell backward. Hansen started to topple onto the corpse. Shill braced him for a moment until Maharg could grab Hansen's shoulders and lift him upright.

Hansen tried to raise his right arm. He watched with amazement as the limb obeyed, but he still had no sensation from the shoulder on down. His chest felt cold and he was shuddering.

The battle paused. The warriors who'd followed Tooley, and those men of Golsingh's whose opponents had fallen in the flank attack, waited uncertainly. Hansen was trying to get his breath.

Malcolm got to his feet behind the Thrasey warriors. His helmet and plastron had been seared black by Tooley's arc. It was only by the red-blue-silver bands on his arms and legs that he could be identified. He hacked down the nearest man from behind.

"General freq!" Hansen gasped to his AI. "Come on, you bastards! Golsingh and Peace!"

He wasn't sure that was the best battlecry for *this* place, but peace was the brightest hope Hansen himself could imagine just now.

And he knew there'd be no peace on this field until every one of the Thrasey warriors was down.

"Strike!" with his display centered on a Thrasey warrior whose arc quivered first toward Hansen's unit, then toward Malcolm.

Hansen slashed; Shill and Maharg cut, together and within a fraction of a second of their leader's stroke. The warrior's helmet burned as Malcolm chopped down the man beside him.

"Come on!"

The whole Thrasey flank collapsed. Warriors turned and ran as Golsingh's troops swept toward them from the front and side simultaneously.

"No-'count merchant kissers!" Malcolm bawled as he strode down the line he was crumpling. "Frekka-paid cowards!"

They didn't look like cowards a minute ago, Hansen thought as he tried to keep up with the veteran.

But the prejudice against merchants' hirelings must be as great *among* those hirelings as it was among warriors who hadn't decided to accept Frekka's offers. So long as they were led by a champion of Tooley's stature, they stood and fought; with their leader down, there was no sign of the willingness Count Lopez' men had shown to fight on after the battle was clearly lost.

Despite the success of Hansen's flanking movement, the battle *wasn't* clearly lost for the Thrasey forces.

The central division around a figure in blue and silver armor ("The Lord of Thrasey," answered a feminine voice when Hansen asked his AI for an identification) had surged into the gap between Golsingh and the headlong advance of Taddeusz' unit. The king had avoided being surrounded only by falling back, and the Lord of Thrasey was pushing him hard.

A dozen Thrasey warriors faced around to meet the threat from the collapsing flank. The foremost were champions from the lord's personal bodyguard, and even the warriors of their retinues, falling into place behind them, looked reasonably well equipped.

Malcolm slowed and stopped five paces from the new line. The rush of easy winners behind him halted at the appearance of a real enemy again.

Hansen put a hand on the veteran's shoulder. "Malcolm," he said. "I'll lead and you back—"

Malcolm pushed Hansen aside with a clang.

A maelstrom of arcs snarled around the leaders. The Lord of Thrasey had led the remainder of his bodyguard in a rush to overwhelm Golsingh before the king's left flank could rescue him.

The melee blazed like the lightning which swirls in the funnel of a tornado, flinging battlesuits and bits of battlesuit out from its lethal core. Golsingh stood in his blue armor and struck with deadly effect, but the warriors to either side of him dropped.

Malcolm shouted wordlessly and charged the waiting line.

"Strike with Malcolm!" Hansen snarled as he lurched forward beside the veteran.

Malcolm's arc crossed with that of a fellow whose armor was decorated in orange swirls. Hansen feinted toward the next Thrasey warrior to the left, then struck at the shoulder of Malcolm's man. The armor burned, flinging the limb in one direction as the man's body toppled in the other.

Maharg parried the thrust of the left-hand warrior and went to his knees with the searing force of the fellow's arc. Hansen's sideways sweep drove the Thrasey warrior back. Maharg stayed down, shaking his head.

The Thrasey survivors backed. Some of Golsingh's warriors pressed forward.

"What are you doing?" Malcolm demanded. "He was mine!"

"Winning!" Hansen snarled back on straight audio. "D'ye want to die? We'll all die if we don't cut the king loose, 'n that means teamwork!"

Malcolm lunged forward, thrusting. His arc slipped past the guard and through the plastron of a warrior hesitating between facing Malcolm and joining the attack on Golsingh. The man was dead and falling, but Hansen struck him anyway because he was moving with the stroke and it was better to follow through than to change his rhythm.

Shill chopped at the body as he followed Malcolm and

Hansen. His arc cut at the ankles of the next Thrasey warrior as his betters—as his *fellows*—whipsawed the victim through both shoulder pieces.

The last of Golsingh's bodyguards fell. Three of the four men with the Lord of Thrasey, all of them champions, turned and faced the threat from the flank.

Thrasey and his remaining warrior slashed at the king. The warrior got home with a blast of sparks that blistered blotches of paint away from Golsingh's helmet.

Malcolm cut at a guard wearing black and white checks. The Thrasey warrior thrust back, not at Malcolm but at Hansen lunging in to double the stroke. Hansen's display blurred and all his hair stood out straight as his muscles twitched.

He almost fell as his display shrank back into bright focus. All three of the Thrasey bodyguards held their blocking position. One of the Golsingh's left-wing warriors had fallen between them and Malcolm.

Two meters away, the Lord of Thrasey was body to body with Golsingh. Their arcs were locked in a shower of blue fire. The warrior with the Lord of Thrasey had lifted his rippling arc weapon for the final blow.

"Come on," Hansen gasped as he jumped forward. The check-armored warrior parried his cut.

Their armor crashed together, jarring the Thrasey warrior back a half-step before the power of his better suit stopped Hansen's rush and began bending him over. Malcolm was dueling with another bodyguard, and there was no chance that—

Shill stepped between Hansen and Malcolm with his palm outstretched. His bolt struck the Lord of Thrasey at the join of his backplate and helmet. Malcolm's opponent swiped sideways, cutting through both knees of Shill's powerless suit.

Golsingh neatly decapitated the Lord of Thrasey.

Shill toppled forward. The bodyguard struggling with Hansen doubled up as Maharg stabbed him through the belly.

Hansen's AI tagged all the figures standing with a spike of blue light. Friendlies, they were all friendlies. Malcolm had finished his opponent when the fool struck down Shill, and Golsingh was hacking with an intensity that was more vengeance than caution at the smoldering ruins of the warrior who'd almost killed him.

Hansen unlatched his suit. He opened the heavy clamshell with hysterical strength that belied his exhausted weakness of moments before. The snowy air was a club, but his body was already shuddering.

The smell of burned meat was even worse when he jerked open Shill's battlesuit.

Shill's eyes were closed, but his nostrils fluttered as he breathed.

He wouldn't be breathing long. The wounds were cauterized by the arc that made them, but the shock of the high voltage and double amputation would certainly be fatal.

Freemen rode in to join the warriors at the moment of victory.

"Furs!" Hansen screamed. His voice cracked. "Furs! Here! Now, goddam you!"

"Fin'ly broke my way," Shill whispered. He was smiling. "Didja see him go down? I killed the fuckin' Lord a Thrasey!"

A freeman leaped from his pony and draped his cloak over Hansen's shoulders. Hansen snatched it off and tucked it around Shill, still cradled in the back half of his armor.

Maharg knelt beside them. "You all right, sir?" he asked. "You all right?"

"Old Shill fin'ly . . . ," Shill said.

His eyes opened. The old man's irises were a brilliant blue that Hansen hadn't noticed before.

"Old Shill fin'ly had some luck!" Shill gasped.

His chest arched. A convulsion drove the remainder of his breath out in a long rattling cough that continued several seconds after the light had gone out of the blue eyes.

Maharg shook Hansen by the shoulders. "Sir?" he said. "Are you all right? You're crying."

≡ 20 ≡

"WELL, LORD GOLSINGH," said the warrior named Aude-mar, "if you pass your right to Thrasey's armor, then the suit should properly go to me."

"We've been over this, Audemar," Golsingh said. His voice was so quiet that Hansen barely heard it over the scrunch of his spade.

"He shouldn't be doing that," Taddeusz grumbled. "It isn't a warrior's business to work with his hands."

"He did a warrior's business this day, foster father."

Hansen freed another block of turf. A pair of slaves set it on a tarpaulin with three others. They lifted the edges of the cloth to carry the lot to the growing mound.

Hansen positioned the spade, then slid it down through the sod. He wriggled the T-handle to clear pebbles caught among the grassroots.

"But when Lamullo fell," Audemar said, "I was the senior warrior in the left division. Therefore I should have the leader's share of booty taken by the—"

"Shut up, Audemar," Taddeusz said.

"Lord Malcolm sits at my left now in banquet, Audemar," Golsingh said. His tone was growing sharper and thinner, like a blade being drawn from a cane scabbard.

There weren't any proper stones with which to raise a mound here, but turf would last as long. More fitting for Shill, besides. Shill hadn't had the harshness of rock; but he'd endured nonetheless.

"Ah, sir?" said Maharg. He looked older now, but that might be only exhaustion. "Would it be all right if I, ah . . . if I dug one myself?"

Hansen straightened, leaving the spade upright in the cut.

He gestured toward the handle. "Keep the corners square," he said, massaging his lower back with both hands.

He looked around critically. "We've probably got enough by now."

There were thirty slaves lifting sod for the mound, but the straggling rectangle Hansen had cut in the prairie was twice the area of what any of the others had managed. Well, the slaves were working because it was their life to work—and their lives if they didn't. Hansen cut sod because—

The mound was two meters high, an oval proportioned eight to three across the axes, much like the proportions of a sleeping man.

"Hope he likes it," Hansen said.

Maharg levered the strip of turf loose and stepped back so that the slaves could remove it. "Shill?" he said. "I dunno."

The young warrior knuckled his forehead. The fine hairs on the back of his right hand had crinkled when the surge of an opponent's arc overloaded his battlesuit. "I never figured North's Searchers would, you know, be interested in Shill."

He looked at Hansen. It wasn't just exhaustion: Maharg had aged. "Nor me neither," he added. "Though with the new armor, that might change. Thanks to you."

"You earned it," Hansen said. "Shill did too."

He looked toward the sky. It was cold, and the wind made his vision blur.

"I recognize your right to appoint whomsoever you please to positions of honor, Your Majesty," Audemar said, his voice hoarse with suppressed anger.

"If you choose to make a warrior of limited status your left-wing commander—and your new Lord of Thrasey!—" Audemar bit the words out "—then that is your option, and I only hope you don't regret it soon. But—"

The sun was low. Because there was a thin slice of clear sky near the horizon, the landscape was brighter than it had been this day before.

Malcolm turned from the battlesuit which stood upright at the head of the mound and walked toward the group around the king.

"—that's for the *future*," Audemar continued. He was about fifty years old, of middle height, and soft rather than precisely fat. "At the time the booty was taken, *I* was in charge—"

Hansen watched with no expression for a moment, then jerked the spade from the soil and also walked toward the king. Maharg was beside him.

"—and that means that the Lord of Thrasey's armor is mine by right unless you claim it yourself. It's a royal suit and even after repairs it will be superior to mine. Theref—"

Malcolm gripped Audemar by the shoulder with his left hand and spun the older man so that his cheek was in position for Malcolm's broad right palm. The slap sounded like a tree-limb breaking.

Audemar would have fallen, but Malcolm continued to hold him. The backhand bloodied Audemar's nose.

Taddeusz started to move. Golsingh stopped him with a raised hand. "Wait," the king said.

Hansen let the spade lie down along his right leg again.

"Listen, you bastard," Malcolm said. He and the man he held were about of a weight, but Malcolm's fury gave bulk to his greater height. "If you'd been worth shit yourself, we wouldn't've had to bury Shill today, would we?"

"That old man was noth—" and the rest of the word vanished in a spray of blood from Audemar's lips as Malcolm slapped him again.

Golsingh stepped between them. "That's enough," he said mildly.

His head turned to Audemar. "Audemar," he went on in a tone of thin steel. "You have been informed of my decision. Further objection to it will be treason. Do you understand?"

Audemar spun and walked off. His steps were uncertain.

"Very good," said Golsingh. The king's eyes met Hansen's. "Then we'll return to last night's encampment and set off for Peace Rock in the morning. There's no point in trying to travel any distance now."

Hansen nodded. "Yes, milord," he said.

His throat was dry. He set the edge of the spade on the ground and drove it in a hand's breadth, so that a slave could easily find it.

"Let's go find somebody with a skin of beer," Malcolm

said to Hansen and Maharg. His voice had odd breaks and catches in it, as if he had crumbs in his throat.

At the head of the mound over Shill's dead body, the late sunlight winked on the blue and silver majesty of the Lord of Thrasey's battlesuit.

≡ 21 ≡

"IT'S CUSTOMARY AFTER a battle, Lord Hansen . . . ," said Krita as she leaned forward to fill his cup.

The breasts wobbling beneath the scooped neckline of her blouse were fuller than the taut planes of her face and her muscular limbs had led him to expect.

". . . for a warrior to describe his own exploits. Not those of a—friend?"

"Shill was my friend, yes," Hansen said coldly.

"Maybe he didn't have any exploits to describe," suggested Unn. "Is that it, Lord Hansen?"

"Krita, girl," said Taddeusz from the opposite corner of the cross-table, "stop chattering while we're trying to plan. And leave *him* alone anyway."

Krita looked at Unn, balancing the beer pitcher on her hip. She was wearing red, while Unn's dress was of linen dyed the same rich blue as Shill's eyes.

"I hear," said Krita, as though she hadn't heard her father speak, "that Hansen was one of Lord Malcolm's greatest champions. And we *know* what a hero Malcolm was—"

Krita bent again, this time filling Malcolm's mug.

Hansen thought the new Lord of Thrasey looked flushed, but with Malcolm's complexion it was hard to tell. Besides, the color might come from drink, the hearth, or the fact that Malcolm was now the man sitting to the King's immediate left.

"—don't we?"

She drew her index finger up the back of Malcolm's wrist. He jerked his hand back as though she'd touched him with a branding iron. Taddeusz clutched the arms of his chair.

"Lord Golsingh?" Hansen said loudly to cut through the

woman's—the women's—deliberate provocation. "Have you given any thought to what I said about Frekka?"

"Have I realized that you were correct in what you told me before the battle?" Golsingh said with a trace of a smile. "Yes, I have."

He looked to his other side. "And you're of the same opinion now too, aren't you, foster father?"

"That Frekka needs to be put down?" Taddeusz said harshly. "Yes, I'll grant that. Burnt down and sown with salt, *I* say—but you've got your own notions there, too, don't you?"

He glared fiercely at Hansen. His daughter shifted so that her back was to the warchief and her mocking, enticing smile played over Malcolm, Hansen, and Maharg.

"We need—" Hansen said.

"*We* need!" Taddeusz snarled.

"Lord Golsingh needs—" Hansen said, raising his voice to shout down the warchief if that was necessary, but Taddeusz was only interjecting "—the trade and manufacture of Frekka to succeed in his plan of unifying his kingdom. What he doesn't need are the present Syndics of Frekka and their games."

Taddeusz drained his goblet. "And Golsingh will take your advice, I suppose?" he said/asked bitterly.

"The king will do as seems good to the king, foster father," Golsingh said in his thin voice.

Taddeusz met his eyes for a moment, then blinked.

"More beer, girl," he growled as he thrust his goblet out to Krita. Unn filled it instead.

"I've looked over your suggestions of which warriors go to Thrasey with Lord Malcolm," Golsingh continued when he was sure his point had been taken.

"And your own requests, Lord Malcolm." He nodded toward Malcolm, who leaned closer in relief at the change of subject. "There are discrepancies." The king smiled. "*Only* discrepancies, I would say. Now. . . ."

The conversation turned to the merits—and otherwise—of warriors Hansen knew only as battlecolors, not names. He relaxed, glad not to have a fight just now. He was bruised and aching, and his eulogy on Shill had drained whatever energy the battle two days ago had left.

Shill died because he trusted Hansen further than he should have.

Maharg got up from the table. He patted Hansen on the shoulder and said, ''Thanks,'' as he left.

Maharg wasn't on watch tonight, and he'd made a female friend since he came back from the battle a hero. . . . Which was Maharg's doing, not Hansen's, not really; but the boy didn't see it that way.

A female friend. . . .

''We've been wondering, Lord Hansen,'' said Krita as she refilled the mug that he seemed to have emptied, to his surprise, ''whether you're one of those men who don't like women?''

''What?'' The question sobered him like a bucket of meltwater.

Unn's eyes were amused, Krita's were laughing.

''Since none of the girls say you've,'' Krita continued, ''shall we say—given them the time. That's so, isn't it?''

''I haven't *had* the time!'' Hansen snapped, flicking his eyes right and left—and right again, to the cross-table; but thank god the bitch had chosen to keep *this* conversation in a low voice.

He grimaced. ''This is the first day since I've, I've been here, that I haven't been training in my battlesuit. *You* know how exhausting that is.''

''Are you ashamed of your tastes?'' Unn asked coolly. ''Some of the male slaves quite like it, we're told. Not that it matters what a slave thinks.''

Krita giggled. ''Some of the warriors, too. And not the least of them, either. Would you like some names?''

''What I'd like—'' said Hansen, standing as he downed the beer in his mug in three quick gulps. And he'd been wondering if *Malcolm* was flushing at this bitch's games! The low firelight was sufficient camouflage now, thank goodness.

''What *I'd* like is a piss and my bed.''

He stamped out of the hall for the former; and, much later, having emptied the skin of beer he'd taken from a servant, he returned and found his bed.

Hansen was awakened by the sound of the bar sliding between the staples of his door, locking it from the inside. There was no light at all.

Hansen swung his body erect at the far end of the bed. He didn't get up because his legs were tangled with furs. He'd do himself more trouble than help by the noise he'd make trying to free them.

In Hansen's right hand was an iron pry-bar, half a meter long. He held his breath and the weapon, waiting for the intruder to make his move.

"Do you have the time now, Hansen?" whispered a woman's throaty voice. "Or should I send you one of the serving boys?"

A woman's voice, the smell of a woman. . . . Hansen's body began to shiver.

The plank bed trembled as she rested her hand on it, then sat down. "Are you afraid?" she murmured.

"No," Hansen lied. "Why are you—"

Her fingertips, then her palms, slid through the hairs of his bare chest.

You bet he was afraid of Krita. She was her father's daughter, headstrong and violent—and surely frustrated in a dozen different ways, ready to light a fuze in order to watch the explosion that would follow.

Taddeusz was out in the hall, slumped in drink over the table. If he even dreamed—

But it'd been too long since Hansen made love to a woman. He hooked the pry-bar over the edge of the bed and reached for Krita.

She wore a robe of thick, clinging material. He fumbled with it for a moment.

"Wait," she said, imperious in the darkness, and pushed Hansen's fingers out of the way. Ribbon-ends brushed him as she untied them; then her strong hands pulled his face down to her breasts. Despite her cool demeanor, Krita's heart was beating fiercely and her nipples were already erect.

They made love with a swift violence that embarrassed Hansen—it had been a *long* time—but thrilled the woman to the point that at climax she bit his shoulder to stifle her cries.

He continued to stroke into her, uncertain as to the etiquette of sex here on Northworld—and individuals were more different than cultures, besides.

Krita murmured in question, then fell into the rhythm again.

Her head tossed and she moaned, "Oh Penny bless me . . . oh bless me . . . oh, oh. . . ."

She buried her face in his shoulder again, this time without biting, and began shuddering through a series of multiple climaxes while Hansen thought of Krita's father and the fact her breasts were flatter and broader than they had seemed when he glimpsed them beneath her dress.

"Oh, gods . . . ," she whispered as she let her body go limp. Her fine hair pooled over his hands. He imagined it in the light of the hearth, black with auburn streaks colored by the glowing coals.

"Why did you come here, Hansen?" she asked. Her fingers kneaded the great muscles over his shoulders, then traced down the knobs of his spine.

"Chance," Hansen said in the honesty of the moment.

He realized as he spoke that his honest statement was almost certainly untrue. North and the Consensus were playing a game, and Nils Hansen was one of their pawns.

But *that* truth wasn't one to speak here.

"But I'm probably the only person on this—" *planet*, but he wouldn't say that "—kingdom who can make Golsingh's dreams a reality. And that's what I'm going to do."

"Then you really intend to help the king?" Krita said. She chuckled. "Taddeusz hates you, you know?"

"Yeah, I'd figured that out."

"He thinks you're a deliberate troublemaker."

Her fingertips lightly massaged the place she'd bitten. Hansen felt it burning. She'd broken the skin for sure . . . but it wasn't anything that'd show with his clothes on. "He thinks you were sent by Frekka to bring down the kingdom."

Hansen snorted. "He wouldn't think that," he said, "if he'd been where the *battle* was being decided the other day instead of haring off on a private war of his own. Golsingh'd be cold meat today if it weren't for . . . ."

"If it weren't for you?" Krita prompted, challenge in her tone.

"If it weren't for Shill," Hansen said. "And Malcolm. But yeah, I was there too. And your father wasn't."

Her body shifted. "Here," she said. "Lie beside me for a moment. Is there enough room?"

There was, so long as Hansen watched his head. The bed was almost as broad as the cubicle itself, but the sweep of the thatch lowered the ceiling on the outer edge.

She ran a hand down his chest to his groin. Hansen's belly muscles twitched. He was always ticklish, but particularly at times like this.

He was as relaxed as he'd ever been in his life. He began to play with the woman's groin.

"I've heard what happened during the battle," she said. Her vaginal muscles sucked greedily at his finger. "The real stories—*oh*—not just the boasting around the table tonight. Oh. *Oh*. Why do you. Blame yourself. For Shill dying?"

Hansen concentrated on what he was doing. Discipline had gotten him through a lot of bad moments, out of a lot of situations that he'd rather not have been in.

"Because he was my man," he said quietly. "Because he did what I ordered him to do and taught him to do, and doing that got him killed."

"And so he died cursing you?" the woman said. "That's not what *I* heard."

"He didn't know what he was saying at the end," Hansen said.

"Don't believe it!" Krita said harshly. She pulled his face down to her breasts again. "Yes," she murmured, "yessss. . . . Bite them—please, *bite*."

Her fingers were like oaken dowels on the back of his head and neck.

"Shill was sixty years old," she whispered into Hansen's ear. "He'd never have been anything. He wouldn't even have had a job here if it weren't for Malcolm, and Taddeusz wanting to keep Malcolm happy even though he doesn't like him."

She'd been manipulating his prick as she spoke. Now she threw her legs over his. The ceiling was in the way. Hansen slid sideways, to where the thatch gave her enough room to mount him.

"You made Shill a warrior, Hansen," she said as she inserted him into herself. "You made him a *man*. If you were a god, you couldn't have served him better."

A fist pounded on the barred door. "Krita?" Taddeusz shouted. "Krita! Come out of there, you little bitch!"

Hansen's hand gripped the end of his pry-bar. "Your idea?" he asked softly.

"Gods no!" the woman gasped as she fumbled for her robe. "No, no. Oh, gods, I'm . . ."

"Hansen, open this door or I'll break it down!" Taddeusz demanded. His fist slammed the panel hard enough to spring the boards. A trickle of yellow lamplight entered the cubicle.

Hansen explored the ceiling with his hand. The thatch was on stringers at half-meter intervals, plenty of room to slip a body through—but there was a mesh of withies above the stringers, and *that* wouldn't pass anything larger than a clenched fist.

"Didn't I say open?" bellowed Taddeusz as the door slammed repeatedly. The bar held, but the panel itself began to split.

"Into the suit!" Hansen whispered as he tucked his pry-bar under one of the stringers and lifted, putting his full strength into the motion.

The mass of thatch shifted, but only a few strands of the tough willow-wand netting popped despite his effort. Hansen moved the bar and tried again. Night air gushed through the temporary gaps.

Half a board smashed in from the door. Taddeusz' big hand reached through the rectangle of lamplight and slid the bar open.

The woman was out of sight.

Hansen swung to his feet and pulled the door open. He wished he'd had time to dress, but he wished a lot of things right about now. He held the pry-bar loosely at his side.

"What's all this about?" he demanded as Taddeusz pushed him backward and Hansen slammed the heel of his foot down on Taddeusz' instep.

The warchief yelped and halted. The hall behind him was full of people. Nobody in the building could've been drunk enough to sleep through that hammering.

Taddeusz carried one of the freemen's lances, gripping it well ahead of the balance. An awkward weapon.

"Where is she?" he said. "I knew she was here as soon as I went up to the room and found her gone!"

"Look," Hansen said, "there's nobody here. Let's move back and discuss this—"

Taddeusz thrust the lance past Hansen, into the furs piled on the bed. The bed platform splintered. Taddeusz was a strong bastard, no mistake.

"Where *is*—" the warchief said as he stabbed again, a horizontal stroke that pinned the furs against the far wall of the cubicle.

"What's going on here?" Golsingh demanded from somewhere back in the crowd. "Taddeusz?"

"Keep back!" Taddeusz snapped. "This is for me."

He scowled, then brightened with surmise. "In the armor, is—"

Hansen stood with his back against the battlesuit. "If you touch my armor without permission, warrior," he said with terrible distinctness, "I will kill you here and now."

He pointed the end of the pry-bar between Taddeusz' eyes, only a hand's breadth away.

Malcolm forced his way through the doorway. He gripped the warchief's right elbow with both hands. Taddeusz shook himself free with contemptuous ease.

"I'll break your neck anyway," Taddeusz snarled.

His muscles bunched, then froze as a voice crackled from the hollow of the hall saying, "Father! What's the matter with you? Are you mad?"

"Look," said the freeman holding the lamp. He pointed toward the thatch that Hansen's desperate efforts had torn.

Taddeusz turned slowly, then burst out of the bed cubicle like a boar charging hounds.

Malcolm exhaled in relief. Hansen was too focused to feel anything. He pushed his friend from the cubicle behind Taddeusz and followed, pulling the broken door closed behind him.

A dozen animal-fat lamps supplemented the dull glow of the hearth. Krita stood near Golsingh. She wore boots and a fur cape on which the snow was melting.

"Where were you, you whore?" Taddeusz demanded in a thick voice.

"Outside, walking with Unn," his daughter blazed. "If it's any concern to a drunken pig like you!"

"You were not, you slut!" Taddeusz roared as he lurched forward.

Golsingh stepped between father and daughter, saying, "Fos—" and Taddeusz stiff-armed him out of the way.

Never hit a man with your bare hand, a man had once told Hansen. An old man, too old to live but too tough to die.

Hansen raised the pry-bar, measuring the distance to the back of the warchief's skull which wasn't as hard as iron whatever he might think—

A figure in a battlesuit stepped into Taddeusz' path. The warchief crashed into the armor, bounced back, and raised his fist in a gesture so vain that even he understood its absurdity.

Taddeusz twined the fingers of both hands around themselves. He squeezed as though choking a dragon.

The battlesuit was Hansen's own.

Had been Hansen's. He'd claimed Tooley's armor after the battle, and his own suit went to—

Maharg's voice boomed from the battlesuit's amplifier, "Excellency? Are you all right?"

The suit's great steel arm extended toward Golsingh who was already picking himself up from the floor.

If Krita was here, fully dressed—and she was—*then who in hell had he been fucking?*

Taddeusz knelt before Golsingh.

"Excellency," he said in a voice choked by emotion. "I don't deserve to live. Slay me, but grant my spirit forgiveness for the insult to which my whore of a daughter drove me."

"Don't—here, get up, foster father," Golsingh said uncomfortably. "Come on, we've all been drinking, and we've imagined things tonight, I'm sure."

The warchief arose. He looked even more like a bear when the lamps woke amber highlights from his beard and moustache. "No imagining, Excellency," he said.

Taddeusz turned and pointed to Hansen. "A joke for you, was it? Drag my name through the cesspit?"

"Father!"

"I wish you no disrespect, Lord Taddeusz," Hansen said carefully. The warchief had lost his lance at some time during the scuffling, but he could still break a man's neck with his hands.

"You'll do me none after tomorrow," Taddeusz said heavily. "Lord Hansen, I challenge you. We'll meet tomorrow at midday."

"Foster father, this is not a thing I wish!" the king said sharply.

The big man glanced at him.

"I regret that, Excellency," he said. "But it happens nonetheless. It's a matter of my honor."

Taddeusz glared past Golsingh toward his daughter. She looked away angrily.

Golsingh shrugged. "So be it, then," he said without raising his voice. "But—if you do this thing, against my express will, Lord Taddeusz . . . you will leave Peace Rock and never return. I swear it."

Taddeusz nodded. "So be it, then," he said.

An opening at warchief—just the kind of move that Hansen needed for his reorganization to work, though a bit early, three months later after Malcolm proved himself, that'd be better. . . .

Except that everybody was assuming Hansen, the catalyst of the change, would be dead after tomorrow's duel.

Golsingh looked around the hall bleakly. "Go to your beds," he ordered. "There's been enough harm done this night."

"Wait," said Malcolm. The veteran was wearing boots and a linen nightshift, damp with the snow that had fallen on him when he ran to the hall at the sound of trouble. His body, from chest through hips, was a solid tube of muscle. 'You can't set the meeting so soon."

Taddeusz looked from Malcolm to Hansen and snorted dismissively. The big man was no longer angry, just determined. "What's the matter?" he said. "Is your friend afraid to die?"

Hansen smiled. He wasn't sure what the answer to that one was. Too much had happened. Been happening.

"He'll meet you in a tennight," Malcolm insisted. "You can wait that long."

Krita had disappeared, but most of the others in the hall, warriors and servants alike, were listening with interest. Golsingh waited with a hard, emotionless expression which Hansen suspected was a mirror of his own.

Taddeusz shook his head. "The challenged has three days

by custom to settle his affairs," he said. "Three days and a half day, then."

Taddeusz looked at Hansen. His visage was that of a man glaring at the turd onto which he'd just stepped. "Or he can run. He can go farther in that time than I'd be willing to chase him."

Malcolm looked at Golsingh. "Excellency? A tennight would—"

The king shook his head. "Lord Taddeusz will have what custom dictates during his remaining stay at Peace Rock," he said coldly. "In three days and a half day, then."

He and the warchief both turned and strode toward the ladder to their chambers above the far end of the hall. They didn't look at one another. When the crowd didn't part quite fast enough, a thrust of Taddeusz' arm slammed a number of people into the wall.

Golsingh turned at the base of the ladder and shouted, "Go to your beds, damn you!"

The crowd scattered to side-chambers and the entrance, murmuring in voices as dim as the glow of the long hearth.

Hansen let out his breath. He was stark naked and the hall was cold. Malcolm stood beside him, and Maharg was returning from having stripped off his armor in his own chamber.

Now that the lamps were gone, the hall was dark. Its framework creaked mournfully as wind pressed the roof.

"Just a second," Hansen said, slipping into his cubicle. He closed the remains of the door before he started exploring the darkness with his hands.

His battlesuit stood ajar. There was no one within the armor, no one hidden in the pile of bedding. The tear in the thatch Hansen had made as camouflage was wider and a real gap, now that somebody with a sharp blade had slashed through the mesh of withies.

The knife must've been in her robe, because it sure wasn't hidden in what she was wearing when Taddeusz started banging on the door. . . .

Hansen pulled on his coveralls. "Come on in here, then," he said as he reopened the door. It wasn't much privacy, but with Malcolm's cubicle to one side and Maharg's to the other, it would do about as well as anything available.

He couldn't see Malcolm's expression in the darkness, but there was a combination of wonder and regret in the veteran's voice as he fingered the torn thatch and said, "Well, laddie, you've got expensive tastes, haven't you? This time it's your life they've cost you."

"I appreciate your confidence," Hansen snapped.

Maharg was standing like a fireplug in front of the door.

"You did a smart thing, putting your armor on," Hansen said to him. He grimaced. "A lot smarter than anything I did tonight, Malcolm. I know that. Question is, where do we go from here?"

"Your only chance was getting the Thrasey armor," Malcolm said, impressively calm and matter-of-fact. "It's a royal suit, and with a good enough repair job, it might stand up to Taddeusz."

Hansen had seen too many officers flustered when the news they had to report was very bad. That got in the way of solutions . . . and damage limitation, when there were no solutions. But as for what Malcolm was saying—

"I've got armor," Hansen said. "And I wouldn't take Shill's suit if it were that or go naked."

"Shill doesn't need it—"

"*I* don't need a suit!" Hansen snapped. "I've got Tooley's suit. And what's Shill's is Shill's!"

"Oh, it's a good suit, is Tooley's," Malcolm said reasonably, as though unaware of the hard edge glinting from Hansen's tone. "As I know to my cost, having been put down by it—and out, it would have been, without you, laddie—and Maharg here; and without Shill, to whom I owe my life as surely as Golsingh does, I think, but he's still dead."

"There isn't time," said Maharg. "To get to the mound and get back, mebbe. But not to get it fixed, no way. That's a three-day job with the head off, you bet."

"Look—" said Hansen, his anger past.

"No, laddie," said Malcolm, patting his shoulder in the darkness. "You listen, because it's as you said: you're a warrior, but not with battlesuits."

Malcolm sat on the bed, drawing Hansen down beside him. "You think Tooley's armor is good," he continued, "and so it is; but Taddeusz wears a royal suit, and that's to yours as my armor was to Tooley that day that would've been my last without your help. And there will be no help in a duel.''

"He took Zieborn down wearing crap," Maharg said. "Villiers' suit, that was crap aginst my old one, even."

"You tricked Zieborn," Malcolm said reasonably, "and very clever it was, laddie; but you won't trick Taddeusz. He watched you then, and for all that he's a bastard, our Taddeusz is as fell and canny a warrior as we'll any of us meet."

"Musta killed more folks 'n bunk in the hall, he must," Maharg agreed sadly.

"So for you to face him . . . ," Malcolm continued. "Remember what it was like for you when Krita matched herself against you—and you wound up wrestling—the *first* time? Now, think what that'll be like with her father and the weapons at full bore."

Maharg snorted with laughter. "Taddeusz's gonna fuck you good!" he quipped.

Hansen found his face grinning even as his mind wondered sourly whether Maharg would think the joke as funny were it his neck on the chopping block.

It also occurred to him that he, and Taddeusz' daughter, and one other woman, were the only people in Peace Rock who didn't believe that Krita had been in Hansen's bed this night.

There was no way Krita could have cut her way through the willow mesh in time to reenter the hall fully dressed at the time Hansen saw her. Which might mean his plans and his life were about to end because of half an hour with some slut from the scullery. . . . But he didn't believe that either.

"All right," he said coldly. "What do you see as the options?"

"Run," said Malcolm flatly. "Or die, laddie. Because you're too big to wear *her* suit—"

"If she'd let me borrow it," Hansen said.

"As she might, women being as they are," Malcolm continued. "And too big as well for Golsingh's, or I think he'd have offered it from what I saw on his face. He's a smart man, our king . . . and a hard one, which is much the same at times."

"Thrasey ain't far enough," Maharg said, dropping the

words into a silence. "Nowhere Taddeusz might hear. No-where in the kingdom."

"And the kingdom will be the worse for it, laddie," Malcolm said softly, "and we'll all be the worse. But that's not so much to bear when you're alive, is it?"

Hansen barked out a laugh. "You don't think I owe it to honor to meet the challenge, then?" he asked.

"Taddeusz would think that," said the veteran very carefully. "And it might be that I would think that, were it me whom Taddeusz challenged. But just as being a warrior is different where you come from, laddie . . . I think honor is different as well. Not so?"

Hansen looked at him. There was no light and no expression at all. Maharg drew in his breath.

"Which is not to say," said Malcolm, "that I ever doubted you were a warrior either, you must see."

Hansen relaxed. "Yeah, I guess I do," he said.

He laughed harshly again. "Look," he added, "the main thing I see is that there'll be time after a night's sleep for anything we can figure out to do. And I'll be in better shape to deal with it then."

Malcolm squeezed his shoulder again. He and Maharg went to their own cubicles.

Dawn streamed through the hole in the roof. The weather had finally broken, and the sky was clear.

Hansen raised his head from the cocoon of furs—blinked—snatched up the pry-bar. There was a meter-long snake, probably disturbed from its winter burrow in the thatch, coiled in the open front of his battlesuit.

He got stealthily to his feet. The snake turned its head.

It had one bright eye and a milky globe for the other.

"Well, Hansssen . . . ," Walker said. "Are you ready to be my man for a battlesssuit? For a sssuit that a god would envy, to be my man . . . ?"

Walker's forked tongue flicked and toyed with something scarcely visible, caught in the latch of the armor.

"I'd need it in three days," Hansen said. "Otherwise—"

He took a deep breath and made the decision that his mind had waited till dawn to confirm. "Otherwise I'll fight him with what I've got."

TECHNO-WARRIORS . . .
ONE ON ONE

The air stank of ozone and burned flesh. The snow softened the outlines of the bodies, but it couldn't hide the smells of death.

Tooley screamed an amplified challenge as he lunged toward Hansen. His arc was a dense blue-white, even though it was extended more than a meter.

"Strike!" Hansen shouted with his arc hovering just above his right gauntlet.

Shill and Maharg had jumped back from Tooley's furious rush. Hansen was alone.

Hansen knew he couldn't block Tooley's weapon, even with his own flux as dense as his suit could produce. He caught Tooley's downward slash and held it momentarily while his body twisted out of the way.

Their armor clanged together . . .

≡ *Northworld* ≡

For Toni Weisskopf
who, like the Black Prince,
won her spurs among scenes of butchery.

≡ 1 ≡

HANSEN SAW THE blast bubble like an orange puffball above the building roofs three kilometers away. He stuck his head out the side window of his chauffeured aircar and heard the *whump!* over the rush of wind.

"Don't get us above—" Hansen started to say, but the car was already sideslipping to lose altitude and take them the rest of the distance to the crime site in the shelter of the buildings. The drivers who rotated through Commissioner Hansen's duty list were the best in Special Units. This one, a human named Krupchak, didn't want to enter the sight radius of the bandits' heavy weaponry any more than Hansen did.

Hansen's visor was split into three screens: the top showing the view from one of the units already at the crime site; the center clear for normal sight; and the bottom running a closed loop from the incident that set up the current situation. Hansen's own viewpoint showed nothing but faces from the ground traffic gaping upward at the aircar which howled above them with its emergency flashers fluttering at eye-dazzling speed.

The Civic Patrolmen on-site were busy blocking streets and trying to evacuate civilians already in what was clearly a combat zone. They weren't interested in the building at 212 Kokori Street where the bandits had holed up, except to keep from being blown away by the shots spitting—and sometimes slamming—from the top story of that structure.

Hansen set his remote to one of his own Special Units teams which had already arrived. Hansen's people (some of them female and not a few of them inhuman despite the complaints from bigots) were for the moment setting up fields of fire to block the bandits if they tried to escape. They were ready and willing to make a frontal assault if the Commissioner gave them that order.

The target was a fortress. Special Units would make a frontal assault on it over Commissioner Hansen's dead body.

Literally.

The structure was part of a row of cheap two- and three-story apartment buildings built long before the twenty-nine-year-old Hansen was born. The windows of the top floor now bulged with the soap-bubble iridescence of a forcefield. A white Civic Patrol hoverscoot stood abandoned outside the building's front entrance.

Kokori Street wasn't a slum. The Consensus of Planets didn't permit slums in or around the capitals of any of its 1,200 worlds; and besides, there were few real slums anywhere on Annunciation. Still, though there wasn't any trash in the street, the buildings' cast facades were dingy and sculpted in curves which flowed according to tastes superseded decades before.

The district's residents generally staffed the lower tiers of the city's service industries—but they *had* jobs, because residence in a planetary capital for periods longer than three months required that a household member be gainfully employed. Here on Annunciation, the Consensus fiat was enforced by the Civic Patrol—backed up by Special Units if necessary.

Ousting unemployed squatters could be a nasty job, but the worst casualties were usually a broken nose or a wrenched knee. *This* job was uniquely dangerous, but there was nobody in Hansen's section (and few enough in the Civic Patrol) who wasn't glad to have it.

The Solbarth Gang. It had to be Solbarth, the criminal whose genius was equalled by his ruthlessness. Inhuman ruthlessness, the news reports said; and this time the news reports were precisely correct.

One of Hansen's people was trying to get an update on the situation within 212 Kokori. Behind a Civic Patrol forcefield barricade parked a nondescript van. A SpyFly the size, shape, and color of a large cigar burred from within the vehicle.

The little reconnaissance drone was scarcely visible until

it arced to within a meter of the building's sidewall. There it exploded as ropes of scintillance.

Whoever was inside had an electronic flyswatter; which figured, if it was Solbarth.

A man jumped from a second-floor window, stumbled, and ran three steps toward the portable forcefield one of Hansen's units had set up at the intersection kitty-corner from the target building. A black sphincter dilated in the villains' protective screen. A blue-white flash cut the runner's legs from under him, long before he reached safety.

The body thrashed.

Just a civilian caught in something that was none of his business. Would've been smarter to hide under the bed until it was all over. But then, if Special Units opened up with the kind of firepower necessary to overwhelm the gang's force-field, the whole block would melt into a bubbling crater.

That wasn't going to happen.

"Support," Hansen said, cueing the artificial intelligence in his helmet. "Is the building's climate control in metal ducts?"

A green light winked even as the Commissioner's last syllable rose in an interrogative.

The AI had accessed the data from Central Records; probably out of Building Inspection, but the exact provenance of the information didn't matter. Every scrap of data about this building, its residents—and the villains believed to be holed up here—had been sucked into a huge electronic suspense file within seconds of when the shooting started. Any extant knowledge that Hansen might need waited at the tip of his tongue.

The trouble was, quite a lot of what Hansen needed to know would be available only in the after-action report on the operation; and Commissioner Hansen might or might not be alive to examine the data then.

"Top to Orange Three," he ordered, letting the AI punch him through the chatter of the unit he'd just watched launch the SpyFly. "Put one into the building's ventilation system. Use a One-Star."

The 1* class drones were old and slow, but they had double-capacity powerpacks and were rugged enough to air-drop with their lift fans shut down.

"Sir, they've turned off the air system 'n the louvers're down!" the Orange Three team leader replied in a voice half a tone higher than normal.

"Then it'll take the SpyFly a bloody while to burn through the louvers, won't it?" Hansen snarled. "So get on the bloody job!"

"Hang on, sir," his driver warned. The aircar bounced to a dynamic halt behind the forcefield barricade at the intersection.

A streak of flame washed from the villains' hideout. The portable forcefield pulsed like a rainbow, but it absorbed the burst without strain.

Regular police fired a sparkle of stun needles, but the temporary opening in the villains' forcefield had already closed. The Special Units teams held their fire the way they'd been ordered to do.

Polarized light cast a blue wash over everything on the other side of the barricade. The legless man halfway to the intersection had stopped twitching. Another plasma bolt licked from the far side of the building, silhouetting the roof moldings with its brief radiance.

Hansen glanced at the video loop running across the bottom of his visor. It displayed the sensor log of the patrolman who'd arrived to investigate a reported domestic disturbance.

The cop had been a little fellow and young, to judge from the image of him recorded in reflection from the building's front door as he entered. He was whistling something tuneless between his teeth. As he climbed the stairs, he checked the needle stunner in his holster.

He'd been a little nervous, but not nearly as nervous as he should've been.

It was all a mistake. The reported loud argument had been in District 9, not here in District 7. An administrative screwup that normally would've meant, at worst, that a family argument blossomed into violence because the uniformed man who could've stopped it had been sent to the wrong place.

No sign of a domestic argument now. Knuckles rapping on a doorpanel; *Who's there?* muffled by the thick panel, and "Civic Patrol! Open up!" sharply from the cop whose equipment was recording events and transmitting the log back to his district sub-station; standard operating procedure.

Maybe if the patrolman had been a little less forceful in his request—

But that was second-guessing the man on the spot, and Hansen wasn't going to speak ill of the dead.

The video image of the door opened. Before the figure within was more than a blur, the universe dissolved in a plasma flare that the victim didn't have time to understand.

Hansen got out of his vehicle. The air smelled burned, from the forcefield and the weapons the villains were using; from the hellfire dancing in the Commissioner's mind.

His jaws hurt. He'd been clenching them as he watched the patrolman die. Hansen's muttered order cleared his visor of both the remote and the recorded images, but the fatal plasma burst continued to blaze a dirty white in memory.

Bad luck for the cop, knocking on the wrong door. And very bad luck indeed for Solbarth.

Four Special Units personnel squatted behind the forcefield they'd stretched between their vehicles. Two sighted over plasma weapons; one had a wide-muzzled projectile launcher; and the fourth, the team leader, carried the forcefield controls, a pistol, and long knives in both of her boots. They were all dressed in light-scattering camouflage uniforms which blurred their outlines and hid anything that an opponent could use for an aiming point.

The team members kept their faces rigidly to the front, pretending they didn't know the Commissioner was standing behind them. "Pink Two to Top," Hansen heard the leader say. "Are we clear to fire?"

The question didn't come to Hansen through the commo net, because the Commissioner's AI blocked out all the idle chatter that would otherwise have distracted him from the real business of solving the problem.

Hansen stepped over to the team leader, put a hand on her shoulder, and said, "We'll get where we're going, Pink Two. Don't worry."

"Sorry, sir," one of the plasma gunners said, though the reason *he* thought he needed to apologize was beyond Hansen's understanding.

Nobody needed to apologize. No matter how good your training was, no matter how much on-line experience you had, there were going to be tics and glitches in a real crisis.

People said things, people forgot SOP . . . sometimes people shot when they shouldn't have, and even *that* was forgivable if you survived it.

Training went only so far. Situations like this went right down into the reptilian core of the brain.

With his fingers still resting on Pink Two's shoulder, Hansen said, "Support. Give me a fast three-sixty of the target site. Left side only."

Hansen's artificial intelligence began walking him visually around the apartment building. Images from other police personnel were remoted to the left half of the Commissioner's visor, changing every ten seconds to proceed around the site in a counterclockwise direction.

A patrolman in an apartment to Hansen's right poured a stream of stun needles toward the gang's hideout. There were brief sparkles on the forcefield and occasionally a puff of dust from the plastic facade. Raindrops would have been more effective than the one-gram needles were at this range.

On a roof halfway down the block, Special Units personnel stripped the tarpaulin from the 4-cm plasma weapon they'd just manhandled from an armored personnel carrier. Two other teams watched tensely from behind the forcefield they'd erected to shelter the gun installation. They knew the weapon could probably batter through the villains' protective screen; but they knew also that the sidescatter of powerful bolts hitting powerful armor was likely to incinerate every unshielded object within a kilometer of impact.

Ten seconds later. A white aircar picked out with gold braid skidded to a halt behind a forcefield manned by Civic Patrol personnel. Holloway, Chief of the Capital Police, got out. He was still trying to seal his bemedaled uniform blouse over his fat belly.

An aide lifted a pair of slug-throwing hunting rifles out of the car and handed one to Holloway. Both men aimed as a police technician spun narrow loopholes in the protective forcefield so that his superiors could fire at the hideout.

No one but Special Units personnel was permitted to use deadly force. No one.

The AI cycled to the next image around the circle. Hansen's mouth was open to bark an order that Holloway, even Holloway, would obey—*or else*—when his right eye saw a whorl gape in the villains' forcefield. Solbarth must be using tuned elements so that merely presenting a weapon opened his shield wide enough to fire. *That* sort of hardware was too expensive even for Special Units.

And the weapon being aimed in Hansen's direction this time wasn't a plasma gun.

"Watch it!" he screamed, and "Down!" to the personnel near him who thought their forcefield protected them from the villains' fire.

Hansen flattened, pushing the team leader out of her crouch and hoping the three men had sense enough to obey without asking questions. There was a flash from the momentary hole in Solbarth's protective bubble.

A ten-kilo war rocket arched down on a trail of thin smoke.

The missile skimmed the top of the police forcefield—which would have halted it harmlessly—and detonated in thunder on the pavement behind Hansen and his people.

The blast hurled the Commissioner's car—was the driver clear?—onto its side. The pavement shattered. Howling shards of missile casing pocked facades for twenty meters in every direction. Bits that struck the inner face of the forcefield hissed and melted as their kinetic energy was transformed into heat.

Hansen's ears rang. The men around him were all right, and his driver was getting out of the aircar with a dazed look on his face.

A rifle bullet whacked the hideout's facade and ricocheted over Hansen's head.

Hansen took a deep breath. "Top to all units," he said in a voice that rattled like tin in his own ears. "Cease firing. All units cease firing. I am Commissioner Hansen, and this site is under the jurisdiction of Special—"

Three bullets smacked the villains' forcefield where it bulged from one of the third-floor windows. The projectiles melted in showers of white sparks. The muzzle blasts of the rifles echoed down the corridor of building fronts like a burst of automatic fire.

"I say again, cease fire," Hansen ordered. "Special Units personnel, enforce my orders by whatever—"

The left half of Hansen's visor had cycled back to a view

of Chief Holloway just as the fat man's body rocked under the recoil of his powerful rifle. Hansen fully expected one of his people to stitch the Chief's ass with stun needles, but he hadn't said that.

Actually, he hadn't gotten the order completely out of his mouth before the back of Chief Holloway's limousine geysered metal and plastic, then collapsed in flames. Somebody from Special Units had put a plasma round into the vehicle.

Well, Hansen's personal motto was that no means were excessive if they got the job done. Holloway hurled the rifle away and curled up in a ball. His aide tried to shield the Chief's body, but the disparity in size of the men made the attempt ludicrous.

The delicate flicker of stun needles hitting the villains' forcefield stopped also.

Hansen stood up. A black spot in the center of a window spat plasma at him. He flinched as the bolt coruscated fifty centimeters from his face.

He drew his own pistol. "Pink Two," he said, wishing he could remember the woman's name. "Get ready to open the screen for me."

"You'll shoot, sir?" the team leader asked.

"For me, damn you!" Hansen shouted. "Me! Not a gun!"
He'd have to apologize later.

"Yessir."

He'd been this scared before, so scared that his palms sweated and muscle tremors made the fine hairs on the surface of his skin crawl. Sure, he'd been this scared.

But he'd never been *more* scared.

"Now," Hansen said very softly. He leaped forward as the forcefield collapsed momentarily to pass his body.

It was thirty meters to the front of the building. Hansen had covered half the distance in ten quick strides when a hole like Hell's anus spun in the bulging forcefield above him.

The Commissioner's pistol snapped two high-velocity projectiles through the opening before the villain within could fire. The mirror of the protective forcefield dulled momentarily as its inner face absorbed the plasma bolt triggered in a dying convulsion.

Hansen was doing *this* job because he wouldn't order any of his people to do it, and because it had to be him anyway.

But nobody in Special Units was better qualified to handle it, either.

Motes of plastic drifted in the sunlight beneath 212 Kokori, bits snapped from the facade by stun needles and shrapnel from the villains' own weaponry. They had one hell of an arsenal in there. This wasn't a police action, it was a war. . . . Or at any rate, it'd degenerate into a war if Hansen's try here failed.

Hansen looked back the way he'd come. Squat figures, mere shadows behind the polarized sheets of forcefields, waited with mechanical passivity.

He was panting, as much from tension as from the sprint. The villains' forcefield bulged from the windows above him. It was driven hard enough to reflect light, not merely shadow it. Solbarth must have his own fusion generator. . . .

But even Solbarth couldn't fight the Consensus.

"Support," Hansen said. "Give me a lower-quadrant remote from the four-centimeter's guns—"

The sight picture, broad field in acquisition mode, from the crew-served weapon directly across from 212 inset a quarter of Hansen's visor. He could see himself as a tiny figure in the corner of the image, staring at the bulging fortress above him.

"—ight," Hansen's mouth said, completing the order that the AI had already obeyed.

He heard the *crack!* of a plasma weapon firing somewhere from the back of the building, but there was no time to worry about that now.

"Solbarth!" he shouted. He tilted his visor up, losing the panoramic image that he'd need for warning if—

"Solbarth!" Hansen shouted again, his voice no longer muffled by the shield in front of it. "This is Commissioner Hansen. I'm giving you a chance."

"Kommissar?" said the voice that Hansen's artificial intelligence had passed to his ear. "Orange Three. We've got the SpyFly in position outside the last set of louvers. Do you want us to burn through?"

"We don't need a chance from you, Hansen," called a cold, clear voice from a window on the third floor. "You'll be old and gray before we run out of supplies."

"Orange Three, not yet," Hansen muttered. He desper-

ately wanted images from within the hideout, but he knew
that this reconnaissance drone would be zapped like the others if it left its protective screen of metal too soon.

Hansen cocked his visor at a 45° angle, open enough for
him to shout past it. He peered at the distorted quadrant of
panorama—which his AI immediately reconfigured to meet
his master's needs.

And why the hell hadn't he been smart enough to *tell* the
machine to do that?

"Solbarth, I'm offering you your lives," Hansen said. He
could hear other muffled voices from the lower floors of 212
Kokori, civilians praying or weeping into their shielding
hands. "It's more than—"

The helmet beeped to warn Hansen and flashed a red caret
over the remoted image on his visor, but his gunhand was
already rising, pointing—taking up the slack on the trigger.
An arm thrust a wide-mouthed mob gun through the window
five meters above the Commissioner's head.

Hansen fired twice. The villain's weapon rang and bounced
off the bloody transom before dropping to the street. There
was a bullet hole through its bell muzzle, and a separate hole
through the wrist which the screaming gunman jerked back
within the forcefield.

"You won't open *this* can with the toys you've brought out
so far, Hansen," Solbarth said, as calmly as if the wounded
man's whimpering was only the whisper of wind. "When you
do requisition what you'd require . . . if you do . . . then this
whole district will be radioactive for a decade."

The bare skin of Hansen's hand and chin stung from the
whiplash muzzle blasts of his pistol. The shadows of Special
Units stirred restively behind their forcefields.

"Solbarth," he called, "if you don't surrender to me *now*,
I'll have the building cut away beneath you. For all I know,
your forcefield may hold; but that won't matter to you, because you and everything else inside the field are going to
be shaking around like the beans in a maraca as you drop into
the sub-basement."

The silence was so deep that Hansen could feel the pulse
of the villains' forcefield through the fabric of the building.

"The lower floors are full of civilians," Solbarth said.
Hansen thought he heard a tremor of color in the gang lead-

er's voice, though 'emotion' would have been too strong a word for it.

"Solbarth," Hansen said, "I know you . . . and you know me. This is a Special Units operation. I answer to *no one* until it's complete. And I promise you, Solbarth, that I'll do exactly what I told you I'd do."

Very softly, almost subvocalizing, he added, "Orange Three, go ahead. Support, switch my remote."

"A starship," the cold voice demanded. "A starship and your word that we'll be allowed to take it and leave, Hansen."

"Your lives, Solbarth," the Commissioner repeated flatly. "And the rest of your lives to spend on whatever hellhole or prison asteroid the Consensus chooses to send you. But I promise you your lives."

The remote quadrant of Hansen's visor suddenly melted into an image of the gang's hideout. All the interior walls of the third story had been removed. The cases of food and water suggested that Solbarth hadn't been entirely bluffing when he'd said they could withstand a siege.

Not years, though. Not the dozen males and three females still moving.

A corpse had been dragged into the center of the room. The moaning man, his right hand hanging by a scrap of skin, still huddled beneath the window at which Hansen had shot him.

The female who'd just gotten up from the protective-systems console to join the argument was a Mirzathian, skeletally thin and over two meters tall. The SpyFly whose sensors were recording the scene made a bright pip on the holographic screen the Mirzathian was supposed to be minding. The touch of a key could have pulsed the drone's electronics fatally, but neither the Mirzathian nor any of the other gang members had time to spend on that now.

Solbarth was a male of average height, with a pale complexion and features of perfect beauty. He was wearing a loose-fitting suit of rather better quality than the clothing of most residents of District 7. He moved languidly, but Hansen's practiced eye could still identify the bulge of a pistol high on Solbarth's right hip.

When Hansen wore a business suit, that was where his own holster rode.

"He won't really spare us!" the Mirzathian shouted.

"He won't really blast all them civvies!" a heavy man with a shoulder-stocked plasma weapon boomed simultaneously.

"He didn't come here," Solbarth said mildly, "*here*—" he gestured down in the direction of Hansen, standing beneath the overhang "—to lie to us. He's Hansen, and he's quite mad . . . but I think he's telling the truth."

"Look, whadda we got to lose?" whined another gunman. "Look, they blast us or we wind up drinkin' our own piss 'n starvin', right? So whadda they do to us worse if we *do* chuck it in now?"

"Wait," said Solbarth.

He leaned closer to the window above Hansen and called, "Commissioner, there's something that you don't know about me. How can I trust—"

"I don't know that you're an android, Solbarth?" Hansen said. His words echoed uneasily, in his ears and weakly through the radio link from the SpyFly that had penetrated the hideout. "Sure I do. The offer stands."

"*You* promise," Solbarth said forcefully. "But the Consensus wipes androids that vary from parameters, Hansen. You can't promise for the Consensus."

Hansen wiped the lower half of his face with his left hand. Sweat glistened on his skin, but his mouth was as dry as the pavement.

"Solbarth," he said, "you're a murdering bastard and I'd've strangled you with my own hands if I could. But I'm Hansen, I'm Special Units, and here I'm in charge. For this moment, I *am* all twelve hundred worlds of the Consensus."

He took a deep breath. "They can fire me for making this deal if they like. But the Consensus will stand by my deal . . . or by god, Solbarth, the Consensus will deal with me. On my honor."

The image of Solbarth turned to face his henchmen. "I think," he said with delicate insouciance, "that we should take the offer."

"*I* say you're fucking crazy!" the Mirzathian snarled. She snatched up an antitank launcher and leaned toward the window.

Hansen wasn't sure he'd ever seen a man draw and fire as swiftly as Solbarth did . . . though Solbarth wasn't technically a man. The contents of the Mirzathian's skull splashed the inner face of the forcefield and sputtered. With their velocity scrubbed away, bits of bone and fried blood tumbled out the window and fluttered past Hansen to the sidewalk.

There were two more shots from within the hideout; the heavy man collapsed around the plasma weapon cradled in his arms. Either he'd been planning to use it, or he'd looked like he had . . . or, not improbably, Solbarth was making a point to the remainder of his gang in the most vivid fashion possible.

Other weapons clattered to the floor of the hideout. A small man covered his face with his hands and cried, "I'm clean! I'm clean! Don't shoot me!"

"Hansen!" Solbarth called without turning his eyes from his fellow villains. "We accept your offer. Warn your men that we're coming out!"

The android's left hand keyed a series of commands into the protective-systems console. The window above Hansen gave an electronic whine. The forcefield went translucent an instant before it vanished altogether.

"All units, hold your fire," Hansen said. "The subjects are surrendering. I repeat, the subjects are surrendering. Blue teams, prepare to secure the prisoners. Orange teams, be ready to move in with the medical staff. There's a wounded prisoner, and we won't know about the residents here until we check."

The SpyFly showed Solbarth gesturing the last of his subordinates down the stairs with a negligent wave of his pistol. The slim android set the weapon carefully on the floor, bowed toward the closed heating duct whose paint had blistered when the SpyFly burned through a hole for its sensors, and left the room.

Hansen couldn't tell whether or not the bow was ironic. Perhaps not.

"Blue teams," Hansen said, "I want you to accompany the prisoners to the detention center after you turn them over to the Civic Patrol. There'll be no accidents along the way."

He swallowed. "Whatever it takes, there'll be no accidents."

Six Special Units personnel jogged from their positions in

the building across Kokori Street. They held both nets and electronic restraints.

The first of Solbarth's men poked his head through the entrance door. His mouth was bent into a smile like the rictus of the last stages of tetanus, and his eyes were glazed with fear. Blue One gestured to the villain as though he were a dog to be petted.

The man glanced aside at Hansen, then bolted into the arms of the personnel waiting to immobilize him. A second gang member scuttled out behind the first.

Hansen was still holding his pistol. He tried to holster it, but his hand was shaking too much for him to manage that operation. Swearing under his breath, he set the weapon down on the sidewalk in front of him and clasped his hands together.

There was commotion at the intersection where Hansen's car lay on its side, but he couldn't tell what was happening since the portable forcefields were still—properly—in place.

Chief Holloway waddled down Kokori Street from the other direction, at the head of a contingent of Civic Patrolmen. Holloway's white uniform was streaked and blackened. His face was maroon. Blood pressure might prove fatal though the nearby plasma bolt had not.

Most of the villains had left the building. Blue One was giving crisp orders to the Civic Patrolmen arriving to accept prisoners cocooned in restraining nets. Some civilians poked their heads from the lower-floor windows, able now to savor the adventure they'd survived . . . and how close it'd been, might they never know!

Hansen was tired. He was as tired as he ever remembered being.

"Kommissar!" cried the team leader whose concern was obvious despite compression of the radio signal and the minute speakers in Hansen's helmet. "This is Pink Two, and something's—"

The warning crunched to silence, though Hansen could vaguely hear Pink Two continuing to shout behind the barrier.

"Commissioner Hansen," said a voice more mechanical than any machine needed to be in a day that AIs could manufacture surds and sonants with greater life than those of any rhetoric teacher. "You are summoned by the Consensus."

Something—a spindle of black *fuzz*, taller than a man—drifted through the forcefield blocking the intersection. There was another spindle beside the first.

Hansen had never seen anything like them.

The portable forcefield sputtered and vanished.

"Not now," Hansen said. The sweat on his palms was suddenly cold. "I've got to—"

Hansen's visor went opaque. His helmet was dead, screens and speakers alike. He took the helmet off.

His hands no longer shook. He didn't glance down toward his pistol, but his toe, with a motion that might have been only a twitch, located the weapon precisely.

Solbarth stepped from the entranceway. The android froze, his blank eyes taking in Hansen and the creatures which slid toward the Commissioner at a walking pace.

The two spindles were hazily transparent. An aircar—Hansen's own aircar, torn but upright again—drifted along behind the creatures, a hand's breadth above the pavement.

No one was aboard the vehicle. Krupchak, the driver, gaped at Hansen from beside the personnel of Pink Two.

"Commissioner Hansen, please get in the car," said the mechanical voice.

It sounded exactly as it had before, even though Hansen was no longer wearing his helmet.

"I had the authority at this site," Hansen said hoarsely. "You have no grounds to remove me without a hearing."

The spindles moved to either side of him. Hansen's skin tingled. Close up they still looked transparent, but he thought he saw something *in* the black tendrils as well as between them.

The vehicle's power door opened. "Commissioner Hansen," the voice repeated, "please get in the car."

Hansen obeyed, shifting his foot slightly so that he didn't scuff the pistol. One of his people would take care of it. . . .

Fifty meters away, Chief Holloway licked his lips. He looked as though he were watching a pornographic display.

The door shut after Hansen. The two spindles drifted through the plastic panels, into the driver's compartment. Hansen didn't see them fold or shrink, but their peaks didn't quite brush the vehicle's blast-pocked headliner.

"Sir, should we—" shouted one of the Special Units personnel as he leaned from a roof with his plasma weapon half-pointed.

"No!" Hansen cried. He stuck his head out the shattered side window and shouted, "No, everybody get on with your duties."

He didn't know what was going on, but he knew that it wouldn't be helped if his own people started shooting.

The aircar slid in a tight circle and accelerated as it started to rise.

"I have full authority from the Consensus for everything I've done here," Hansen said, knowing that in truth, he'd always claimed whatever authority he needed to get a job done and trusted that he could make it stick after the fact.

That had always worked. Until now.

"The Consensus is not interested in your actions here, Commissioner Hansen," said the voice. The words sounded in the Commissioner's mind, seeming to have nothing to do with the creatures which were escorting him. "The Consensus has need of you on a planet called Northworld."

The car had risen to 300 meters and was moving at a speed that made the wind howl through the many shrapnel holes. Other air traffic was avoiding their arrow-straight rush.

Hansen frowned. "What's Northworld?" he muttered.

The creatures—or the voice—must have been able to hear him despite wind noise, because Hansen's mind rasped with the words, "The Consensus will inform you of what you need to know, Commissioner Hansen. In good time."

For the first time in his life, Commissioner Nils Hansen realized that there might be more to the Consensus of Worlds than simply the bureaucracy of control of which he himself was a part.

≡ 2 ≡

NORTH CAME OUT of the Matrix, gasping and wheezing as he always did.

Hanging in the Matrix, the world that connected the Eight Worlds, was like drowning in ice water. The infinite series of minute events forced itself into his being, through him; chilling his flesh, freezing him, threatening to grind *him* out of existence in an avalanche of nine-times-simultaneous discrete realities.

It would almost be better not to be a god.

"But that is a lie, North," said Dowson with the dry precision which was all that remained to him since emotion had been cut out of him with his body.

"Who are you to speak of truth and lies, Dowson?" North said. "All you know are facts."

"Facts are all there is to know, North," replied the disembodied brain suspended in a vat of nutrient. The words washed across North to ring coldly within his skull, but they were not as cold as the Matrix. . . .

He shuddered again and looked up at the roof of his palace, shards of sunlight frozen into groins and vaulting that could cover an army.

"There's another one coming," North said. "From outside, from the Consensus."

The liquid flowing through Dowson's vat kept up the same soft susurrus it had whispered for ages. "What will you do with these?" asked the non-voice as colored waves which sprang from a cone of ice beside the vat. "Find them a plane of their own?"

"There *are* no unoccupied planes, Dowson!"

"None that you know of, North," the brain replied. "None that I know of either."

For a moment, North imagined that the pause was one of sadness, but Dowson's words were as emotionless as ever when he continued, "Send them to the lizardmen, then. Let them destroy one another."

North's laughter bellowed out in response to the bitter joke. The sunlit building trembled and quivered with shadows. North stretched his long, sinewy arms high above his head, and the air cleared.

"The others will need to know," Dowson warned.

"The others will want to know," North corrected. "I'll summon them."

His right hand twisted in the air. Motes of light sprang away as though condensing from the atmosphere; a score of sparkling blips that drifted in widening circles until they touched the walls of the palace, spat, and vanished on their missions.

"They're only sending one this time," North said, trying to control the shudder which remembering the Matrix induced in him. "A man."

"You'll kill him?" Dowson asked, carelessly, uncaring.

"His name is Hansen," said North. "And he will serve my purposes."

≡ 3 ≡

HANSEN'S CAR WAS speeding toward a large building on what had been the outskirts of the capital twenty years before. Now it was a bland residential district, not dissimilar to the one from which Solbarth had spun his webs of theft and murder.

The building was marked as Consensus property on the maps Hansen had viewed in the course of his duties, but there were many Consensus buildings in any planetary capital. A warehouse, Hansen had thought; and he would still think the great three-story block was a warehouse, except—

Except that two *creatures* had ordered the Commissioner of Special Units into an aircar that they were driving straight into the front wall of the building.

Hansen opened his mouth to protest—and closed it again, because there was nothing he could say that the spindles didn't know already.

The warehouse was an old one, built of clay and a plasticizer which hardened after extrusion. That technique created a solid structure of surpassing ugliness even when new.

The aircar was about to hit the dark dun building at 200 kph. The smear Hansen made would scarcely be distinguishable from the stains and earth tones already an indelible part of the wall's texture.

He forced his muscles to relax. So be it. A pedestrian in the street looked up in amazement.

The aircar shot through the 'wall.' Hansen felt a momentary chill. They were in a lighted tunnel whose circular sides made the drive fans rumble.

"Where are we?" Hansen demanded. The noise of the damaged car was even worse in this enclosure than it had been in the open air, but he knew the spindles could hear him if they wanted to.

No answer rang in his mind. They shot past a pair of cross-tunnels. Half a dozen workmen carrying unrecognizable tools glanced up at the aircar. One of the faces turned toward Hansen was inhuman: blue, scaled, and as expressionless as those of its companions.

"Where are we *going*?" Hansen cried. He didn't even expect an answer.

He'd been a powerful man, a few minutes ago. In some ways—in some circumstances—the most powerful man on Annunciation.

He looked at the things beside him in the car and wondered whether any man in the Consensus really had power.

The spindles were shrinking. When Hansen first saw the creatures, they had been taller than he was; now they were only about the length of his thigh. They sputtered like electronics on the verge of failure, and the scenes within the fabric of their bodies were becoming increasingly clear.

Hansen looked away.

The tunnel ended in a white-tiled rotunda which appeared so abruptly that Hansen felt the car braking before his eyes focused on the change in scenery. Two figures waited for them, both human—

Not human. Both of the figures were male androids. One was as beautiful as the dawn, while the other was a squat, hideous travesty of humanity with thick, twisted limbs. They might very well have come out of the same production batch.

The rotunda had a high, domed ceiling. There were eight archways leading from it—all of them closed by bronze doors, including the arch by which the aircar had just entered.

"Please get out, Commissioner Hansen," said the voice in Hansen's skull. The aircar bobbled a few centimeters above the floor instead of settling with the shut-down fans.

"This way, please, sir," said the handsome android. He had to shout to be heard over the racket the car made.

The android was speaking with his mouth. At least *that* was a change for the better. . . .

Hansen got out of the vehicle. It sped off into—through—another doorway.

The spindles who'd escorted the Commissioner had shrunk

to hand's breadth height. They were giving off sounds of sizzling, fiery anger as they disappeared.

The rotunda was almost silent when they and the aircar
were gone.

"This will only take a moment, sir," said the misshapen
android, raising the flared nozzle of the apparatus he carried.
"Please hold still."

"What are you—"

"Please hold still," said the handsome android as the nozzle hissed an opalescent bubble which wobbled and grew
without detaching itself from the apparatus. The android
reached around Hansen and guided the edges of the bubble
like a couturier with a swatch of cloth.

"Now, sir," said the ugly android, "if you'll step carefully
onto this . . . ?"

Hansen lifted his feet so that he was standing on the doubled thickness of the bubble's lower edge.

He understood now. They were blowing him a temporary
atmosphere suit, a membrane of polarized permeability. Oxygen could pass in, while carbon dioxide and other waste
gasses passed out no matter what the composition of the encircling atmosphere.

A useful tool for chemical emergencies or even fires, though
the membrane didn't block heat. Temporary suits could keep
people alive in hard vacuum for as long as the oxygen level
within the bubble remained at a breathable level.

The hideous android smiled as he continued to extrude the
material. Hansen supposed the expression was meant to be
friendly.

The handsome attendant took a palm-sized device from his
belt. He gathered the flattened bubble over Hansen's head in
his slim hands and touched the edges with the tool, mating
them with a faint sputter.

The seam was a quiver of light when Hansen moved and
made the bubble tremble. His mind told him falsely that his
lungs had to struggle to breathe. He controlled his expression, but he could feel his heart rate rise.

"That's right, sir," said the ugly attendant. "Now, if you'll
just walk this way . . . ?"

The attendant had shut off his apparatus. Now he gestured
toward one of the archways. His skin had the utter pallor that

some androids tried to conceal with cosmetics; but whatever his skin color, this creature couldn't have been anything that sprang from a human womb.

Hansen obeyed, walking deliberately so that the flexible membrane could billow ahead of his motion. He could see and hear normally, except for a slight shimmer in the air and the hint of distortion at the seam.

The Commissioner's senses were overloaded with hormones from the gunfight, from the capture that should have been the crown of his career no matter how much longer he served the Consensus—

From all that had happened since.

"Why is this happening to me?" Hansen shouted. "Why are you doing this?"

The handsome attendant shook his head blandly. He'd put the sealing device back into its belt pouch. "Don't worry, sir," he said. "Just step through the portal."

Would the bronze doorleaves open, or would—

Hansen stepped through what had seemed to be solid metal. There was an instant of chill. He thought he saw the crystalline pattern of the atoms themselves, but then he was through the door and standing in a darkness more intense than that of the core of his brain.

Light bloomed, a flush of pink so faint that for an instant Hansen thought the illumination was an accident of his optic nerves—synapses tripping to relieve the oppressive black.

The color was real. He could see again.

Almost-color sublimed in all directions from a stalagmite of ice that grew out of a floor as smooth as a bearing race. Hansen couldn't see any walls, but the ball of light—fading as it expanded—swelled across a dozen other cones of ice.

Hansen braced himself. When the pink glow touched him, a voice in his mind said, "There has been a crime, Commissioner Hansen."

Other stalagmites were scaling away drifts of color as weak as the nimbus of sunlight about a butterfly's wings. Each was a separate pastel, each so pale that only by comparison could they be differentiated.

"I don't belong here!" Hansen cried. "If there's been a crime, let me out of here and I'll deal with it."

Hansen could see that there was no door behind him now, nothing but vacancy and a plain like a mirror.

Green ambiance washed over him. "There was a world," said a different voice in his mind, mellifluous and a trifle arch. "It had been charted. Humans could live there, we thought—"

Orange light. A voice like a whip. "The Consensus thought. Captain Rolls led a unit to do a final examination. They—"

Pink neutrality again: "They vanished. A crime has been committed."

Motes of light drifted upward like fog without finding a ceiling. Hansen tested the floor with his toes. It was solid, unyielding. It felt cold, even through his boots and the double insulating layers of his airsuit.

Almost all of the cones were glowing now as they discharged their burdens of thought and near-light.

"Listen and learn, Commissioner Hansen," said blue certainty in the Commissioner's mind. "We sent another team under Captain North, trusted personnel who had dealt with crises on a dozen other worlds to be colonized. Faithful—"

"Faithful servants of the Consensus," quivered a red voice. It reminded Hansen of the lip-smacking tones of politicians who demanded tough measures but who'd never stood in an alley after a firefight and realized how little there was to a human being after the life goes out of him. "North had cleansed worlds, seeded them—changed weather patterns, raised continents, crushed all opposition to the Con—"

"The Consensus," whispered violet. "North reported that he had succeeded again, that we should send a colony at once, that all was prepared for settlement. He said that we should call the planet Northworld, that it was his right that the planet receive his name."

Blue fog drifted over Hansen. "We sent the colony, because—"

"—because he was a faithful servant," rejoined the red tones. "Ruthless and skillful, a servant to the needs of the Consensus. But North and his team had not returned from the planet, as they reported, and the new colony—"

"The planet vanished," said pink light. "There has been

a crime, Commissioner Hansen. The colony has been stolen, the planet has been stolen."

"Northworld has been stolen," thundered Hansen's mind in the organ tones of all dozen shades of light at once. "You will determine why, and you will cure the problem."

The plain on which Hansen stood was boundless, but he no longer thought it was empty. There were shapes in the far distance, hinted bulks as huge as storms on a gas giant.

"This is nothing to do with me," Hansen cried with fatalistic recklessness. "The colony wasn't sent from Annunciation, North wasn't—*was he?*—from here. I have my duties. Let me return to my duties."

Light like yellow sunshine washed over him. If glaciers could laugh, the sensation in Hansen's mind would have been that cold laughter. "Your duties are to the Consensus, Commissioner Hansen," said a voice. "The Consensus demands that you deal with this event. You have been chosen from among—"

"From among many," said violet light. "From among all the planets of the Consensus, from all the peoples. . . ."

"Records have been searched," said the cold blue voice. "The Lomeri settled the world in past ages—"

"The lizardfolk settled Northworld in past ages," said pink, "but no Lomeri were there when the exploration unit arrived. There has been—"

"There has been a crime, Commissioner Hansen," purred a pastel so faint that it might have been either brown or mauve. "When Rolls' exploration unit landed, they found a waterworld with necklaces of islands—"

"Island necklaces and no other land," the yellow light said. "But North reported a world with forty-six percent of the surface area land."

"And now the world is gone and North is gone, and they have taken with them the colony," said pink. "There has been a crime, and you must solve it—"

"*Cure* the crime," insisted the red voice. "Deal with the criminals with the full rigor of the Consensus, for the will of the Consensus is the law of the universe—"

"For all the universe except Northworld," resumed blue. "*That* world does not recognize the Consensus, nor do the Lomeri—"

"The Lomeri who were lizards and who have been dust," rasped the orange voice, "for a thousand millennia before there were men. And before the Lomeri there were other settlements, we are sure of it—"

"The Consensus is sure," whispered violet, "though that past is a far past even for the Consensus."

"Far even for us . . . ," the voices of color murmured in unison.

Hansen felt the chamber shiver like a sigh. His feet were becoming cold, and it was not merely his imagination that the membrane around him sagged. It was voiding the carbon dioxide exhaled without a corresponding influx of oxygen.

"This isn't my job," Hansen said. "I don't—"

He paused. He was at the center of a glowing ambiance that continued to expand indefinitely, like the ball of plasma generated by a nuclear weapon between the stars.

"Send a fleet, s-sirs," he continued, afraid to choose a term for the entities which spoke here with him. "I'm a man, a cop. I don't find planets. You need a—"

"There was a fleet," said a voice as scales of light shimmered away from the brown/mauve stalagmite. "A fleet and a fleet—"

"—and a fleet," echoed the pink voice. "Humans in the first fleet, and they vanished—"

"Though drones," said blue, "had penetrated the area where Northworld should have been, and the drones reported nothing. Therefore we sent—"

"The Consensus sent a second fleet," said the red voice, "crewed by androids and ready to destroy anything it met in the dead zone, the region—"

"The region that had flouted our majesty, our Consensus," resumed the violet voice. "And when the androids vanished without warning, without report, we sent a third fleet that was a great machine in itself but which lived and thought, though—"

"Though not as men think, and not part of the Consensus," chuckled the yellow voice. "And it vanished, Commissioner Hansen, as though it had never been. . . . Though machines that are no more than machines ignore the area and pass through it."

Hansen felt the pressure of thoughts, of words, all around

him. The airsuit was no protection. His whole body was becoming numb.

"Fleets have failed," said the red light, "so we are sending you. We will arm you, Commissioner Hansen—"

"But the fleets were armed," shivered tones of deep green light. "You will be alone, so you may penetrate the defenses unnoticed—"

"Penetrate the mystery . . . ," brown/mauve murmured.

"You are the best for the task," boomed all the colors together. "On all the planets of the Consensus, in all the Consensus."

You are resourceful/Commissioner Hansen is resourceful/ The Kommissar is resourceful, rasped/purred/said the voices pounding Hansen's mind.

And then, in a single thought so smooth and steely that it could have been Hansen's own—and perhaps it *was* Hansen's own thought—

"Commissioner Nils Hansen will execute the will of the Consensus. . . ."

≡ 4 ≡

THE LIGHT THROUGH the varied crystalline roofplanes was brilliant without being dazzling. Some of the score of figures seated around the walls used the rays to ornament themselves; others formed the light into shrouds and hulked as shadows within opalescent beauty that hid their features better than darkness could have done.

North sat in the high seat and glowered at his peers. His left eye didn't track with his right; there were limits to power, even North's power, and the freezing paths of the Matrix had exacted a price as he learned them.

"This latest probe by the outsiders doesn't matter," said Rolls from his place near the doorway. He was almost as tall as North and enough heavier than the man in the high seat to look soft . . . until one looked more closely. "Any of us can take care of that—"

"My *pleasure*," said Rao. A smile of anticipation licked over his broad, dark face.

The curtain of light beside Rao rinsed away for a moment as Ngoya reached over to stroke her husband's thick wrist and silence him. Rao wasn't interested in—wasn't capable of understanding—what Rolls and many others of the team regarded as major issues. Ngoya was often embarrassed for her husband, since she in turn failed to see that Rao's single-minded simplicity was also his greatest strength.

"What matters," said Miyoko, pointing an index finger at North to emphasize her words, "is the threat to Diamond. You can't think of sending this invader to Diamond until we at least understand—"

"We don't *know* there's a threat," objected Saburo, not so much in disagreement as to calm his sister. He glanced uneasily at North, trying to read meaning into the craggy patience of the man who had led both his own team and the exploration unit of which Saburo was a member ever since—

But 'since' implied duration. Saburo composed his mind, then his face, and nodded apology to Rolls.

"There is a threat to Diamond," said Rolls, "whether or not we can see where it comes from."

He looked up at North, then across the hall to Eisner, and continued, "I'll admit that *I* can't see the source of the threat."

Eisner nodded her crisp agreement; North and North's face said nothing.

"I don't see what the problem is," Penny said. "I don't see why we're here at all."

Penny was playing with her appearance. As she spoke, she changed from a petite redhead in her early twenties to a tall, black-haired beauty whose face promised experience as well as passion . . . and back again to the redhead. A curtain of light provided a mirror, and the jewel on Penny's breast glowed with the power it gave her desires.

"On Diamond," Eisner said, in another of the attempts to inform which exasperated her fellows as much as Penny's care of her physical form bothered Eisner, "the inhabitants—"

"Yes, yes, I know," Penny snapped, briefly flirting with an older image, still redheaded. "They're having nightmares, terrible nightmares, and that's all very sad—but there *can't* be anything really wrong going to happen with them, because we're the only ones who can touch them or Ruby."

She looked around the room challengingly. "And if we did, the balance would fail, and we'd all—"

Penny made a moue of distaste and a dismissive gesture with fingers which for the moment were long and aristocratic. "Not that anybody would *do* that."

Fortin stretched and smiled. His white skin and perfect features were a legacy of his android mother, but the twisted subtlety of his mind was his own . . . if not from the genes of North his father.

"Who can fault the wisdom of our Penny?" Fortin said.

His lilting sarcasm cut all the deeper because what Penny said *was* true, though none of them doubted the reality of the danger except Penny, who didn't care; and Rao, who couldn't imagine it; and Dowson, who saw no threat in the Matrix and who lacked the fleshly baggage of emotions from which to create a hobgoblin that the data didn't support.

"I still don't think we should chance setting an intruder down in Diamond until we have a better idea of what's going on," Rolls said calmly.

"Of course," said Eisner as much to herself as to the assembly, "if the intruder were put in Diamond, we might learn more about the threat—"

"We might learn he *was* the threat!" Miyoko snapped. "Put him in Ruby. They'll take care of him!"

"Or set him on the plane of the Lomeri," her brother added. "So long as he's coming from outside the Matrix, we have absolute control of his destination. It makes no sense to take a risk—" he nodded to Miyoko "—even though the risk is still speculative."

"We'll set the intruder in Diamond," said North, speaking for the first time during the assembly he had called, "because only in Diamond can we be sure that all of his weapons will be stripped from him—" he smiled "—without harm."

"What do we care about hurting him?" Rao asked. "I mean, it's all right with me, but he's just an outsider. Isn't he?"

He looked around his fellows to make sure that there wasn't some point he had missed. Ngoya patted his arm.

North nodded. "I understand your position, my friend," he said, "but I've seen far enough into the Matrix to be sure that this Hansen is no threat to Diamond."

"But still—" said Miyoko.

"And I," North continued, "have my own reasons for wanting him unharmed for the time. Surely *I* needn't be the one to apologize for not killing, eh?"

"Well, do what you want, then," said Penny, who had finally fixed on slight, red-haired youthfulness. "You're going to anyway. I don't see why you even bothered to call us here."

Fortin began to laugh, because Penny was again perfectly correct. . . .

Rolls waited to meet Eisner in the doorway of North's palace as they left the assembly. She smiled at him, but the expression went no deeper than her thin lips.

"He sees something in the Matrix," she said, flicking her head back to indicate their leader and late host. "Do you?"

Eisner's hair was the color of a gray-draggled mouse; a few wisps which had escaped from her tight bun wobbled abstractedly.

Rolls shrugged. "North plays games," he said. "If there were something to see, you or I would know it. But still. . . ."

Neither of them spoke for a moment. Their eyes glanced over their fellows leaving the assembly; some of them concerned, some not.

Rao had hitched to his cart a pair of frilled ceratopsians from the plane where the Lomeri ruled. Most of the beasts which whim led others to ride or drive gave the dinosaurs a wide berth, but Saburo's huge hoglike dinohyid exchanged angry grunts and foot-stampings with Rao's much larger animals.

Eisner nodded. "Good day," she said and turned.

"Let me take you back," Rolls said. "You don't need to walk."

"I don't *need* to do anything," the woman corrected crisply. "None of us do." Eisner was thin and looked small at the moment, but only Rao and North failed to shrink when they stood next to Rolls.

"But yes," she added. "All right, I don't need to walk."

Rolls whickered to his giant stag and let it nuzzle his hand for a moment before he mounted. The beast had cast its horns and looked oddly naked. Still, it was awkward to bridle a creature whose horns spread a meter and a half to either side.

Everything was whim—for Rolls, for all of them since North had discovered the turning of the Matrix which gave them each whatever they most wanted. . . .

Rolls leaned over and lifted Eisner up ahead of him. The stag's spine was higher and sharper than a horse's, so the saddleframe had to be built out stiffly to give a comfortable seat. Horses were better adapted as riding animals, aircars were a far more efficient way to get around; but the most *practical* means of transportation for Rolls, for any of them, was the choice that provided the most amusement—and a practical level of aggravation.

It had been hard at first to imagine that there were any negative aspects to godlike power.

Eisner tried to straddle the spine the way Rolls did, but he turned her side-saddle and put his arm around the small of her waist to support her. She met his eyes and said coolly, "Still your games, Rolls? You might have learned by now."

Rolls shrugged. "The saddle was designed for me, so you'll find this more comfortable, Eisner," he said. "More practical, if you wish."

He clucked to the stag. It turned obediently and slid by the fourth stride into the long-legged canter that Rolls found its most comfortable pace.

Eisner sniffed, but she didn't object further to Rolls' touch. Neither did her abdominal muscles soften beneath his hand.

Rolls kept the contact well within the bounds of what was necessary for the task. His easy-going charm was effective because a real concern for others underlay it.

Rolls smiled to himself. One might almost say that concern for others ruled him.

The grassland swept by beneath the stag's measured paces. The rounded roofline of Eisner's palace appeared in the near distance.

"Do you remember," Rolls said, "when duration had meaning?"

Eisner shifted to meet his eyes; her left thigh slid over his. "Time still has meaning, Rolls," she said. "Time means everything dies. Even us. . . ."

Eisner had looked older than her years when Rolls' unit arrived on the planet it was to survey. Power had not given her youth, neither in her face nor in the mind which, more than age, had shaped the lines of that face.

Obedient to its training rather than specific command, the stag drew up before Eisner's palace, a windowless dome. Rolls held out an arm like a steel bar to support the woman as she lowered herself to the ground.

She looked up at him and said, "We created Diamond and Ruby as bubble universes, bound into the Matrix by our united minds."

Rolls nodded. "A whim," he said. "A desire to create the perfection that we—"

He swung his leg over the saddle and lowered himself beside Eisner. "—fail to achieve in ourselves."

Rolls pretended to be unaware of the wariness in the woman's eyes at the implication that he intended to enter her palace.

She grimaced. "All right," she said and stepped toward the door. It opened in response to her presence. Eisner kept no human servants.

"If one of *us* destroys Diamond," she continued, "our minds fall out of balance with the Matrix and . . . All of us. But only we can harm Diamond."

"If that were the case," Rolls said as he ducked to follow Eisner, "then Diamond wouldn't be in any danger. As perhaps it is not."

Though the ceilings within Eisner's dwelling were full height, the woman had pointedly constructed the door transom to clear her head by a centimeter. Eisner had few visitors; and, she would have said, little need for them.

"There's Fortin," Eisner said as she turned. "Fortin is insane." The door behind Rolls remained open, a reminder and invitation to him to leave.

"Fortin is very clever," Rolls said. "And yes, he's usually destructively clever. But he doesn't want to die before his time, Eisner. All our time."

He looked at the books, racked in a jumble of varied sizes and bindings. Computers were a better way to access information, and the Matrix itself was all knowledge if one had the patience to prowl its twisted, freezing pathways. Eisner used both, constantly, because there was no end to learning . . . but books were a symbol, and symbols had a particular reality here on Northworld.

"There's something we don't see . . . ," Eisner murmured.

"We're changing, Eisner," the man said as he watched his hostess through the corners of his eyes.

"We don't change," Eisner snapped, crossing her arms over her chest as she turned her back on Rolls. Her breasts, as unremarkable as her face and hair, were hidden beneath the loose folds of the coveralls she habitually wore. "We're old and we're getting older, but we don't *change*. We don't have the power to change ourselves—"

Rolls touched the woman's shoulder. "You know what I mean," he said.

"—except for Penny with her necklace," Eisner continued.

Her voice, never particularly attractive, cut the phrase like a hacksaw. "She can change."

"Penny got what she wanted," Rolls said. Rather than try to turn Eisner to face him, he stepped around her.

"You have—" He gestured with his left hand. "You wanted knowledge. You wouldn't trade that for Penny's necklace, would you?"

"No, no," Eisner agreed, forcing herself to lower her arms, though she met her guest's eyes only for a moment. "I have exactly what I want, of course. . . ."

"But we don't have to limit ourselves to one thing," Rolls said. "Eisner, we have *all* powers, we're like gods. But we're focusing down to—" his hand described an empty circle "—to caricatures, like Penny and her appearance."

"And her men, you mean!" Eisner said.

Rolls' expression softened to see the pain in the woman's eyes. "That's all part of the same thing, Eisner," he said gently. "You know that. There's no reason that we can't change things back. Become—"

He reached out slowly, his fingers curled to cup Eisner's breast.

"—complete human beings again."

Eisner slapped his hand away and turned her back again. "I don't want that!" she said.

In a voice almost too faint to hear, she added, "And you don't want me, not really."

"I *do* want you," Rolls said. "I want you to be—"

"Go on!" Eisner said, facing Rolls to gesture imperiously toward the door. "Get out. Your sympathy is quite unnecessary."

"Whatever you wish," the big man said as he obeyed; but he paused, hunched in the doorway, to add over his shoulder, "There's still time to change, Eisner."

As the door swung closed behind him, Rolls heard her cry, "There's nothing to change!"

There was no doubt in her voice; but Rolls thought he heard sadness.

≡ 5 ≡

"THERE ARE NO abnormal emanations from the target zone," said the artificial intelligence controlling Hansen's intrusion capsule.

In its current mode, the capsule's radiation on all spectra was as close to zero as Consensus technology could arrange. That meant Hansen had no radar, no lasers—no emission rangefinding of any sort. He was dependent on the target to reveal itself when the intrusion capsule got close enough.

If North had managed to blank out a planet as thoroughly as Consensus scientists had shielded this capsule, the two were going to intersect with what would seem to be a hell of a jolt from Hansen's side.

"On a dark stormy night . . . ," Hansen sang.

Hansen had a pleasant voice, but he couldn't carry a tune even on a good day.

". . . as the train rattled on. . . ."

A good day was one on which Hansen wasn't scared and strapped into a seat with only the dim blue numerals of the console to illuminate his surroundings. In low-observable mode, the AI shut down all non-essentials so that there was as little energy as possible to be trapped within the hull as heat.

It was out of his hands. There was nothing to expect from the next few moments except death, and there wasn't a damned thing he could do about it. He'd been shot at before, but it wasn't like that. Then he'd had a gun in his hand or at least the chance of getting to a gun. . . .

". . . one young man with a babe in his arms," Hansen sang tunelessly, "who sat there with a bowed down head."

His palms were sweaty, his skin prickled, and he figured

he knew now what it was like to be under artillery fire where life and death were at the whim of entities in the invisible distance.

"The calculated time of arrival is five seconds—" said the artificial intelligence.

There was no lack of data for the calculations—

"Four—"

—because the Consensus handlers had watched three fleets vanish at the intersection point.

"Three—"

The voices in the mist might think an intrusion capsule—

"Two—"

—could slip through where a fleet couldn't, but Hansen didn't believe that.

"One—"

If it wasn't impact and instantaneous death waiting, what—

"N—" said the artificial intelligence, the first grunt of "Now!" before it cut off and the console display went dead black.

Hansen listened to the sound of blood coursing through the veins of his ears.

The next line of the song went, 'The innocent one began crying just then . . .' Hansen would've kept singing to show the bastards *somewhere* that being trapped in limbo until his air supply failed didn't terrify him; but his mouth was too dry to form the words.

The hull of the capsule quivered. One of the hull plates shifted like a shingle that had rotted away from the staple holding it to the wall.

Light bathed Hansen through a crack that widened as the plate fell off completely. The capsule's three-layer coating of absorptive materials had already sloughed like the carcass of a beached jellyfish.

The console displays were still dead.

Hansen should've been dead also. The amount of heat or other radiation it would take to make the capsule disintegrate would carbonize a human being before he knew what was happening.

Not that Hansen *did* know what was happening.

Three more hull plates fell away, clanging against one another and, more mutedly, on the ground beneath.

Hansen still couldn't see much, just blue sky with some impressive cumulus clouds in the distance. He hit the quick-release plate in the center of his restraints and rose with a neutral look on his face.

Hansen was more than 200 meters in the air, on top of a huge building. He was looking out over the neat patterns of farmland, and—

The floor of the intrusion capsule gave way and dropped Hansen thirty centimeters to the ground. That shouldn't've been unexpected, the way the upper hull was crumbling, but *every*damnthing was a surprise just now. The read-outs and touch-sensitive panels on the console all had a frosted look as though they were withering under extreme heat.

Particularly surprising was the fact that he was alive.

The capsule had—landed?—on a promenade around the building's roof. Behind Hansen was the quarter-sphere sheltering the audience section of a 3,000-seat odeum.

Two men and a woman came from a door in the back of the much smaller quarter-sphere intended to cover the performers. Apart from miniature figures in the fields below, these were the first living beings Hansen had seen since a trio of androids strapped him into the intrusion capsule.

"Can we help you, sir?" called the older man in the center of the group.

Hansen stepped out of the collapsing ruin of his capsule. The fallen hull plates had a porous look, and the monomolecular carbon frame members were beginning to sag under their own weight. He'd envisioned a lot of possibilities for what would happen on this mission, but not this one.

Not anything as survivable as this one, if it came to that.

He bent his mouth into a pleasant smile to match that of his questioner and said, "Ah, my name's Hansen. Ah, this is going to sound silly, but is this Northworld?"

Hansen wore what looked like standard exploration-unit coveralls until one checked at the level of the weave and found the battery of hidden weapons and sensors. Besides the coveralls, he had a satchel holding three separate changes of clothes, each one a direct copy—in appearance—of an outfit that one of the later colonists was known to have carried to Northworld.

His options didn't include sandals and loose, flowing robes cinched at the waist with a belt of soft fabric—which was what the three locals greeting him wore.

"Well, that isn't our name for it, Mr. Hansen," said the other man—still older than Hansen by a decade, if appearance was anything to judge by. "We call it Diamond, but since we believe we're in a spacetime bubble of our own, we may well be a minority in our opinion."

"We're so *glad* to see you," said the young woman who touched Hansen's arm in a gesture of welcome and perhaps reassurance—for one or both of them. "We'd been afraid that it was, you know . . . something to do with the Passages."

Her fingertips felt warm even through the cloth. She had long brown hair and was very attractive, primarily because of her lively expression.

This place might well *be* a bubble of phased spacetime; certainly it wasn't Northworld, a barren wilderness until its settlement three standard months before. The crops below had been in the ground longer than that, and Hansen couldn't even guess how long it must have taken to construct the city-sized building on which he now stood.

"You were expecting me, then?" Hansen asked, keeping his tone mild. The promenade was paved with a rubbery layer that responded comfortably beneath his boots.

"Well, not you precisely," said the old man.

"My name is Dana, by the way," interjected the younger man. "And these are Gorley—" the other man "—and Lea."

"And as Lea said," Gorley went on, "we're delighted you're here—"

"Both for yourself," added Lea, "and because you're not. . . ." Her face quirked in embarrassment, and her hand squeezed Hansen's biceps.

"But particularly for yourself, Mr. Hansen," the older man went on. "We never received a visitor before."

"As to whether we knew you were coming," said Dana, "and please—you mustn't take this as an insult—but. . . ."

"You are disruptive, you see," explained the woman. "Here in Diamond, because of the, ah. . . ."

"Well," said the older man, "your weapons, Mr. Hansen."

He pointed with the paired index and middle fingers of his left hand toward the remains of the intrusion capsule—now a silhouette in ash as if a quantity of cardboard had been burned on the promenade. "I'm afraid that the vehicle in which you arrived was itself a weapon."

All three of the local citizens looked apologetic. "And you see," the younger man finished, "weapons don't exist in Diamond."

"Anything can be—" Hansen snapped before he got control of his tongue. Even if what he'd been about to say were true—and it certainly *was* true where he came from that anything could be used as a weapon if the will to do so existed—that wasn't an attitude he wanted to stress to his present hosts.

"But with the weapons gone," Lea said, "we hope that *you'll* be able to stay. Would you like to see the village?"

"Or perhaps you're hungry/he's hungry?" the men said in near unison.

"I—" said Hansen. He looked at his hosts and decided to be perfectly honest—because he didn't have enough information to lie; and anyway, because he preferred the truth.

"I'm not hungry," he said. "But I'd like to get out there—" he gestured toward the surrounding fields "—just to prove this isn't some kind of stage set."

Lea giggled and hugged herself closer to Hansen. Both men smiled also. "Of course, of course," Dana murmured.

"And I'm wondering a little where everyone else is . . . ?" Hansen added.

Contact with Lea wasn't as pleasant as it should've been, because Hansen noticed his coveralls gave too easily at the pressure of her soft body. The equipment woven into Hansen's garments seemed to have vanished. His intrusion capsule was now fluff which drifted over the edge of the building on the light breeze.

"We didn't want you to worry," said Dana.

"We thought you might be startled by a crowd," said Gorley.

"But *everyone* wants to meet you," said Lea, "not just here but everywhere in Diamond."

As she spoke, an aircar curved neatly around the odeum

from a landing site on the opposite edge of the roof. Simultaneously, loosely organized groups of people began approaching from either direction along the promenade.

All the newcomers, including the vehicle's driver, dressed in a similar fashion, but there was wide variety in the color and textures of their garments. The crowds contained many children, some of them infants being carried or led carefully by the hand by their parents.

"Hello, Mr. Hansen," called a little boy, waving a small bouquet.

The aircar touched on the walkway near Hansen and rotated slightly to face its nose outward toward the edge of the roof before it settled finally. The vehicle hummed instead of howling; Hansen couldn't see fan ducts.

These might be gentle people, but they weren't stupid—and they weren't without technology. The whole city-building— very likely the whole of Diamond, planet or universe or whatever it was, was listening to what Hansen said and reacting to it immediately.

"We thought you might prefer to ride," said Lea, nodding toward the car.

"Though we can take the elevators if you'd like," said Dana.

"Or walk," said Gorley. "We'd be more than happy to walk with you."

The old man looked fit enough to manage the walk despite his age, but Hansen wasn't sure *he* wanted to try the long staircases, even going down.

The crowds had halted a comfortable, non-threatening ten meters from Hansen and his companions. More people were still coming around the curves of the promenade.

"No, the car'll be fine," Hansen said, letting Lea guide him into the open vehicle.

"Goodby, Mr. Hansen!" called the little boy, waving enthusiastically.

"We'll have a proper gathering in the common area later," Gorley said.

"If that's all right with you, Mr. Hansen, of course," Dana interjected.

"Yeah, I . . . ," said Hansen. He didn't know enough to ask questions.

"But everyone's so excited," Lea said. "We all wanted to see you in person as soon as we could."

The car lifted to clear the turbulence around the building's edge, then dropped in a curve toward the fields. The irrigation ditches between rows of grain were dry at the moment, but a large reservoir reflected the cloud-piled sky in the near distance, ready to flood the ditches if needed.

"How long has Diamond been settled?" Hansen asked.

The driver throttled back, slowing the car as he steered for a dike between fields. The vehicle was admirably quiet, but it seemed to have surplus power even with five of its six seats filled by adults.

"Our records go back ten thousand years," said Dana.

"What?" Hansen snarled. "That's three times as long as there've been human spacecraft!"

"We didn't mean to distress you, Mr. Hansen," Lea said softly.

"You understand, of course," said Gorley with an apologetic look, "that time within our bubble—if our scientists are correct—doesn't necessarily travel at the same rate as that of the outside universe . . . of which our ancestors may have been a part."

"Though," Dana said, "we don't have any record of existence anywhere but here, in Diamond."

"I'm sorry," Hansen said.

It bothered him that these people kept apologizing to him when hell, either he was at fault or nobody was. He got out of the car and walked toward the rows of grain.

Diamond wasn't an elaborate stage set. Hansen's boots sank into the turned earth. The air was fresh with the scents of growth, and a cloud of small insects rose from the shade beneath the leaves as he reached into the grain.

The crop was still green, the grainheads unformed. Hansen stroked the fine-haired leaves.

His outfitters had given him a ruby ring in a massive gold setting for the middle finger of his right hand. The stone was now as dull as a chip of cement, and Hansen was quite sure that the one-shot laser which the ruby focused no longer functioned.

He turned back to his hosts. They had waited beside the car in attitudes of hopeful attentiveness.

"Do you have criminals on Diamond?" he asked abruptly.

"Oh, no, Mr. Hansen," Lea replied.

Hansen smiled lopsidedly. "Then I'm damned if I know what good I could ever be to you," he said as he took his seat in the car again. "But I guess I'm here anyway."

"Oh, Mr. Hansen," Gorley said, "you can't imagine how wonderful it is to us to have a visitor! We weren't sure that it was possible to enter or leave Diamond."

"May we return to the village, then?" Dana asked. "Or perhaps you'd like to see the animals?"

"The village is fine with me," Hansen said. There was a mild low-frequency vibration through the frame of the aircar for a moment as the driver raised his power. "You know, I'd sort of figured you were vegetarians."

"Ah, well, we are," explained Gorley diffidently. "But we use milk and wool, you see."

The car climbed as swiftly as it had dropped minutes before; he'd been right about the vehicle having plenty of power. "You've been trying to get out of your bubble, then?" he asked.

"Oh, goodness, no!" said Dana in amazement. He blushed in embarrassment. "I *am* sorry. We just—we're happy here."

"It's the knowledge that we miss," explained Gorley. "It's all very well to speculate about our existence, but proof that there *is* an outside universe is quite marvelous."

Lea bent close and kissed Hansen's cheek. "We do hope you'll be comfortable in Diamond."

Instead of returning to the section of promenade where Hansen's capsule had appeared, the aircar circled the building and dropped onto a purpose-built docking area where hundreds of similar vehicles were already parked. "The community is gathering in the common area," Gorley said. "That seemed simplest."

"But if it makes you uncomfortable to be on display, even briefly," Dana said, "of course your peaceful enjoyment is far more important to us."

"To all of us," Lea agreed and nestled closer to her guest.

There was a bank of at least twenty elevators, each of them sized to hold half a dozen people. Cages and shafts alike were of a material whose crystalline transparency had been slightly

dulled by dust and use. Again, Diamond hadn't been somehow raised as an elaborate hoax to fool Hansen.

The aircar's driver waved and got into a separate cage.
Hansen didn't see the controls—or, for that matter, the elevator's drive and suspension apparatus—but he and his three
guides dropped to a level forty meters beneath the roofline
and got off when the door rotated open.

The whole area was open except for the eight massive pil-
lars which housed the elevators as well as supported the
building's upper stories. Plants grew around the outer edges
and around the lightshaft in the center.

The ten-meter ceiling kept the space from looking packed,
but it was full of people who waved and cheered when Hansen got off the elevator. He wasn't sure he'd ever seen a crowd
that big with a *happy* ambiance to it.

"We have a little dais built for you, if you don't mind,"
Dana said, bending close to speak directly into Hansen's ear.

Lea gripped his hand with friendly firmness as she led him
up a short flight of steps to a chair on a plastic platform. "If
you could say a few words, that would be wonderful," the
young woman said as she motioned Hansen to the seat.

Even so they weren't all going to be able to see, Hansen
thought; and then he noticed that the crowd of gaily-clad
citizens was moving in a clockwise rotation, bringing forward
those from the other side of the huge room and taking away
those who'd already gotten a close look at their visitor. There
was no apparent pushing or concern.

"Ah—" he said.

The room stilled save for the whisper of sandals on the tile
flooring.

He certainly wasn't going to sit. He felt like an idiot. Lea
started down the steps. Hansen grimaced, wishing he'd
grabbed her earlier so that he at least wouldn't be alone here
in his—'ignorance' was an insufficient word for how he felt.

"Ah," he repeated, "ah, I don't know how I came to be
here, but I hope that—"

The sunlight through the open sides of the common area
dimmed as though shutters had been drawn all around the
building. People screamed.

Hansen glanced around him. The threat was everything but
palpable, and he was exposed on top of the dais.

He was in his element.

Short-boled palms and bromeliads fringed the exterior of the common area. While the sky beyond darkened in pulses like the throbbing surf, the broadleafed plants were sucked into shadowy, fanged silhouettes. The sun brightened again, and the normal foliage returned.

Shadow humans appeared in the common area when the plants grew serpent doubles also.

Amid the crowd's weeping and wordless cries, Hansen heard from hundreds of throats *a Passage/another Passage . . .* and over and over again, *May it be swift/May it end/end/end. . . .*

For a moment, the great covered park was what it had been when Hansen first saw it: bright, clean, and filled with thousands of healthy people, though their faces were now streaked with tears and terror. Then it changed again, and Hansen saw an armored vehicle that must have weighed hundreds of tonnes.

The tank glided toward Hansen in a false silence while the shadow figures and vegetation shuddered with the noise that such a monster must have made in any medium denser than vacuum. It sprouted missile batteries, guns, and swatches of wire mesh which could have been either antennas or a form of defense.

The tank proceeded at a walking pace which nothing in the park or its own shadow world slowed or affected.

The folk of Diamond keened and clutched one another, keeping their faces down and their eyes closed.

There was no place to run. Hansen picked up the chair—extruded plastic, light if not quite flimsy . . . and probably just as effective as any other man-portable weapon against a monster like the tank which bore down on him now.

Lenses and vision blocks winked with gray highlights that didn't come from the sun of Diamond. None of the tank's guns were aimed at Hansen, but attachment lugs on the bow-slope would gore him back until he and they sailed off the edge of the building. Even on the dais, he had to look up to see the top of the turret and the multiple weapons' cupolas.

Hansen swung his piece of furniture at a vision block on the upper left of the bowslope.

The plastic chair whistled at and through the knobbly armor

without touching anything material save the air. Hansen overbalanced and almost fell off the front of the dais. Daylight had
returned, and with it the rich, soft colors of Diamond.

"Oh, Mr. Hansen . . . ," someone murmured behind him.
Hansen turned. Lea had started up the steps to the dais again
and paused, staring at the chair in the visitor's hands.

Anything's a weapon if you want it to be one.

Hansen put the chair down carefully, feeling embarrassed
. . . though there wasn't any need to, god knew. What he'd
done made as much sense as anything could in a crazy situation like that.

"Oh, Mr. Hansen," Lea repeated. "I'm so sorry."

She stepped closer to him and reached out her hand. Hansen glanced over his shoulder; the whole crowd was watching
him, but there was an evident sadness in everyone's eyes.

What he'd done made sense where Hansen came from; but
this was Diamond.

He felt—cold wasn't the word, but a sensation as deep as
if freezing water were drawing all the warmth out of his body.
There was a thin film between Hansen and everything around
him. He felt the pressure of Lea's hand but not its warmth.

"We're so sorry," she said through a corridor of mirrors.
"It isn't a fault in you, Mr. Hansen, but weapons don't exist
here in Diamond."

She raised onto her toes to kiss him. He couldn't feel her
lips. Everything was becoming gray. He remembered the capsule in which he'd arrived, ash that divided into dust motes
as a breeze swept it gently from the promenade.

"Goodby, Mr. Hansen . . . ," called a distant, childish
voice.

"And you are a weapon . . . ," whispered words that were
only a shadow in Hansen's mind as he felt the structure of
Diamond interpenetrate him completely and leave only nothingness.

≡ 6 ≡

ROLLS FOUND FORTIN with his back to an outcrop, looking down the slope and through the shimmering discontinuity to a forest on the Open Lands, the surface which could be reached from any of Northworld's other planes. Armed figures groped among the dimensionally-distant trees, an army searching for the foe with whom it would fight to decide . . . nothing or everything, a matter of perception.

Fortin was tossing pebbles. They quivered when they struck the discontinuity. Fortin's arm wasn't strong enough to hit the warriors from his vantage point, but his tiny missiles flicked snow from the tree branches.

"Planning to visit the colonists?" Rolls said, seating himself beside Fortin. North's son had surely seen him climbing from the valley below; if he chose to ignore Rolls' approach, that was merely a ploy—and as such to be ignored.

"Perhaps," said Fortin without looking around.

He threw another stone. It sparkled and switched planes. By adjusting their vision, the two men could focus on either the stream a thousand meters below in their reality or the snow-wrapped forest and ignorant army. "Do you care, Rolls?"

Rolls chuckled. Seen from this angle, Fortin's face had the cool perfection of a well-struck medal. "What you plan is no concern of mine, Fortin," he said. "You know where my interests lie."

Fortin turned at last to face him. "Whatever I do," he said, "you'll know."

Rolls shifted slightly. "That's right," he agreed easily. "You—do things. I observe. Eisner learns."

The granite ledge on which they sat was flaking; Rolls reached beneath his buttocks to sweep aside some sharp-edged bits. Fortin picked up one of them, looked at it, and dropped it again instead of flinging it through the dimensional barrier.

"Why are you here?" he demanded.

Rolls smiled. "I'd like," he said, "to borrow Penny's necklace."

Fortin began to laugh. He had a tenor voice, as smoothly pleasant as his features—and as cool. "Then you'd better ask Penny, hadn't you?" he said, looking down for the stone he'd just cast aside.

"I thought perhaps you might help me," said Rolls.

"Did you?" the half android remarked without interest. His index finger dug at the ledge, trying idly to worry another bit loose.

"I . . . want to borrow it for only a moment," Rolls said, trying to keep his voice clear of the concern he was beginning to feel. He had no way to coerce Fortin, and a claim on the halfling's friendship would be as empty as claiming to be a friend of the Matrix itself.

Though the Matrix was not perverse.

"It's nothing to me how long you want it." Fortin said. "Or what you want it for." He met Rolls' eyes again.

Rolls grinned. He was willing to bargain with Fortin; for a moment, though, he'd been afraid that there was nothing he could provide that the other wanted.

He should have known better. Schemes filled Fortin the way maggots did a three-day corpse. There was sure to be a scheme which impinged on Rolls or what Rolls could do. . . .

"Yes," Rolls said, "I can see that." He settled himself against the crag, closing his eyes to feel the sunlight warm their lids.

"I've been thinking of visiting Ruby, you know," said Fortin in a voice as coolly distant as if it came through the dimensional barrier. "It seems to me that Ruby might have something to do with the problem of nightmares on Diamond."

"Waking nightmares," Rolls said, opening his eyes and looking without expression at his smaller companion. "Yes, you might very well be right."

"But I would rather," Fortin continued, picking his words with the care of a climber negotiating a cliff face, "that my visit to Ruby didn't come to North's attention. My father doesn't—"

A look of fury momentarily transfigured Fortin's face, though his features were no less perfect for the purity of the emotion they displayed. "My father doesn't trust me."

Rolls laughed, an easy, deep-throated sound. "Nobody trusts you, Fortin," he said.

The anger left Fortin's visage, leaving behind a coldness like the blue heart of a glacier. "Because my mother was an android," he said.

"Because you're Fortin," Rolls said, still smiling. He'd never been a good liar, and acceding to godlike powers had leached away even the impulse to say less than the absolute truth as he saw it.

And Rolls saw very clearly indeed.

"Maybe it's in the genes," he added, his expression untroubled by Fortin's wintry glare. "After all, Fortin, nobody really trusts North, either."

Fortin turned away. He drew in a deep breath and pretended to look for another chip of stone to throw.

"I can't prevent North from seeing whatever he chooses to see," Rolls said. "But he observes for reasons . . . and I observe because it's my life."

For a moment, a look as bleak as a snowfield wavered across Rolls' soft, handsome features.

"*I* won't be the one to inform your father that you're visiting Ruby," he said.

Below and beyond them, scouts rejoined the army. A trumpet call quavered through the discontinuity and the wind skirling past the crag.

"All right," Fortin said. His voice and visage were carelessly without expression again. "If you can occupy Penny outside her room—and without her necklace—for half an hour, say—"

Rolls chuckled again. "That should be possible," he agreed.

"—then I'll see about 'borrowing' it for you."

There were two armies visible now. To the men on the crag, they seemed to be fighting as though mirrored in the flat surface of a pond.

≡ 7 ≡

HANSEN FELT THE shock of landing before he knew he was alive. The ground was solid enough to knock his breath away.

He could see again. He still existed—or existed again.

Hansen hadn't fallen far. In fact, he'd just gotten his feet tangled during the moment—or however long; maybe he didn't want to think about that—in which Diamond forced itself through the space of Hansen's being. The sun *here* was a little past midpoint.

He was on a forty-meter bluff, overlooking a considerable floodplain forested with scrub conifers as well as willows. The river which had carved the bluff was now an occasional glint through the trees a kilometer away. On the far horizon was a conical mountain from which trailed wisps of yellow vapor.

There was snow on the leaf mould and in the creviced bark of the trees around Hansen, but the air didn't seem particularly cold. A fieldmouse gnawed audibly nearby, rotating a pinecone with tiny forepaws to bring hidden seeds in range of the glittering incisors.

Hansen wasn't on Diamond. He could be quite sure of that, because riders carrying lances and crossbows were picking their way from left to right through the trees below.

A trumpet called from nearby to the right. A living creature out of sight on the left answered the horn with its own louder, angry echo. Two of the riders turned their shaggy, big-headed ponies and trotted back the way they'd come. Their fellows, perhaps a dozen of them, checked their weapons and resumed their careful progress through the trees.

Hansen looked at his laser ring. The stone remained as dull as it had been on Diamond, and even the metal had the false sheen of plastic.

The band crumbled as he tried to work the ring off his finger. He dropped the bits on the snowy ground in disgust.

One of the horsemen below took a curved trumpet from beneath his fur jacket, set it to his lips, and blew a three-note call.

Hansen sighed. He wasn't trained to survive alone in the woods. The sooner he brought himself to the attention of the men below, the better . . . though of course, 'better' might amount to a swift death instead of a slow surrender to cold and hunger.

"Don't be a fool, Hansen," squeaked the fieldmouse. "Swear yourself to my service. You'll never survive here without my help."

Hansen rubbed the trunk of one of the pines. The outer surface of the bark rasped as it ground away beneath the ball of his thumb, exposing the russet layer within.

"Mice talk here, then?" Hansen said conversationally. So long as he squeezed the treetrunk, he could keep himself from slamming his fist into it in frustration at this further madness from which he was now sure he would never escape. . . .

"Faugh!" the mouse said. "Such a form is useful when I visit the Open Lands. You might not even think me alive in your terms, Hansen."

The little creature tossed the cone aside. Half the scales had been nibbled into fibrous sprays. They looked like the blades of a turbine whose epoxy matrix had disintegrated under stress.

"I'm a machine," said the mouse, cleaning its whiskers with its paws. "You can call me Walker. On my plane of Northworld the sun is red, and even the shoals of horseshoe crabs which used to couple on gravel beaches have died. There is no life besides me and my fellows—if we live."

Another horn blew; a second group of horsemen rode into sight among the trees below. Several crossbows fired. The flat *snap!* of the bows' discharge sounded like treelimbs cracking under the weight of ice.

Men shouted. Hansen didn't see anyone fall, but the conifers hid most of the details.

He was shivering; perhaps it was the cold. "You're a time traveler, then?" he said to the fieldmouse. The beast's left eye was as dull as the ruby which had powdered like chalk as Hansen removed his ring.

"You still think in terms of duration, Hansen," Walker said. "Don't. This is Northworld."

He paused for a moment to lick the creamy fur of his belly in firm, even strokes of his tongue. "I'm from a different plane of the Matrix. There are—" the mouse voice took on a didactic singsong "—eight worldplanes of the Matrix, and the Matrix which is a world. But those who live *in* the Matrix are mad."

The riders on both sides were falling back. A riderless pony rushed to and fro among the trees, neighing and shaking cascades of snow from the branches.

Men on foot, stepping heavily with the weight of the full armor they wore, moved through the forest in a ragged array. They didn't appear to be armed, but whenever one brushed a low treelimb, wood and snow spluttered away in a blue crackle.

Similar pops of electronic lightning suggested that more armored footmen were approaching from the other direction, but the line of contact would be at some distance to the right of Hansen's present vantage point. He began walking in that direction, keeping a grip on saplings because he was paying less attention to the bluff's edge than he ought to.

Walker hopped along beside him. "Swear yourself to my service, Hansen," piped the fieldmouse voice. "You're nothing and nobody without my guidance. But be warned: oaths have power on Northworld."

Scores of fur-clad horsemen like those who'd acted as skirmishers followed a few meters behind the ragged line of footmen. The latter's armor was painted in brilliant colors, no two patterns alike. Hansen estimated that there were about 150 men in the force advancing from his left, with only a third of them in armor; but the trees made certain counting impossible.

Several horns called. Fifty or sixty equally garish armored men came into sight from the trees to the right.

A small gray bird, crested like a titmouse, landed on a branch beside Hansen. It rapped the seed in its beak three times to break it open. The bird's head flicked as it swallowed the kernel, letting the husk flutter over the edge of the bluff.

"That's the army of Golsingh the Peacegiver," the bird said, twitching its beak in the direction of the newcomers. "Those others there—" it bobbed in the direction of the force to Hansen's left "—they're Count Lopez' men, though he's bedridden and can't lead them."

Hansen looked at the bird. One of its eyes was bright; the other had the yellow, frosted look of weathered marble.

"My word *always* counts, Walker," Hansen said harshly. "I'm not giving it to you."

Lopez' mounted force suddenly sallied through the loose ranks of his armored footmen. Snow and dirt flew from beneath the hooves of the ponies.

When the riders were twenty meters short of the leading clot of Golsingh's footmen, crossbows snapped on both sides. Several of Lopez' men tumbled from their saddles, but their own missiles were directed at the armored footmen.

It appeared to Hansen that the quarrels sizzled and dropped just short of the armor. Several, probably metal-shafted, vanished in showers of orange sparks.

A single footman stumbled, then fell backward in the snow. His heels drummed briefly. The fletching of a missile projected from his left armpit.

Walker made a *tsk-tsk-tsk* sound, as dismissive now as if he were in human guise. His beak sawed in the direction of the fallen man. "A hireling," the bird explained. "Shoddy armor; no chance at all."

He turned his one bright eye on Hansen. "But more chance than you have, Kommissar. Unless you put yourself under my control and direction."

Hansen gathered a blob of saliva on his tongue. He grimaced and swallowed instead of spitting.

Golsingh's lancers had also ridden through the loose array of their own footmen and were struggling with mounted opponents in a chaos of shouting and ringing metal. Hansen couldn't imagine how the fur-clad riders told one another apart after the first shock had mixed their lines.

The foremost group of Golsingh's footmen, twenty or so of them, broke into a stumbling run. Their leader was a huge man in red and gold armor. The nearest horsemen bellowed afresh and tried to disengage.

The man in red and gold pointed his right arm and splayed

the middle and index fingers of his gauntleted hand. A blue-white arc snapped in a ten-meter parabola from the fingers with a noise like sawing stone. It touched three horsemen in a long whiplash curve, igniting their garments and cleaving away the head of one man as surely as an axe could have done.

Hansen was sure that at least one of the victims had come from Golsingh's side.

"That's Taddeusz, Golsingh's foster father," Walker said with another avian sniff. "The warchief as well. He thinks that war is for warriors, and freemen are more trouble than use."

Taddeusz and his clot of footmen—warriors—continued to pound forward. Saplings burst into flame when arcs touched them in broad slashes, but the freemen had spurred their ponies out of the way so that no more of them fell.

A gap was opening between Taddeusz' group and the nearest of the remaining friendly forces. A few other warriors began to trot from Golsingh's line, but they seemed motivated by personal excitement rather than a desire to hit the enemy as a coordinated force.

Taddeusz and a green-armored warrior from Lopez' army plodded together with a rippling crash of electrical discharges. They met in an alder thicket. Hansen couldn't see the moment of contact, but lightning swept the slender stems away in time for him to watch the Lopez warrior pivot on his right foot and fall.

There was a black, serpentine scar across the green breastplate. Smoke or steam oozed from the neck joint of the armor.

Taddeusz strode on. His arc was condensed to a quaver that reached less than a meter from his gauntlet. Another of Lopez' warriors cut at the warchief with an arc extended into a whiplash. It popped and sizzled, wrapping Taddeusz in its blue fire; clumps of snow puddled around the red and gold boots.

Taddeusz took a step and another step, each in slow motion as though he were walking in the surf. His opponent suddenly tried to backpedal. He was too late. Taddeusz' right arm slashed, and the dense electrical flux from his gauntlet sheared into his opponent's helmet.

Circuits blew all through the damaged suit. Taddeusz blanked his arc for an instant, then snapped it back to life as he moved on.

His victim toppled. A wedge-shaped cut bubbled halfway

through the sphere of the helmet, as though it had been struck by something more material than directed lightning.

A dozen fires struggled fitfully among the scrub trees. Sapless wood tried to sustain ignition temperature against the cold and snow.

Hansen moved sideways to keep Taddeusz in view. A crevice in the face of the bluff blocked him.

He cursed. It was three meters across. There was crumbling soil on the opposite side, but also saplings that'd provide handholds if he needed them.

A rocky, 70° slope jolted down to the embattled floodplain if he missed his hold.

Hansen jumped, knocking the saplings away with his chest as he landed a safe meter beyond them. A twig cut his cheek. He was beginning to feel the cold.

Lopez' men were closing on Taddeusz from all sides. A dozen or so of Golsingh's men still followed their warchief. They closed up and formed a circle as Lopez' resistance stiffened. Smoldering armor lay along the course they'd cut into the enemy, the detritus of their success.

You could get more organization by rolling two handsful of marbles together. "Damned fools!" Hansen snarled. "If that's all they know about war, they oughta stick to knitting."

He wasn't aware that he'd spoken aloud until a red squirrel balanced on a branch above him took the half-gnawed hickory nut from its jaws and said, "They know that they are warriors and heroes, Hansen. Since you know nothing of Northworld, you must give your life into my keeping."

"Go away," Hansen said, restraining an urge to sweep Walker over the bluff edge.

He concentrated on the fight instead. He'd felt a fierce rush of anger—but he knew his emotion was directed at the *butchery*, the *stupidity* going on below.

Hansen was a craftsman, and controlled violence was his trade. The armies below were composed of murderous buffoons.

Two of Lopez' men moved against Taddeusz simultaneously. Taddeusz cut at the one on his right; the warrior tried to block the warchief's arc with his own. There was a moment of explosive dazzle and a shriek like that of bearings freezing up. The warrior attacking Taddeusz from the left slashed at the warchief's helmet.

Taddeusz stumbled. The opponent to his right staggered away. The man's red-striped armor had lost the sheen of electronic polish, but the fellow managed to run three steps before he fell. A pair of fur-clad freemen jumped from their ponies and started dragging the warrior to a safer distance.

One of Taddeusz' party leaped between the warchief and his opponent's descending stroke. Both warriors froze as their arcs crossed. Another of Lopez' men punched Taddeusz' defender in the side with an arc which blazed on entry and was still spluttering when a finger's breadth of it poked through the opposite side of the armor.

Taddeusz got to his feet. Only two of his men were still standing; both of them promptly fell under multiple attacks. The warchief cut low, severing the thigh of the nearest opponent.

Two of Lopez' men struck at Taddeusz from behind and the sides. He spun, sparkling like a thermite fire but still moving with deadly precision. His short-curving arc carved through a helmet and the arm a desperate warrior had raised for protection.

Taddeusz extended his arc into a blue dazzle ripping a full three meters from his hand. He slashed it through the air as he turned and turned again, clearing the area around him. He was ringed by at least twenty of Lopez' warriors, but each time some of them moved to attack, the warchief's sudden movements sent them scampering away.

The remainder of Golsingh's army had begun to catch up with their warchief. Several of Lopez' warriors turned to meet the new threat. Hansen's nostrils wrinkled with the sharp bite of ozone, even at his distance above the fight.

There was something else. Something quivered on the verge of visibility across the battlefield. Black shutters opening, or a great crow splaying its wingfeathers between the sun and death below. . . .

But not quite.

A warrior in silver armor raised his right gauntlet toward Taddeusz, palm outward.

The warchief's arc lashed toward the man. Before the cut could land, an unconfined discharge leaped from the silver gauntlet to Taddeusz' chest.

The thunderous report sounded like a transformer exploding. Both suits of armor lost their luster. Taddeusz' arc weapon shrank to an afterimage on Hansen's retinas. Lopez' men moved in for the kill.

The remainder of Golsingh's army, led by a figure in royal blue, swept across the circle of their opponents. One of Lopez' warriors paused in the middle of a stroke aimed at Taddeusz and tried to run. Several others were struck down from behind.

Warriors began kneeling with their arms raised. Lopez' freemen hopped back onto their ponies and trotted away, harassed by Golsingh's horsemen.

Hansen noticed that the arc which touched the man in silver met no more resistance than it would from a sapling. It cut the warrior in two at mid-chest.

Walker tossed away the remains of his nut and sniffed. "The first rule of war," he chittered superciliously, "is never to fire a bolt. It takes minutes for your suit to build up power again."

Lopez' men were taking off their armor. The suits opened down the left side like gigantic clamshells. Each suit's arms and legs remained attached to the backplate, but the helmet and body armor split to allow the warrior access to his suit.

Dismounted freemen knelt beside Golsingh's fallen warriors. In some cases the victim was able to stand after he'd been lifted out of his armor.

Golsingh's baggage train arrived at the battlefield in a bedlam of trumpets and crackling brush.

"Well, I'll be damned," Hansen muttered.

"You'll surely be lost unless you put yourself under my protection," the squirrel retorted primly. "You would have joined Lopez' army just before the fight, wouldn't you? And where would you be *now*?"

There was a remuda of saddled ponies in Golsingh's train, but the baggage animals were elephants covered with long black hair. Their tusks had been sawn off close to the jaw and capped with copper bands.

The beasts would've been mammoths, if Hansen were standing on Earth a million years before . . . and very possibly they were mammoths here on Northworld—whatever nightmare Northworld turned out to be.

The animals were guided and accompanied by a hundred or more men on foot—but certainly not warriors. Whereas the freemen were dressed in furs, not infrequently picked out by streamers of bright cloth, this lot looked like so many bales of dingy rags plodding through the snow.

Hansen looked at the squirrel. "Servants?" he said.

Walker flicked the brush of his tail. "Slaves," he replied.

Most of Golsingh's men were getting out of their armor also. Pairs of slaves attended each warrior and carried the empty suits to bags of rope netting hanging from the flanks of the mammoths.

Hansen was shivering uncontrollably. He looked at the slope, wondering whether he could climb down directly in his present state or if he needed to find a gentler descent.

The warrior who'd worn the royal blue armor stretched as he stepped clear of his suit, then walked over to join Taddeusz. The warchief's armor had for the most part regained the luster it lost when the bolt of raw energy struck it. There was a black star-burst in the center of the gold and scarlet plastron.

"King Golsingh," Walker said. "He has dreams, but he's too soft to make anything of them."

Slaves were stripping the corpses of warriors; no one seemed to pay any attention to the handful of dead freemen. Birds were already circling the battlefield. The corpses of Golsingh's men were laid over a pile of faggots sawn by the few warriors still wearing their suits. Lopez' men lay where they'd fallen.

All the armor, damaged as well as whole, was loaded onto the mammoths who stamped angrily and hooted at the smell of blood. A score of Lopez' warriors had been captured. They were herded together, under guard by freemen, and watched the proceedings with evident disquiet.

It wasn't going to get warmer on the bluff, and the drop wasn't likely to become less steep. Hansen lowered himself over the edge, keeping a grip on a treebole until his boots found purchase. So far, so—

"You're a fool," the squirrel chittered. "They'll pay no attention to you. Or worse."

Hansen glanced over his shoulder. Warriors were mounting the ponies brought on leads, and the line of mammoths was plodding off in the direction from which they'd come.

Taddeusz and Golsingh were arguing. The warchief shouted

an order. One of the warriors still wearing armor stepped toward the line of prisoners.

One of Hansen's boots slipped. He dropped a step, then slid twenty meters in a half-controlled rush.

Hansen didn't have to be watching to know what the vicious sizzle of an arc weapon meant. Because the captured warriors had no helmets to muffle their voices, their screams were clearly audible. Crows called in raucous answer.

Halfway down the slope, a fair-sized pine grew in a crevice. The bluff below that point was at a fairly safe angle. Hansen let himself slide, angling to catch the tree and hoping that Diamond hadn't rotted the tough fabric of his coveralls the way it had his weapons.

It was a near thing in another way: he almost slid past the tree. The bark tore his palms as he grabbed and the shock strained his shoulder muscles, but those were small prices to pay for not fetching up against the granite outcrop twenty meters farther down.

Bits of rock pattered as Hansen clung to the tree and panted. Golsingh had just mounted his pony. He said something to Taddeusz and pointed toward Hansen.

The pyre piled with the corpses of the winning side was ablaze and beginning to roar. The bodies of the captives smoldered on the snow. Birds were landing on them.

Taddeusz shouted a series of orders. A pair of lancers rode toward the warchief. The warrior who'd just acted as executioner halted in the process of getting out of his armor.

Hansen dropped to the plain in a series of calculated hops, knoll to rock to clump of trees stunted by periodic flooding.

He flexed feeling back into his hands, but he'd never been much good without weapons. Anyway, if it came to a real fight, he was more meat for the crows.

"Lord Taddeusz!" Hansen shouted. "Lord Golsingh, I'm a traveler from a far land, drawn to Your Excellence."

He hoped the locals here spoke Standard. The colonists of course had . . . and the folk of Diamond, albeit accented . . . and the mouse/bird/squirrel that called itself Walker, for whatever *that* was worth.

The clear solidity of the sky and trees pressed in on Hansen. If all this was real, then what was he?

"Who are you, then?" Golsingh called in Standard, walking his pony a few strides closer to Hansen.

The beast sidled, presenting its left shoulder to Hansen as it advanced. The king frowned and tugged at the left rein, turning the pony's head without straightening its approach.

Golsingh was of average height, though he looked small next to his warchief. Taddeusz might better have mounted a mammoth than the pony which struggled beneath his weight. The king's neck and hands were well muscled, but his swarthy face had a fine bone structure. Hansen got the impression of a slight man who had trained himself to athletic prowess.

Whereas Taddeusz was a bear . . . and Nils Hansen was a hound, with flat muscles and a hound's utter disdain for the way cats play instead of killing.

Hansen smiled, and he probably shouldn't have, because Taddeusz said brusquely to a freeman, "Kill him!"

The man lowered his lance and clucked to his pony. Hansen continued to walk forward. A short pine tree just ahead and to his right was the best shelter available. He'd run for it when the lancer charged, but until then—

"Stop!" Golsingh shouted to the freeman. Hansen halted also, unwilling to look as though he were disobeying a royal command.

"Taddeusz," Golsingh continued, "remember that I am your king."

"Excellency," replied the big man, "I'm just—"

"The battle is over," Golsingh snapped. "*I* am king, and I will give the orders now."

Taddeusz nodded in contrition. "I apologize, my son," he said. "I had only your safety in mind."

Golsingh smiled. "As always, foster father," he agreed, nodding back to the bigger man as a mark of honor.

Both men had enveloped themselves in fur cloaks and caps when they took off their armor, so it was hard for Hansen to judge their ages at twenty meters' distance. Golsingh was probably in his mid twenties, Taddeusz two decades older. The warchief's weathered complexion and grizzled russet hair would look much the same when the man was in his sixties, but the brutal force he'd displayed during the battle suggested a lower limit to his age.

Or else Taddeusz had been Hell itself on a battlefield when he *was* in his prime.

"Lord Golsingh," Hansen said, "I'm a, ah, a warrior who's come from the far reaches of—" *why not?* "—Annunciation to, ah, join Your Excellence."

"Is this a joke?" said Golsingh, looking at his foster father with a puzzled expression. One of the slave attendants who huddled as they awaited their masters' pleasure began to laugh.

A crow glided from a treetop and landed nearby on the one corpse the victors hadn't bothered to strip: the warrior whose armor hadn't stopped a crossbow bolt. The bird cawed in amusement, fixing Hansen with its one bright eye.

"Yes, he's probably Lopez' buffoon looking for a new place," Taddeusz said. He added in dismissal—no longer angry, because the intruder was no longer worth his anger, "Go back to your master and tell him to have himself at Peace Rock within a tennight or we'll burn him and everyone else in his miserable village alive."

Taddeusz and Golsingh both wheeled their ponies.

Hansen's face went flat. "If you're looking for a buffoon," he shouted to the riders' backs, "then you could start with the fool who led your right flank into that half-assed charge. It was god's own luck he didn't lose you a battle you should've had on a platter!"

The horsemen drew up; Taddeusz' pony stutter-stepped as the warchief twisted to look over his shoulder. The freemen lifted the lances they'd laid crosswise on their pommels for carriage.

"I'll handle this, Excellency," Taddeusz said.

The wall-eyed crow danced from one foot to the other on the dead man's chest, clicking its beak in mockery.

"I tell you I'm a warrior!" Hansen said. "I can help you more than you imagine in planning your next battle."

"You lot," Taddeusz said, pointing to the four slaves. "Serve him out."

He nodded to Golsingh again. "Come along, Excellence," he said. "We don't want to fall too far behind the column. You never know what's lurking in these woods."

The horsemen trotted off together, spurring clods of mud and snow behind them. The slaves, drawing single-edged knives from beneath their rags, moved toward Hansen.

"A warrior has armor and attendants," cawed Walker. If the slaves heard the words, they gave no sign of it. "What do you have except your own foolishness, Kommissar?"

The riders were out of sight among the trees. "Look," Hansen said to the slaves. "This isn't your problem. Why don't you guys just wait a few minutes—"

The nearest of the slaves rushed him.

Hansen scampered back. The knife looked dull, but its wielder slashed with enough enthusiasm to manage the job if he got close enough.

"Look," Hansen called, "somebody's going to get—"

"I git his boots!" the slave cried to his fellows. All four of them were plodding after Hansen at the best speed their rag-wrapped feet could manage on the slushy ground.

Hansen jogged in the direction Lopez' surviving freemen had retreated. Only his mind was cold now. The defeated men had scattered equipment as they fled, and—

A shadow sailed past his head with a caw and a snap of its wings. It landed on a fallen branch ten meters ahead, then hopped so that its black beak was toward Hansen.

Walker's claws rested not on a branch, but rather on the stock of a crossbow. . . .

"You don't deserve help!" the crow called as it sprang airborne an instant before Hansen snatched up the weapon.

"I don't *need* help, Walker!" Hansen snapped as he turned to face his pursuers.

And that was true enough. He would've found something. Though maybe not this crossbow, a little off the track he was following and half-buried in snow. . . .

The slaves paused doubtfully when their victim turned to face them.

"Naw, it's all right," said the one in the lead. "It ain't cocked, and anyhow, he don't have arrows."

Hansen lunged, smashing the speaker in the face with the crossbow's fore-end, then using the tips of the bow to right and left like a pickaxe to the chests of the next two slaves. The second stroke caught only rags as the target leaped backward, squawling in justified terror.

The crossbow weighed over ten kilos, combining a meter-long hardwood stock with a stiff steel bow. Anybody who doubted Hansen was armed with *that* in his hands was a fool and a—

Hansen buttstroked the man with the broken face, knocking him over the body of his fellow. The other two slaves were running. Hansen ran after them.

—dead man.

"Oh, you're a fine warrior to fight slaves!" Walker cried. "Are you proud of yourself now?"

Hansen stopped. His legs were trembling, and he could only breathe in great sobs.

Walker was right. There'd been four of them . . . but trash like that wasn't what he'd trained for, *lived* for.

Hansen began walking back toward the battlefield, getting control of his adrenaline-charged muscles by moving them. When he was sure the surviving slaves were gone for good, he dropped the bloody crossbow.

The suit of abandoned armor was still where it had fallen. The crow lighted on it as Hansen approached.

"I can show you where a fine suit, a king's armor, can be had," Walker said. "Do my will and I'll reward you."

"Will this work?" Hansen demanded.

He knelt beside the body. The casing appeared to be mild steel, though there had to be complex electronics within. There was a single large catch, directly beneath the crossbow bolt projecting from the left armpit.

"Badly," Walker cawed, hopping to a sapling so slender that it bobbed beneath the crow's weight. "You won't dare face a real warrior in flimsy junk like this."

The helmet was a featureless ball. From a distance, Hansen had assumed there were concealed eye and breathing slits. He'd been wrong.

"Don't tell me what I dare," Hansen said. He released the sidecatch and flopped the suit open.

The man within had voided his bowels as he died. The stench hung in the cool air like a pond of sewage.

Hansen pulled the dead man from the armor with as much dignity as his need for haste and the corpse's stiffening limbs permitted.

The warrior had been old, with a pepper-and-salt moustache and only a fringe of hair on his head. The bolt was through his lungs, and he'd hemorrhaged badly from his mouth and nostrils. At least they were much of a size, Hansen and the dead man. . . .

"How do I make it work?" he grunted as he lifted the body clear.

Walker stopped preening his lustrous, blue-black feathers for a moment. "The suit powers up when it closes over a man," he said disinterestedly. "A living man, that is. But you're a fool to trust yourself to it, Hansen."

Hansen clucked in irritation. The suit could be stood empty on its spread legs—the warriors he'd watched had stripped in an upright position—but the piece was too heavy for Hansen to lift alone. It'd better have servos to multiply the effect of its wearer's motions.

He braced his hands on the edges of the thorax armor and thrust his booted feet into the leg openings simultaneously. *They put their pants on one leg at a time . . . ,* he thought with a grim smile.

The armor still stank. He lay back in it and fitted his arms into the arms of the suit. It'd stink worse in a few minutes if Hansen died in it also; and the smell would matter just as little either way.

"Walker!" he said. Would he be able to speak and hear with the suit closed up? "How do I make it throw an arc?"

The crow cocked its head. "Point your fingers and say 'Cut,' " it said. "Spread them wider to lengthen it."

Artificial intelligence controlled, then. How did you get AI and crude feudalism together? "And to fire a bolt?"

"The first rule of—"

"Bird!"

"Caawk!" Walker said. Then, "Point your palm and say 'Shoot.' "

Hansen closed the armor. When the latch clicked, a display lighted in front of his eyes and tiny fans began circulating the foul air.

He got up. The visual display was streaked with raster lines and seemed to be compressing 180° into the width his eyes would normally allot to ninety.

"Reduce field fifty percent," Hansen said automatically, before his conscious mind could remind him that this crude unit might not have verbal controls—or any controls at all.

The forest expanded to normal width and depth—a narrow window on the world, but the best display for walking.

Fast walking, if he could manage it. He had a lot of time to make up.

He took a step, then another, and raised his pace into a clumsy jog. There was enough delay in the suit's response to Hansen's movements that he thought at first he was going to topple. The dynamic rigidity of the joints was just great enough to save him from that embarrassment.

All exposed points of his body began to chafe. The armor was lined with suede at some points, with hide at others, and for some of its area with cloth scarcely better than the rags in which the slaves were clothed.

Hansen could feel a finger of cold air below his left arm, where the arrow-hole marked the suit. He didn't think he'd have to worry about arrows, though—

But that reminded him. As he clumped along, following the muddy, surprisingly narrow, track the mammoths squeezed into the bottom land, he thrust out his right arm, pointed his fingers, and said, "Cut!"

An arc—blacked out on Hansen's display—sizzled from his gauntlet. It licked a small pine tree into resinous flame.

Hansen fell on his face. When his suit shot out the arc, the legs didn't have enough power remaining to drive him at the speed he expected.

The arc continued to lash the leaf mould into sluggish fire. *How did he—* "Stop!" Hansen shouted. "Quit!"

The weapon cut off.

As he got up again, Hansen didn't see Walker, but from the closeness of the voice, the crow must have been sitting on his shoulder as it said, "A better suit would not have done that. A royal suit, like that which I offer you as my servant, could strike with both hands and still run faster than an unarmored man."

'I'll manage,'' Hansen said.

He began to jog again, then broke into a measured trot. He was flaying the skin from his knees, shoulders, and jutting hip bones.

He'd worn hard suits before, but rarely—and even less often in a gravity well. Motors in the armor's joints carried the weight and drove it in response to Hansen's muscles; but the muscles had to initiate the movements, and there was always a minuscule delay. He felt as if he were trying to run in a bath of soap bubbles—except that soap bubbles wouldn't've galled him.

Hansen concentrated on each next stride. His display fogged with his gasping exhalations. He didn't notice that the trail was rising until he broke out of the trees and saw, on ground that rose still higher across a swale, a palisaded village from which rose the smoke of scores of hearths.

The riders and mammoths of Golsingh's train straggled across the low ground, halfway down and halfway up the other side. A freeman at the rear of the line blew his curved horn furiously, pointing toward Hansen with his free hand.

Three of the warriors around Golsingh and Taddeusz at the bottom of the swale began getting into their armor.

Hansen slowed cautiously. He visualized himself skidding on his faceplate toward the men he wanted to impress; the image diverted some of his tension into a laugh.

A thought occurred to him. He centered the arming warriors in his display and muttered, "Visor, plus ten."

Hansen's helmet immediately gave him the requested magnification. The images were fuzzy, but he could see that the warrior donning the red-silver-blue armor was an octoroon, and that all three were powerful fellows of about Hansen's own twenty-nine years.

"Resume normal vision," he said, sucking his lips between his front teeth as he considered the situation.

This armor was crudely built, but it had a surprising range of capacities. Hansen was fairly certain that the warriors who'd struggled so clumsily in battle didn't know or didn't care about most of the things their suits could do. That gave him an advantage.

God knew that he was going to need one.

"Lord Golsingh!" Hansen shouted as he strolled toward the waiting army. His armor quivered with the amplified sound of his voice. "I came here to serve you. If there's no place in your service at the moment, then I'll empty one for myself!"

Hansen didn't know anything about the culture of Northworld—but he knew organizations and pecking orders. He'd failed at the start with this lot because they didn't respect him. He wasn't going to fail again because of a lack of arrogance.

After all, it wasn't as though arrogance didn't come naturally to him.

The three warriors had their armor on now. The suits were painted in patterns of black and silver; red, silver, and blue; and lime green with a phoenix emblazoned in gold on the plastron. All three men were big, and their armor was of obviously high quality.

As opposed to what Hansen was wearing: a piece of junk which had once been striped orange and blue, but which now was marked more by rust than by paint.

The shaggy line of mammoths continued to slog onward, but horsemen as well as most of the slaves began to collect at the bottom of the swale. It was the only place for a kilometer in any direction where there was enough flat, clear space to serve for a dueling ground.

Hansen walked on, matching his pace to that of the baggage train. The mammoths moved deceptively fast, covering two meters with each slow stride. Their droppings steamed in the mud, offering Hansen's lungs a tang of crushed hay.

Golsingh's army waited for Hansen. Most of the riders had dismounted, though the king and Taddeusz still sat on their ponies, looking over the heads of the three warriors in brilliant armor.

"That's Villiers' suit," somebody announced. "He's stolen Villiers' suit off his body."

"Cut," said Hansen. An arc spurted at an angle from his right hand. His fingers adjusted its length to quiver just above the muddy ground. He continued to walk forward against his suit's greater resistance.

"Villiers never did anything right," another voice guffawed. "Not even die."

"Lord Golsingh," Hansen shouted twenty meters from the armored warriors, "I challenge whatever champion you choose for a place in your service."

Taddeusz turned to Golsingh. "This is a slave," the warchief said.

"He's dressed as a warrior," Golsingh responded, quirking a smile at Hansen. "And of course he boasts like a warrior.'' The king had short, curling hair and a down-turned moustache. ''I think he deserves to die like one.''

Taddeusz shrugged. ''Zieborn,'' he said. ''Kill him.''

The warrior wearing a phoenix stepped forward. A long arc sprang from his right gauntlet and swung toward Hansen in a curve.

Hansen stopped dead. He squeezed his right index and middle fingers together so that the arc at their tip shrank to a coating like St Elmo's Fire, the greatest flux density of which his suit was capable. He felt a tingle in his right arm as he blocked the attack, but it was Zieborn's arc which failed momentarily with a pop.

The bigger, better-armed warrior boomed a curse. He stepped forward with his arc weapon ablaze again, shortened to the length of his forearm.

''Off!'' Hansen ordered his own AI and lunged toward his opponent with all his suit's power concentrated on movement.

Zieborn must have expected Hansen to backpedal—or flee, subliminally thinking of the armor as the poor excuse for a warrior who'd worn the suit most recently. Golsingh's champion swiped horizontally.

Hansen was already within his opponent's guard. He grabbed Zieborn's right wrist with his left hand, shouted ''Cut!'' to his AI, and carved upward in a shower of sparks from belly to throat.

The painted phoenix sputtered away from the armor in a gout of ash and gold leaf. The underlying metal pitted but did not burn.

Zieborn's electronic armor was proof to the worst punishment Hansen's arc could deliver; and the other man's arm was forcing his weapon toward Hansen's face.

''Off!'' cried Hansen and shifted his suit's full strength into his grip on Zieborn's right wrist.

Hansen had survived because he was very quick and—when he had to be—very strong. He was very possibly stronger than the king's champion now, just as he'd out-thought the man and jumped into a clinch before the other could respond.

And it didn't matter, because the crucial factor was the amount of power available to the armor—not to the human muscles within the suit.

Hansen's display overloaded with the intensity of the sizzling arc and blacked out. The weapon made a sound like a crow laughing. Its negative image forced itself inexorably toward Hansen's eyes like the tongue of a dragon.

He braced his right hand against Zieborn's armored neck and pushed, with no effect on what the warrior was doing. If Hansen twisted away and tried to run, his opponent's arc would extend and cut collops from the back of Hansen's flimsy suit. So—

Receptors crackled and a quadrant of Hansen's display went dead. The edge of Zieborn's tight weapon had touched Hansen's helmet.

"Shoot!" Hansen cried. The jolt left him blind, deafened, and tingling all over as if he'd been living in the heart of the lightning.

But Zieborn's snarling arc hadn't come through his helmet, destroying Hansen's eyes with a metallic plasma even before the electricity itself converted flesh to traceries of carbon.

Hansen reached down to his left side, forcing his suit unaided against the friction of all its powerless joints. He tugged the catch open, then pulled the plastron away from the backplate. Sunlight flooded in.

So did the smell of burned flesh.

There was a babble of voices, angry or amazed in tone, but Hansen didn't bother to process the words until he'd struggled free of the armor. Being trapped in the suit with its ventilation system and all receptors as dead as so many bricks was a more claustrophobic feeling than he had expected.

But Zieborn was dead too. His suit had lost its luster, and in the center of its neck joint was a hole no larger than a worm bores in an apple. Smoke drooled from the hole and from the louvered vents beneath the arms. That was why the air smelled like a bad barbecue.

The other two armored warriors waited impassively, but a freeman pointed his crossbow at the center of Hansen's chest. The quarrel had a four-lobed steel head.

"Put that fucker down or I'll feed it up your asshole!" Hansen snarled. The menace of his voice slapped the freeman back a pace, lifting his weapon as his mouth fell open.

Hansen's suit and his opponent's remained frozen and upright where they stood. A chickadee fluttered by so close that a wing brushed the hair which sweat plastered to Hansen's head. It lighted on top of Zieborn's helmet and said in a tiny voice that only Hansen seemed to hear, "The second rule of war is that in war, there are no rules."

"Lord Gol—" Hansen said. His voice broke. His throat was dry, dry as bleached bones.

"Lord Golsingh," he said, "I claim a place with you."

"We know nothing of this—" Taddeusz said to his king with a face as red as a wolf's tongue.

"And I claim," Hansen continued in a rasping, savage voice, "the armor of this man I killed in fair combat."

"We know," said Golsingh to his foster father, "that he can fight."

The king looked down from his pony toward Hansen and went on, "Your first request is granted . . . Hansen, wasn't it?"

Hansen nodded. He wondered if he was expected to bow.

"Your second request is not granted," Golsingh continued with a cool, vaguely detached expression. "Zieborn's armor goes to his eldest son, as is proper."

Hansen felt his face harden. He'd learned the importance of good equipment here, if he'd learned nothing else this day.

"But I think you've proved your right to a suit of comparable quality from the loot we took from Lopez," Golsingh went on. He glanced toward the curve of his retainers.

"Get him a horse, someone," the king snapped imperiously. "And get this gear loaded up. The women are probably worried about what's going on."

A pair of slaves pushed forward with a saddled pony, perhaps the one Zieborn had ridden until he was ordered to deal with the intruder.

"Oh," Golsingh said, "and bring Villiers' suit as well. It doesn't seem to have been as valueless as we'd assumed."

$$\equiv 8 \equiv$$

ONE OF THE human servants held up a mirror of polished ice. Fortin checked the set of his saucer hat, adjusted the brim slightly, and stepped into the discontinuity around which the central hall of his palace was built.

On the other side of *this* twig of the Matrix lay a swamp shadowed by giant ferns in the plane which his ancestors—

—his mother's ancestors—

—inhabited. This time, however, Fortin's destination was not so much a part *of* the Matrix as apart *from* it. For a moment, Fortin heard the boom of something in a warm pool swelling its throat in a mating call, while his eyes were still locked with those of his servant, impassive until the Master was well and truly gone.

Fortin let his mind step sideways . . .

And his feet were on solid ground, beneath the sullen sky of Ruby. A company of soldiers in battledress stood at attention before Fortin. The guns of a dozen huge armored vehicles were trained on him without even a vague attempt to be discreet about their caution.

A communications specialist stood beside the officer in command of the drawn-up company. The officer keyed the handset flexed to the com-spec's radio and said, "This is Bonecrack Three. The Inspector General has arrived. Out."

The officer stepped forward and saluted Fortin sharply. "Sir!" he said. "I'm Major Brenehan, in charge of your escort. We're very glad to have you with us again."

Fortin responded with a deliberately languid salute which he knew would infuriate Brenehan—infuriate anyone in Ruby, with its total dedication to precision and lethal efficiency. He wanted their help, but he couldn't keep from insulting them. It made him *hate* himself—

But then, Fortin hated himself anyway, most of the time. At least most of the time.

He smiled at Brenehan, flicked a non-existent bit of dust from the breast of his uniform, and said, "Very good, Major. I wish to confer with the High Council at their earliest convenience."

"Yes sir," said Brenehan. "At once, sir."

The major took the handset again and began speaking a series of codewords into it. The infantrymen remained at attention.

The tanks continued to point their main guns at the spot where Fortin had appeared, and where he continued to stand.

There was a pause in the radio conversation.

"You're very security conscious," Fortin said with a smile.

Brenehan looked as if the visitor had commented on the fact that they didn't smear their faces with pigshit. "Yes sir," he said guardedly. "We are. Of course."

The radio chattered to Brenehan. He replied in a series of precise monosyllables, his eyes on Fortin. Finally he nodded and returned the handset to the com-spec.

"Very good, sir," the major said. "If you'll come with me, we'll take you to the meeting site."

The infantry fell out of formation in response to an order Fortin didn't notice. Brenehan nodded toward an armored personnel carrier grounded behind the troops, then began striding to the vehicle without looking around to see if the visitor was following.

"What if I wanted to meet the Council at General Headquarters?" Fortin asked, speaking louder in order to be heard over the rising note of the APC's lift engines.

"I don't think that will be necessary, sir," Major Brenehan said.

He offered Fortin the jumpseat near the door, where the commanding officer usually sat. A platoon of infantry piled aboard the vehicle behind them. The remainder of the company loaded onto the other three APCs. They took off with a roar of fans even as the last trooper slammed the door behind her.

There was a joystick attached to the seat. Fortin gripped it and toggled the switch that should give him a full holographic display—where they were, where they were going, and maps of any other region of Ruby he chose to view.

Nothing happened. Very security conscious, even with the Inspector General. . . .

"But if I *did* want to visit General Headquarters?" Fortin pressed, knowing that it was his self-destructive impulse working again.

"You'd have to take that up with the Council itself, sir," said Brenehan. He stood beside the seat which would normally have been his, bracing himself against the armored ceiling as the vehicle pitched and bucked. The soldiers facing outward in a double line were robotically impassive as they checked and rechecked their weapons and other gear.

Fortin smiled at him. "I'm impressed by the way you always pick up my arrival," he said.

"Well, sir," Major Brenehan replied with a smile of satisfaction, "any disruption to Ruby is a potential threat. And even you, sir, if you'll pardon my saying so . . . are a disruption."

The flight to the rendezvous point took twenty minutes, but Fortin suspected that part of the time was spent in direction changes which only security required. The instant the car touched down, its sidewalls hinged flat with a *bang/bang* and the platoon of infantry lunged out with their rifles and multi-discharge energy weapons pointed. The accompanying APCs had also grounded and were disgorging their troops.

They'd landed on a volcanic plain, patterned in grays and greens by lichen. Other troops were already in position, nestled into crevices between the ropes of cold lava. Fortin noted that the waiting troops were equipped with crew-served weapons as well as the lighter hardware which his escort/guard carried.

There was no sign of the Council, just troops.

Fortin rose with dignity and walked toward the other position. Brenehan's men—the Inspector General's men—ported arms and fell in to either side of him. Some of the devices being pointed at Fortin were scanners rather than weapons, peering into the visitor and his equipment to make sure no threat was intended.

There was no question about where the priorities in Ruby

lay: the Council was greater than the Inspector General—but Security was greatest of all.

A colonel stood, gestured Fortin within the perimeter, and spoke into a radio like that which followed Brenehan. Then he saluted Fortin and said, ''Good to have you with us, sir. It'll be just a moment more.''

There was a heavy drumming from the western sky. Another squadron of armored personnel carriers swept in low and fast. Most of the APCs landed in the near distance, but one crossed the perimeter and dropped only meters from where Fortin stood. Its fans blew hot grit across his face and uniform.

A door in the side of the vehicle opened. The uniformed woman within looked like a hatchetfaced leprechaun. ''Sir?'' she said. ''We've brought a mobile command post. If you'd care to join us?''

Fortin stepped inside and met the stares of the five members of the Council who waited in a formal at-ease posture around a central table/display console. The ceiling of the command-post vehicle was twenty centimeters higher than that of a standard APC; even Marshal Czerny, as tall and thin as North himself, bent forward only slightly.

Marshals Czerny, Kerchuk, Tadley—the tiny, sharp-featured woman—Moro, and Stein. They wore the gorgets of their supreme rank, but their camouflaged battledress contrasted with the pearl gray of Fortin's parade uniform.

The arrogance of those in Ruby amused Fortin—and frightened him. *If you'd care to join us?* after they'd danced him to their tune—and would continue, in one way or another, no matter what the Inspector General said, to do whatever they felt was necessary.

He could order the Council to commit suicide *now,* in front of him, without explanation—and they would obey. But if his orders threatened Ruby, or might threaten Ruby—if the Inspector General absolutely required to be taken to General Headquarters . . . then obedience would be very slow indeed, and all possible administrative means would be taken beforehand to limit the potential damage.

Arrogance, but the arrogance of duty. Nothing came before that: not life, and certainly not the Inspector General. The folk of Ruby *believed* with a frightening intensity, while their visitor believed in no one, in nothing, except perhaps in his own godlike cleverness.

"Sit down, comrades," Fortin said, gesturing his hosts to the seats around the display but continuing to stand himself. "I have a technical problem for you."

He smiled with chill humor. "I think you might find it amusing."

Czerny nodded sharply, part agreement, part prodding.

"Let us postulate for the moment," Fortin continued, "that Ruby is a segment of phased spacetime in a larger universe—"

"Yes, yes," Stein murmured. "We accept that."

"—but that you are balanced *within* the matrix of that universe with a precisely opposite bubble universe."

Moro's chubby fingers were gliding across his keypad. The air before him quivered with a holographic display, intelligible only from the aspect of the intended user's eyes. "Balanced in what sense, sir?" he asked/demanded briskly.

"In every sense, Marshal Moro," Fortin replied.

"Our military equals, then?" Tadley said.

"Quite the contrary," said Fortin, reveling in the glow of interest replacing caution in the eyes of those watching him. "Your *opposites* in the arts of war. Your perfect balance."

A gust of wind traced across the lava flats, curling fiercely enough to make the vehicle tremble. Wisps of air with a sulphurous tang crept through the vehicle's climate control.

"So . . . ," said Moro, his fingers still, then dancing again. "So. . . ."

"If such a target existed," said Fortin, "how would you go about attacking it?" He smiled again.

"A number of the possibilities which occur to me now . . . ," said Kerchuk. His voice was rich and cultured in contrast to his scarred, brutal face; he had only one arm.

". . . would involve support for the operation from outside Ruby," he continued. "Are we to postulate that, sir? And if so, what are the param—"

"Under no circumstances are you to postulate outside assistance, Marshal Kerchuk," Fortin said sharply. "This operation is to be planned for execution by resources available within Ruby alone."

"On the face of it," said Moro as he stared at his display

rather than the visitor, "an impossible task. The operational unit's first requirement, of course, would seem to be exiting from Ruby—from the universe."

"And even if that problem could be solved—" said Stein.

"It *can* be solved," interjected Tadley. "A way can be found."

Stein looked at her. "Your confidence does credit to your optimism, Marshal," he said caustically. He raised his eyes to Fortin again. "Even were that problem solved, if we and this postulated target are *truly* in balance—"

"Then it will flee through general spacetime at precisely the rate at which our operational unit pursues," said Kerchuk with a broken-toothed grin. "An interesting problem indeed."

"There's also the difficulty of *locating* the target," Stein mused aloud.

"No difficulty at all," Tadley snapped decisively. "If they're really our—other selves, shall we say—then locating us locates them as well."

Even Stein and Moro nodded agreement with that.

"If I may ask, Inspector General . . . ," said Marshal Czerny in a voice like stones rubbing. "What is the purpose of this proposed attack?"

Fortin hesitated a moment. "The total destruction of the objective," he said crisply.

"Yes," said Czerny, licking his lips. "I supposed it might be that."

"This will take study," Tadley said. "We'll refer it to Contingency Planning and see what they come up with."

"I think," said Marshal Czerny, "that the matter will go directly to the Battle Center rather than Contingency. Although we will treat it as contingent unless and until we receive an execution order."

He raised an eyebrow toward Fortin.

Fortin smiled again. "Yes, that will do quite well," he said. "I'll return to see what you have determined."

He paused. "It's necessary to identify all potential threats in order to defend against them, of course," he added.

"Of course," murmured the voices around the display.

All of them were grinning like sharks. All six of them.

≡ 9 ≡

"WELCOME TO PEACE ROCK," said Malcolm, the powerfully built warrior who'd worn the red-blue-silver armor as he'd watched over Hansen's duel with the late Zieborn. Malcolm had a *café au lait* complexion and a rich baritone voice that was musical even in its sarcasm.

A mammoth raised its trunk and hooted loudly as it walked through the gate in the outer 'defenses,' merely a wooden palisade. But then, stone and reinforced concrete would be no better protection against the warriors' arc weapons.

"It was Blood Rock under Golsingh's old man," said Shill, who seemed to be one of Malcolm's hangers-on; a crabbed, older warrior one short step up from Villiers, whose corpse and armor had been abandoned on the field. "Golsingh changed it, because he's gonna bring peace to the whole kingdom. *He* says."

"Don't matter," said Maharg, a hulking young warrior and also under Malcolm's vague protection. "There's plenty work for us while he's bringin' peace."

"This is the capital?" Hansen said. "This is the *king's* capital?"

Peace Rock was a village of mud streets and houses whose thatched roofs arched over meter-high drystone foundations. It stank of beasts—mammoths, ponies, and huge bison with polled horns, stabled within stone fences—and of excrement, obviously from the population as well as from their livestock. Women and children, their varied status indicated by the quality of their clothing, greeted the returning army.

Peace Rock's only substantial building was in the center of the community: a hall forty meters long and almost half that in breadth. Hansen judged the roof to be ten meters high at the peak, but its thatched expanse swept down to waist height at either side. Smoke from an open hearth boiled out beneath both end gables.

Slaves had begun unloading the mammoths and collecting the ponies for feed and grooming. Many of the freemen were disappearing into squalid huts with women in tow. Nothing like an afternoon of slaughter to bring men to the need for reaffirming life in the most basic fashion possible. . . .

Hansen nodded to the hall. Dozens of male and female servants—and a pair of young women, one blond and the other black-haired, who were too beautiful and beautifully dressed to be less than nobles—waited at the entrance to greet Golsingh and Taddeusz.

"Is that Golsingh's palace, then?" he asked the trio of warriors whom he'd permitted to take him under their wing. Actually, he, Shill, and Maharg were all under Malcolm's wing.

"That's the hall," said Malcolm. "You'll sleep there, until you find a woman with a hut of her own."

He looked sharply at Hansen. "Why, do you do it differently in Annunciation?"

Hansen shrugged. "Not really," he said noncommittally.

His coveralls had lasted the run and struggle in the battlesuit, but they weren't sufficient garb for a winter evening. Where the skin was chafed, Hansen's limbs burned in the cold. He was going to need additional clothing—furs, like those the freemen and warriors wore—heat, and food, all very quickly, or exposure was going to finish what Zieborn had attempted.

The richly-dressed blond woman put her arms around Golsingh and kissed him. As if that slipped the leashes of the others gathered before the hall, the servant women broke ranks into the returning warriors like a covey of quail lifting.

Malcolm patted Shill and Maharg on the shoulder and said, "Later, gents." He strode forward and lifted a buxom redhead off her feet as she threw herself into his arms. A touch of embroidered hem showed beneath her fur cloak.

"Lucky bastard," Shill muttered, but there was more pride than envy in his voice.

"We'll do all right," Maharg said, looking around the

crowd. " 'specially tonight, since there'll be some bunks cold otherwise.''

A woman with an infant at her breast and a child of three clinging to her dress suddenly began to wail in heartbreak. Maharg watched her, flat-eyed.

The black-haired noblewoman took Taddeusz' hands in hers and dipped her head. The warchief bowed back to her.

Hansen frowned. "His wife?" he said. "Taddeusz' wife, I mean?"

"Krita," explained Shill. "His daughter. Don't touch her."

"Won't have much choice 'bout touching her at battle practice," said Maharg with a note of gloomy memory. "Fancies herself a real warmaiden. Wouldn't be surprised she goes for one of North's Searchers."

"North?" said Hansen, suddenly shocked by memory of the mission that had sent him *here*. "There's a man named North here?"

"No, no," said Shill in aged peevishness. "The god North. Where did you say you came from?"

"Look," said Hansen, "if I don't get near a fire, it won't *matter* where I came from. Can we go inside? Somewhere?"

Maharg shrugged. "Why not?" he said and stamped toward the entrance to the hall.

Golsingh, Taddeusz, and the women who'd greeted them were already going in, talking with animation. The blond paused for a moment in the doorway and looked back over her shoulder at Hansen.

"Unn, the king's wife," said Shill grimly. "And if she don't wear armor much the way Krita does, don't let that fool you. She's a tough one too. And she don't want anybody tryin' t' put one over on Golsingh."

Hansen snorted. "If Golsingh wanted to listen to me," he said, "I just might make him a real king. But I don't guess that'll happen."

The interior of the hall was dimmer than the twilight outside, but it was warm—which was rapidly becoming the only thing in the world that Hansen cared about.

The center of the long room was a hearth. Board cubicles, each with its own door, ran down either sidewall. Between the hearth and the cubicles, a U of trestle tables was arranged with benches on their wall side. Two carved chairs supplied the cross-table at the far end in place of a bench.

The whole thing was barbaric and pre-technological; whereas the warriors' armor was extremely sophisticated—though idiosyncratic.

And there was a god named North somewhere, for a man-hunter named Hansen to find and to deal with.

Golsingh and Taddeusz seated themselves on the two chairs. To Hansen's surprise, Krita and Unn took cups of jeweled metal from servants and offered them to the leaders instead of joining them at the table.

The face of Golsingh's blond wife was as cool as the surface of a forest pond which hides all the life beneath its reflection. Taddeusz' dark daughter Krita had high cheekbones and eyes like fire glinting from a hatchet blade. She wore a sleeveless tunic of blue brocade, cinched with a belt of gold. Her sinewy arms had calluses at the wrists and elbows, places where Hansen's armor had rubbed him raw.

Hansen had been busy enough taking stock of his new surroundings that he hadn't paid attention to the way his companions hesitated beside him while other warriors seated themselves at the benches. Servants stood on the inner side of the U—where the hearth must've been damned uncomfortable against their calves. They were slicing joints and ladling stewed vegetables onto plates.

Shill muttered something and scuttled toward a bench about halfway between the chairs and the door. Hansen followed, hungry enough not to realize that something beyond open seating was involved.

Maharg hung back. "Malcolm's not here," he said.

The benches were filling. Shill glanced over his shoulder, hesitated—but carried out his original intent. Maharg grimaced as he seated himself to the older man's right—throne—side; and Hansen squeezed in beside Maharg.

"How do I get proper clothi—" Hansen began as a female servant set a plate covered with broiled meat—half-burned, half-raw—and stewed vegetables before him.

The man to Hansen's right turned and gripped him by the ear. "What do *you* think you're doing here, you slave's whelp?" the man demanded.

The corner of Hansen's eye placed the carving knife—too

far—and the serving fork—just right, as the servant froze in surprise. The warrior who held him was big, young, and very angry. Hansen didn't know the etiquette at Peace Rock, but he did know that in a fraction of a second, Nils Hansen would be discussing the matter with the survivors, over the body of the man beside him.

"I think," said Malcolm, taking the other man by both ears from behind, "that he's the guy who took your brother one-on-one, Letzing. Which you—" Letzing's fingers relaxed as Malcolm twisted "—couldn't've managed in a million years. So what're *you* doing up-bench of him?"

Malcolm lifted Letzing deliberately from his seat. Everyone in the hall was watching, but no one attempted to interfere.

Letzing stumbled as Malcolm walked him backward off the bench. "You wouldn't do this to me if my brother were here!" he cried out unexpectedly.

Malcolm let him go and said brutally, "Zieborn's not here. He's dead. Want to try me tomorrow and join him? Want to try me tonight?"

Letzing was broader than Malcolm and almost as tall, but you didn't need Hansen's experience to realize that it would be the contest of the axe and the firelog if Letzing accepted the challenge.

Letzing knew that too. He turned away and stamped across to a seat on the other side of the hall—and well down the bench. Malcolm took his place, looked at Hansen, and said, "Well, we're the bold lad, aren't we? But if Maharg doesn't mind, I certainly don't."

Maharg forked a slice of meat into his mouth and said mushily, "Aw, it don't matter. I figured I'd let him sit beside you this once, is all."

The meat was unseasoned, tough, and cut into larger chunks than Hansen was used to putting in his mouth. He chewed and stared at Maharg until the powerfully built young man met his eyes.

Hansen swallowed. "And then again," he said deliberately, "maybe this is how it's going to stay."

Maharg flushed and took a spoonful of turnips and potatoes. He didn't reply.

Malcolm guffawed and accepted the cup handed him by the

redheaded woman he'd embraced on returning. "Quite the lad," he repeated.

The food was not so much bad as boring, and the beer that was the only available drink had a musty undertaste. Still, Hansen was hungry enough to have chopped a piece of one of the draft mammoths if nothing else were available. He concentrated happily on his meal.

While the warriors ate, slaves carried suits of armor into the hall and placed each in one of the cubicles along the sidewalls. Malcolm nudged Hansen and said, "That's yours," pointing to the quartet of slaves who had just entered with a russet and black suit.

"The arm's cut off," Hansen said, trying to keep the concern out of his voice.

"Don't worry," Malcolm explained. "It's a good suit. We'll carry it to Vasque the Smith tomorrow and get it repaired."

"It's a *damned* good suit," muttered Shill.

Maharg turned on the old warrior and snarled, "So why didn't *you* ever challenge Zieborn and get a suit just as good, ha?"

"Maharg," said Malcolm quietly.

"Yeah, well," said the younger man as he went back to his food.

Taddeusz' daughter took a silver pitcher of beer from a servant and walked down the runway between the fire and table. Her soft shoes made no sound on the hall's puncheon floor. Golsingh, Unn, and—with dawning fury—Taddeusz watched her progress.

She stopped in front of Hansen. He looked up in surprise.

"Krita!" the warchief shouted.

Krita bent and filled Hansen's cup.

"I want to meet the new hero," she said in a clear voice that rang in the sudden silence. "The wolf in Villiers' clothing."

"Some would say," Unn called with equal clarity down the length of the table, "that it's a coward's part to slay a man with a bolt."

Hansen went cold. He looked in Unn's direction, but he saw nothing except a blur of blond hair and his own cold fury. "Zieborn wouldn't say that, milady," he said loudly.

A warrior across the hall snorted. "That's tellin' her, buddy!" he shouted. The whole room rocked with laughter as heavy fists pounded the tables in amusement.

Krita raised an eyebrow and walked back to the other end of the room.

Taddeusz stood up. The hall quieted.

"I served my king this day as no other man has done," the warchief boomed in what Hansen realized after a moment was a set speech. "Alone I strode among my king's enemies—" *nearly true, and nothing for a sensible man to boast about* "—and smote them down by the scores. Cerausi, the warchief of Count Lopez, a mighty hero, dared stand against me. His armor was silver and blue. He struck at me—"

Hansen began to nod. He was exhausted; the fire warmed him, and much of his blood supply was in his belly, converting the heavy meal into strength for the morrow.

He looked around covertly to see how the other warriors were reacting to Taddeusz' speech. They were just as tired as Hansen, and most of them had been much less sparing with the beer. Several had already collapsed in place. Servants worried the plates and remains of food out from under them.

Hansen heard dogs yelping outside, but at least they weren't being allowed in the hall during the meal as he'd rather expected would be the case. Reassured that the worst he was likely to do would be within the bounds of propriety here, Hansen slid his dish out of the way and concentrated on keeping awake.

After Taddeusz finished his speech, the warrior at the head of the bench to the king's left rose and rambled off on a boast of his own. No one seemed to listen to him—or, for that matter, to any of the warriors who followed him with equally boring harangues. As soon as one warrior sat down, the next—across the hall—got up, even if they'd been snoring on the table a moment before.

It was noticeable that the farther down the benches the speakers were, the shorter and less circumstantial their boasts tended to be.

The man across from Hansen stopped in the middle of a sentence that hadn't seemed to be going anywhere. He didn't so much sit down as flop when his legs gave way. A servant handed him a refilled cup.

Maharg elbowed Hansen. "Well, go on!" he said.

"But—" Hansen said. He stood, shaking his head to clear it. All right, he hadn't been in the battle, and he wasn't going to brag about killing Zieborn . . . or anybody else. Zieborn hadn't been the first, or the twenty-first; but that had been the job of Special Units.

"I won't tell you what I've done," Hansen said, raising his voice over the sound of snores and servants clearing dishes. "That's little enough so far, here in your country. And I won't boast about what I'm going to do in the next battle or the next hundred battles. But—"

Hansen turned to the cross-table. Taddeusz was—no, the warchief *wasn't* asleep, for his eyes snapped firmly shut when Hansen stared at him. Golsingh was watching; and Krita, and Unn. . . .

"But Lord Golsingh, if it's your true desire to bring peace to all your kingdom—peace that stands, not a battle here and a feud there, always and forever, for you to stamp out and go on to the next—"

The king was nodding. The women's faces didn't change.

"Then I can show you how to do it."

"That isn't a warrior's part!" Taddeusz shouted, raising his head from his crossed arms. Golsingh looked at him with a frown.

"I'll do a warrior's job when there's fighting," Hansen snapped. "But I'll let you do a king's job, Lord Golsingh— if you really want that!"

He sat down abruptly, before he said too much—if he hadn't already. The beer's unpleasant taste covered a surprising kick.

Another warrior rose and maundered unintelligibly.

Hansen fell asleep while the last warriors spoke.

Clashing metal—a dropped cup—awakened him. The hearth had burned to coals, but there was still enough light to see forms hunched at the tables. Half the room was empty, but many of the warriors were continuing to drink and mumble to one another.

"Malcolm, where do I bunk?" Hansen asked, hoping he'd correctly identified the man to his right.

A servant stepped between the coals and Hansen. "More beer, hero?" she asked.

Not a servant. Krita.

"No," Hansen said curtly. "And you can call me a hero when you believe it yourself. Not now."

The black-haired woman laughed. "How good are you, Hansen?" she asked.

"Good enough," he said. "As good as I—"

He paused. "I'll tell you this, lady," he said in sudden decision. "I'm the best there is. That's how good I am."

He turned his back on her throaty chuckle. He was pretty sure he remembered which cubicle he'd seen them carry the russet and black armor into.

Malcolm put a hand on Hansen's shoulder. "That one," he said, pointing to a doorway.

"Thanks."

"Quite the lad," Malcolm said. "You know, boy—"

Hansen paused at the doorway and looked back.

"—I'm not sure I'm going to want to know you," Malcolm finished.

And he chuckled as he sat down on his bench again, but Hansen was pretty sure the comment had been more than a joke.

≡ 10 ≡

THERE WAS JUST enough sunlight percolating through the walls of the bed cubicle for Hansen to see his breath in a chill cloud.

Hansen straightened his arms; the heavy fur bedclothes resisted. He groaned and swung himself out of bed at once, because it wasn't going to get better—and if he didn't have the guts to face the morning, any morning, then he'd spent his life in a variety of the wrong businesses.

The parts of Hansen's body that didn't ache jabbed when he made them move. Twenty-nine was too old for this crap; he ought to leave it for the new crop of bright-eyed nineteen-year-olds who healed fast, who didn't know how badly they could get hurt—

Who hadn't seen enough other people die to realize that they would be among that number very soon themselves.

On the other hand, Taddeusz had been in the heart of the battle, and he was damned near old enough to be Hansen's father. Which probably proved that older didn't necessarily mean wiser . . . and that Hansen wouldn't be ready to hang it up at Taddeusz' age either.

Things had bitten him in the night. Hansen told himself he'd get used to that. He'd better. The jakes here were an open pit with a crossbar and a perfunctory windbreak—damned cold last night, and he'd get used to that too; though he figured either to find or invent a chamber pot before evening.

Hansen's battlesuit stared blankly at him from the foot of his bed.

Hansen opened the door of his cubicle to let in more light. The latch was a bar set in heavy staples, an unexpectedly sturdy arrangement given the flimsy construction of the bed-chamber itself. Slaves, sweeping the night's debris into the hearth with straw brooms, dropped their voices when they saw one of the warriors was up—and chattered again when they saw it was Hansen.

Only Hansen. Well, he'd been a newbie before, in the Civic Patrol and later when he transferred to Special Units. If he survived the next few months, he'd have as much respect as he wanted.

Hansen examined his new battlesuit. It was a noticeably more solid unit than the one from which he'd ejected Villiers' corpse. The difference was not as much in the weight of the metal—equating mass with sturdiness was an error out of which he'd trained himself long before—but in the fit of the various sections.

The lining was thick suede. It wouldn't keep his skin from chafing, but it was probably as good a material as could be found for the purpose here. Hansen found to his surprise that it wasn't slick with dry, clotted blood down the left side, because the arc that burned off the former owner's arm had also cauterized the blood vessels.

The severed piece lay on the floor in front of the rest of the suit. Hansen rotated it in his hands, looking at the line of bubbled metal and the core of integrated circuits, shattered and blackened by high-temperature cutting.

Repairing *this* wasn't a job for a smith on a feudal back-water. It would require technicians of exceptional compe-tence—

And by watching the work done, Hansen might just find the path to North and the answers the Consensus had sent him to find.

The door of the cubicle next to Hansen's opened. "You look cheerful," said Malcolm, though the way he said it in-dicated that he'd noticed more than humor in Hansen's grin.

"What are you doing here?" Hansen asked in surprise. "I assumed you'd be . . ."

"Nancy, you mean?" Malcolm said with a smile of his own. His features were as perfect as his voice, and his tawny complexion looked almost golden in the diffused sunlight. "I was on duty last night—we sleep night and night in the hall, here at Peace Rock. Taddeusz is very firm about that."

Hansen nodded. "Something we can agree on," he said.

Malcolm smiled more broadly. "It isn't considered good form to entertain your friends in your chamber here," he went on. "But it's been known to happen, particularly the night after a battle."

"You, ah . . . ," Hansen said. "I'm not sure. . . . Do you have formal ranks here? That is, what's *your* rank, for instance?"

"Where do I sit at table, do you mean?" said Malcolm with a puzzled expression. "But you saw—"

He grinned again. "Ah, you drank more than I thought. I've been on the lower end of the left side, but after yesterday's battle I'd decided to move to the middle—even before you put yourself in my train."

So that was why Malcolm had been so friendly. He was himself an ambitious outsider, trying to build status by increasing the number of warriors under his protection.

"Not everybody would say I was a desirable supporter," Hansen commented aloud.

"Not everyone would," Malcolm agreed, nodding. "What do you say, my bold laddie?"

Hansen met the veteran's eyes and said, very deliberately, "I say that in a year, you'll be sitting in Taddeusz' seat. If you want to."

Malcolm looked around sharply to see if any of the slaves were within earshot—a precaution Hansen had taken before he spoke.

"I think you've just convinced me that the others are the smart ones," Malcolm said.

He nodded toward the damaged armor. "Let's get your suit repaired," he added. "And let's you not talk about things that don't concern either of us."

"All right," said Hansen. He got a grip on the suit. "Where do we go with—"

Malcolm swatted his hands aside. "Where do you come from?" he said in amazement.

He turned to the cleaning crew. "Hey!" he called. "You lot! Get over here and carry Lord Hansen's armor to the smithy."

Good humored again—Hansen's stated plans had frightened Malcolm, but the notion of a warrior doing scut work had offended him—the veteran warrior smiled and said to Hansen, "There should be some furs in Alyn's chest—at the head of the bed."

He gestured into the bed cubicle. "Knock the lock off if there is one. Alyn won't mind where he is now, whether North took his soul or Hell did."

There were furs—and they smelled—but they were warm and the bright sunlight was cheering, although not particularly hot. Hansen wondered idly what season he'd arrived in. It wasn't a question he thought it'd be a good idea to ask.

The smithy turned out to be a long shed against the back of the palisade. Wicker baskets of rock—ore, presumably, but not smelted metals—were piled around the walls. There wasn't a hearth in front of the building as Hansen had expected, and the open fire within was no more than necessary for heat.

Four grunting slaves set the armor just inside the doorway. A fifth started to lay down the arm he carried, but Malcolm stopped him with a snap of his fingers. "Not yet," he said. "Vasque, we have a project for you."

There were already three men in the smithy: a bald old fellow with a wizened face, and two lads in their late teens. The old man was seated. One of the youths stood, looking uncertain, and the other lay on a couch, snoring stertorously, beside a table heaped with sand and gravel.

The old man glared. "Then it'll have to wait."

"Wrong, Vasque," said Malcolm. "The king directs that Lord Hansen here be outfitted properly. The king's honor is involved."

"Faugh," muttered Vasque. He stepped to the suit and ran his fingers over first the plastron, then the sheared metal along the cut. The sleeping youth was muttering to himself.

Hansen couldn't judge the status of the smith and his apprentices. Vasque wore a gorgeously-embroidered tunic—though there was a cracked leather apron over it. Even the youths were dressed rather better than many of the warriors.

"Not much of a suit," Vasque said. "Dilmun's work, I wouldn't be surprised, and he was never much."

"Dilmun's good enough to dress the Lord of Thrasey," said Malcolm. "And as for this suit, there were three arcs on it together before it failed."

"On a good day, I suppose Dilmun might be all right," Vasque admitted grudgingly. He took the severed arm from the slave and worked the elbow joint with his hands as he peered at the cut. "Well, we'll see."

The sleeping youth groaned loudly and threw out an arm. After a moment, his eyes opened. The other apprentice helped him sit up on the couch.

Vasque handed the arm back. "Go on, boy, go on," he said to the apprentice, making shooing motions with his hands. "There's king's work to be done."

He turned to the slaves. "Lay it down by the couch, you. I'll take care of it now."

As the slaves laid the damaged suit full-length on the floor, the two youths positioned the arm by it so that the cut ends joined. Vasque himself stepped outside. He came back with his leather apron laden with bits of ore.

"Might need more than this," the old man muttered, "but I think not, I think not. . . ." He arranged his chips and pebbles around the severed arm with as much care as a florist creating a wedding bouquet.

As the master smith worked, the apprentices poked into rubble piled on the table. The youth who'd been sleeping came up with the forearm of a battlesuit. The rock heaped over it was pebble-sized on top, but the portion around the piece itself was fine dust that made Hansen sneeze.

Vasque lay down on the couch the apprentice had vacated. One of the youths took a polished locket on a thong from around his neck.

"Keep back, boy . . . ," the smith murmured.

His eyes, focused on dust motes dancing in the light, glazed and closed. The apprentices watched with critical interest, while the slaves gaped with amazement as great as that which Hansen tried to conceal.

Asking what in hell was going on would be just as bad an idea as trying to learn what the season of the year was. Besides, Diamond had come pretty close to Hansen's idea of what heaven would be—right down to the fact there'd been no room for *him* there.

That meant Hell wasn't a word he wanted to take in vain on Northworld either.

Vasque was shuddering in his sleep. Hansen gestured toward him. "Is he any good?" he asked Malcolm in an undertone.

"You won't wake him," said Malcolm in a normal voice, as though that were the only reason someone would want to discuss the matter in a whisper. "And yeah, he's very good."

The veteran smiled impishly. "Almost as good as Dilmun, I'd say. You'll have a suit to be proud of."

Malcolm took the piece of armor from the apprentices and looked at it critically. "Who's this for?" he demanded suddenly.

The youth who'd been on the couch said, "Well, it's for stock, milord."

"For practice," added his fellow.

On closer examination, Hansen saw that the portion of armor wasn't complete. It was shorter than most adult male forearms; and, while there was a raised border on the wrist end where the piece would join the gauntlet, there was no corresponding reinforcement toward the elbow. The core of circuitry in a ceramic matrix was white against the heavy metal of the exterior and the lighter cladding of the inner face.

Malcolm handed the piece back. "Keep practicing," he said coldly.

The ore shifted around Hansen's suit. The chunks on top of the pile slid as dust puffed away. As Hansen watched, a fist-sized lump he thought was magnetite crumbled as though in a hammermill. Bits of it drifted down through the interstices of the pebbles beneath it.

One of the apprentices bobbed his head in approval. "Look, he must be four centimeters away from the join," he said. "Great extension!"

Malcolm sniffed. "The important part," he said, ostensibly to Hansen, "isn't how far a smith can reach through the Matrix for material but how well he stitches the result together. *That's* the craftsmanship that keeps you and me alive, Lord Hansen."

"That and skill," Hansen remarked coolly.

He hadn't seen Walker since the duel the day before. That was someone whom he could question without worrying about raised eyebrows.

Of course, while Walker could be a machine from the end

of time, as he claimed; or simply a series of talking birds and animals, as he appeared—the likelihood was that the little voice was an aspect of Hansen's psychosis, like everything else around him. Maybe Commissioner Nils Hansen had been shot in the head as he ran toward Solbarth's hideout. . . .

Half the gravel piled on the shoulder of the battlesuit powdered and slipped to a flatter angle of repose.

Vasque shuddered like a swimmer coming out of cold water. His apprentices stepped toward him, one of them with a skin of wine or mead, but the older man waved them away. "There!" he gasped. "There, Lord Malcolm. Tell me about Dilmun *now*.

"Although," he added as he got to his feet and only then accepted the container of drink, "I checked the whole suit while I was in the Matrix, and it's not so very bad after all. . . ."

"How do we test it?" Hansen asked.

Malcolm smiled. "I get my suit," he said, "we go out to the practice ground . . . and I see just how good you are, laddie."

It wasn't an especially nice smile; but then, neither was the grin that bared Hansen's teeth.

≡ 11 ≡

THE PRACTICE GROUND was outside the palisade, on a broad, flat stretch of meadow that had been trampled to gluey mud. A bad surface for comfort, but one which accurately reflected the sort of filthy conditions in which wars had been fought from time immemorial. There were fir posts set up at three-meter intervals around the perimeter; many of them had been burned in half.

Hansen was already pleased with his new armor. His displays were crisper by an order of magnitude than those of Villiers' suit, and the limbs moved in response to Hansen's movements without nearly as much lag time.

Of course, getting there and being able to see what he was doing were by no means half the battle.

No other warriors were on the practice ground, but Hansen and Malcolm had attracted a scattering of spectators, both freemen and slaves, on their walk from the hall. A female slave called an offer that Hansen didn't quite catch, but the laughter of the others hinted at the nature of the words.

"All right," said Malcolm. "Let's make sure we're both on practice setting, shall we?" The words had buzzing undertones as they reached Hansen through the speaker on Malcolm's helmet and the headphones in Hansen's.

The veteran's right gauntlet sprouted an arc. He turned and slashed. The weapon scarred a post to the heartwood but didn't blast it apart the way Hansen had seen trees disintegrated during the battle.

He could guess, but: "What's the codeword on your suits?" he asked.

"Huh?" Malcolm responded like a bumblebee. "Practice, of course. I thought that was standard everywhere?"

"Practice," Hansen said, then, "Cut." His arc sizzled into the post, cross-cutting Malcolm's mark to within a degree of perpendicular.

He smiled. Malcolm cut at his head.

Hansen hadn't expected the attack—*my fault,* his mind cursed as he threw himself backward and tried to raise his arc weapon to block Malcolm's. He didn't succeed in either attempt. Malcolm's arc slipped under Hansen's flailing guard and cut across his neck joint.

Hansen's armor froze. His display vanished and left him in blackness lighted only by the afterimages on his retinas.

He wasn't dead. He could feel his heart beating in claustrophobic fear.

"Well," demanded Malcolm's distorted voice, "reset your suit."

Ah. . . . "Reset," said Hansen, hoping that was the key word—though he was becoming increasingly impressed by the flexibility of the suit's artificial intelligence. Light dawned—literally. Hansen's display flooded him with images of morning. He saw Malcolm waiting a pace back, arms akimbo.

Hansen flexed his left gauntlet and cried, "Cut!" as he lunged. Malcolm shifted and slashed down at his attacker, but he hadn't been expecting Hansen to strike from the left. Hansen's thrust struck home at the veteran's hip joint.

There was a shower of sparks. Hansen's arc snuffed unexpectedly, but Malcolm's suit went dull and his empty gauntlet quivered to a halt in mid-stroke.

Hansen had fallen into a three-point stance. He pushed himself erect and backed a step, waiting for Malcolm to reset his armor. "Cut," he muttered, flexing his right hand to be ready for the next attack.

This was work, was heavy exercise. His armor weighed over a hundred kilos. Though that wasn't dead weight so long as it was powered up, inertia gave the suit the resistance of a brick wall for the instant before its servos took over the work from Hansen's muscles.

A long arc twinkled from Malcolm's gauntlet. In practice mode, the discharges were at only a fraction of war power, and interlocks cut off the weapon as soon as its touch had shut down an opponent's armor. It was at least as safe as fighting with buttoned epees, though no doubt accidents could happen.

And it was a good time to explore the capacities of the armor itself.

"Display energy levels," Hansen ordered, wondering what the artificial intelligence would make of the command—and delighted to see Malcolm's suit not as painted steel but as a mosaic in which the visual spectrum mapped electrical activity across the surface of the suit.

The arc sprouting from the veteran's right hand pulled from indigo through violet. The gauntlet itself was a bright blue, while the remainder of Malcolm's limbs and torso rippled mostly in the yellow and green. The helmet peak was nearly orange, and another orange blotch wavered across the plastron generally at mid-chest level.

It looked like . . .

"Off!" Hansen said, and the hot spot on Malcolm's armor vanished as soon as Hansen's weapon did.

God almighty! Malcolm's artificial intelligence tracked Hansen's arc—and raised the defensive charge of the spot the AI thought most at risk.

The veteran's knee joints streaked orange as power fed to the servos. Malcolm started a lunge but Hansen, alerted by the display, drove forward to anticipate the attack. His left hand slid along Malcolm's right wrist and forearm, and his right hand speared toward the veteran's throat.

Forgot the arc.

"Cut!" and the crackle of harmless sparks ended almost as soon as they'd begun. Malcolm fell over as his circuit breakers tripped. His suit blurred into the dull red background.

Hansen stepped back and reformatted to standard optical display. He was taking deep, gasping breaths. His suit's air system strained between each wheezing exhalation to clear condensate from the displays.

The surface of Malcolm's armor quivered as the veteran reset it. There was no definable change from a suit that was powered up to a cold one, but the difference in appearance was as great as that between a living man and a fresh corpse.

Malcolm rose to a four-limbed crouch but paused there. "How did you do that?" he asked.

"It's the display," Hansen explained. His suit's steel casing vibrated every time he spoke. "Look, let's stop this for a minute and I'll show—"

Malcolm gave a brief nod of his armored head. The spectators were turning their heads. Hansen turned also and saw the figure in gleaming black armor striding down the path from the settlement.

"Show *me* what you can do, stranger," the figure called.

Ordered. *Small—as much shorter than Hansen as he was shorter than Malcolm. Wasn't in the battle the day before. A battlesuit of exceptional quality. . . .*

"If you wish it, milord," Hansen said deliberately as the black figure stepped through the line of posts that marked the edge of the practice ground.

"Not 'milord,' you fool!" the figure's harsh mechanical voice snarled. An arc sprang from the right gauntlet.

"Display energy levels," Hansen murmured. The figure before him shimmered in cold blue. *This was going to be* . . .

"Yes, milady," he said aloud. "Krita."

Instead of striding toward Hansen, Krita's hand twisted and shot her arc across the four meters separating them. He didn't have time to think about defense before his displays went dark and left him with his own moist breath.

"Reset," Hansen muttered. "Cut."

He spread his fingers, giving him a broad fan of spluttering discharge. Krita waited, spurting and shrinking the weapon vertically from her right hand. At its peak, the discharge fountained ten meters in the air.

A very good suit indeed.

Hansen stepped forward. Krita's weapon lashed down at him. He caught the blow and shrank his own arc to a tight ball as he took another step—

The arc from Krita's left gauntlet slashed across his knees.

Falling in a dead battlesuit was very similar to being rolled off the porch in a garbage can. It wasn't likely to be fatal. . . .

"Reset. Cut."

Default setting on Hansen's display was standard optical. He didn't bother to switch it over to show energy levels; Krita's battlesuit operated at such a high order that there'd been no significant change in the display when she attacked.

Although—

Hansen rose to a crouch and lunged forward as if to tackle his opponent around the knees. He thought that by leading with his helmet, the focus of his electronic armor, he might be able to get close enough to use his own arc effectively.

A contemptuous sweep of Krita's hand swatted him down. His scalp and the back of his neck tingled, even at the arc's reduced charge level. Hansen grounded face first.

He squatted. His display was fuzzy. He wiped the faceplate of his helmet with his steel palm.

Blobs of mud dribbled from his gauntlet like raindrops blowing across the windshield of a moving vehicle. His display cleared. The suit's electronic defenses worked on fouling; they just took a little time.

Krita laughed. She stood three meters from Hansen with her hands on her hips.

Hansen had cut his chin, and he thought his nose was bleeding.

"Cut," he said, flexing his right hand. He snapped the long arc across his opponent's ankles.

Mud hissed away as steam and dust. Krita laughed again, without moving.

"Off," Hansen said and lifted the palm of his left gauntlet toward the woman's throat as he charged.

At this range, a bolt might or might not have been effective enough to end the duel; one had, after all, shut down Taddeusz' battlesuit under similar conditions. Krita'd probably watched Hansen kill Zieborn; certainly she'd had an opportunity to finger the hole the stranger burned through Zieborn's armor and life. . . .

The threat shocked her into a defense response: limbs rigid, arc weapons shut down; her AI concentrating all the suit's energies on the point the bolt would strike.

There was no bolt. Hansen hit the woman with a crash like anvils meeting, gripping her by both wrists. Even at this range the black battlesuit was probably proof against Hansen's arc—

But his mass and the momentum of his rush carried her backward a half-step until Hansen twisted and threw her over his knee. Krita skidded a meter in slick mud, her limbs flailing.

Hansen stepped back and let his arms hang at his sides.

There was no way he could prevent Taddeusz' daughter from taking whatever revenge she chose, but by standing braced he could at least keep from falling over again when she tripped out his circuit breakers.

Krita got up. Her suit streamed mud as if she were under a firehose.

Black fury. . . .

She turned and stamped back toward the palisade. One of the fir posts was in her path. Instead of changing direction, she lashed out with an arc that exploded the base of the post into blazing splinters. A patch of mud hardened to scorched adobe.

Malcolm split his armor and twisted his torso free. "My, my, my," he murmured, watching Krita go.

Hansen opened his own suit also. The outside air turned his sweat into a cold bath. His breath rattled through his open mouth; he hoped his nose wasn't broken.

"My, my," Malcolm repeated. He looked at Hansen. "You know," he said wonderingly, "I think you deserve each other."

"Why wasn't she fighting?" Hansen asked. "You know, yesterday?"

Malcolm looked at him oddly. "Women don't go to war," he said. "Not . . . not here." His face hardened. "Not anywhere I want to be, either."

Hansen withdrew his arms from the battlesuit and massaged his shoulders. The woman in black armor had disappeared into the palisade.

"That's a waste," he said, though it wasn't quite what he meant; and anyway, he wasn't sure what he meant. Cultural factors didn't make a lot of sense here on Northworld—or anywhere else Nils Hansen had been or heard of.

"North has his Searchers," Malcolm said, "and if it were in our Krita's gift, she'd be one of them, you bet."

"Searchers?" Hansen said.

His mind was suddenly back in gear. While he fought Krita, he'd been locked into the notion that only the next microsecond mattered. "Searchers. That's the—black shutters opening and closing? During the battle yesterday?"

"Black wings, yeah," Malcolm agreed, wary again.

"Some people say that, I've heard. Nothing I know about myself."

His mouth quirked in a false smile. "Nothing I like to talk about much, to tell the truth."

So there was a way to North . . . maybe.

Hansen thrust his hands back through the armholes and prepared to close his suit over himself again. "All right," he said. "Let's get to it. There's a lot I need to learn about this suit before I use it for real."

Malcolm laughed. "Well, you don't have very long to manage that, do you?"

Hansen started to pull the clamshell shut. "Eh?" he said as he strained against the dead weight of the armor. It gave slowly, pivoting like the door of a cell across his view of Malcolm.

"Didn't you know?" called the veteran's voice. "The Lord of Thrasey defied Golsingh also. We'll be—"

Hansen's suit slammed shut. His display flickered to life, and the conclusion of Malcolm's statement buzzed with static.

"—fighting him in three days."

≡ 12 ≡

THE PALACE IN which Penny lived was a thing of curves and pointed turrets joined by sweeping walkways. Balconies jutted from beneath arched windows, and flagstaffs streamed pennons in the breeze. The walls were slabs of pink marble with pearly inclusions, while the grilles and railings were pure yellow gold.

A central spire, slim and twice the height of any other portion of the palace, swelled at the top into an onion-domed suite.

"I always find it breathtaking," said Rolls dryly from the saddle of his giant elk.

"Indeed, my lord," said Fortin. He walked at Rolls' left stirrup and wore Rolls' livery as though he were one of the thirty human retainers accompanying their master on his visit to Penny.

Rolls looked down at the half android. They'd chosen slouch hats and capes of bright orange velvet for the retainers on this operation, a costume which hid the wearers' form and features. Penny's human servants wouldn't recognize Fortin, but she herself would if she saw him clearly. Even now that they'd reached the critical stage, Rolls remained sure that there was little chance of that happening.

Trumpeters on the lower balconies of the palace blew a greeting in sequential notes while flags of gold on pink— matching their livery—fluttered from their instruments.

The gate was also golden. The doorleaves, molded with cavorting cherubs, opened with glassy precision as Rolls and his entourage approached them. Hundreds of Penny's servants were drawn up in the entrance hall.

Rolls dismounted. Like his retainers, he wore orange—but

briefs that were little more than a jockstrap and matching sandals. He'd been proud of his body before—before North, before godhead. If he was past his first youth and carrying ten kilos more than ideal, then it still was a body that justified pride.

For the moment, the important thing was that all eyes be on him and not on his servants—as was proper in any case.

The trumpet calls ended when Rolls and his entourage entered the hall. String instruments played by hidden servitors took up a melody so saccharine that Fortin murmured to Rolls, "Now the little cupids fly down from the ceiling, don't they?"

The entrance hall had coffered walls with tall sconces on the verticals and mirrors on the sunken central panels. Another set of great doors stood at the top of a pink marble staircase at the far end of the hall.

The music built to a crescendo. The pulses of light rising through the transparent sconces dimmed.

Rolls continued to walk forward. His servants fell off to either side and milled behind the lines of Penny's pink-clad folk. "Good luck," he murmured as the caped-and-hatted figure to his immediate left broke away.

"Good luck to *you*, my friend," Fortin whispered back. "Our Penny expects her standards to be met. . . ."

When Rolls passed the center of the room, the gold doors above the staircase swung open in silent majesty. The vague, mirrored glows of the sconces exaggerated the vast size of the hall.

Penny stood at the head of the stairs, a statuesque vision of beauty and passion. Her hair was black, her complexion as white as bleached flour. Penny's dress and elbow-length gloves were the same brilliant scarlet as her lips, and a single bright jewel gleamed at her throat.

"Greetings, Lord Rolls," Penny called in a throaty contralto. "It has been long since you visited us."

She pouted. In the same voice, but with utterly different intonation she added, "I thought you didn't like me any more."

"You know how jealous I am, my darling," Rolls said as he advanced to the foot of the stairs.

In this outfit, with his hairy, muscular body, he looked like an apeman approaching the mistress of the plantation. Penny would probably find the contrast piquant.

"But I found I couldn't keep myself away from you."

Of course, Penny found most things piquant when they touched on her areas of interest.

She extended a gloved hand to him. "You know the others mean nothing to me, darling," she said—and giggled, spoiling the effect.

Rolls took the first of the six steps normally, swung his long leg up the next two together, and mounted to the landing in a rush as Penny threw open her arms and allowed him to sweep her off her feet in a passionate embrace.

"Oh, Rolls," she murmured with her eyes closed. "You know I've missed you, honey."

It bothered Rolls that sometimes he had the feeling that Penny was much more intelligent than she seemed. Than she *played*, forming herself into a one-dimensional caricature. . . .

But then, that was what they all did, since godhead, unless they fought the tendency the way Rolls did.

And perhaps even if they did fight.

Rolls nodded upward and lifted his eyebrows. "Ah, can we . . . ?" he asked. The strings had resumed playing, but in whispered undertones of sweetness.

"I thought you'd never ask," said Penny haughtily.

She linked her arm with his and led him back through the gold columns. The doors closed behind them, shutting off the music and the sound of servants chattering as soon as their masters' backs were turned.

The room beyond the doors was a circular foyer, not as large as the entrance hall but huge in its own right. The floor was paved with marble. Around the walls roses had been trained into secluded arbors. Light flooded through high windows.

Rolls' bright sandals whisked on the stone as he led his hostess toward the transparent lift across the room.

Penny glanced down at herself. "How do you like this?" she asked critically.

Rolls paused and kissed her, resting his left hand on her shoulder and his right, caressingly, in the small of her back.

In this form, Penny was supple and tall enough that her head reached his chin when they both stood erect.

"Now?" she said, urgent, questioning, hopeful. "Or in the roses?"

She nodded. As she did so, a pair of servants entered the foyer through a door hidden in the foliage, saw their mistress and her guest, and bolted back out of sight.

"No," Rolls said. He didn't have to fake the interest in his voice. "I have an idea."

He led her by the hand to the lift tube, their strides lengthening with each step.

The lift appeared to be an empty three-meter shaft until Rolls and Penny stood on it. The air beneath their feet hardened and they began to rise. A foreshortened figure in pink livery walked across the foyer, unaware of their rising presence.

Penny stroked Rolls' bulging groin. "I thought perhaps . . . ," she said, and as she spoke the figure in the air beside Rolls was shorter, slender, and nude except for the necklace.

"Or even—something unusual?" and she was fat, though her breasts were heavy rather than pendulous. Her hair was black for a moment, then blond, and finally a rich chestnut. She cocked an eyebrow at Rolls.

The lift rose through the ceiling of the foyer and into the shaft of the central tower. Individual rooms opened onto a hall which circled the shaft.

There were railings here. The lift was for Penny, her peers, and those whom her whim chose. It was a straight drop to marble for any ordinary human servant who stepped into the shaft.

Rolls leaned forward and kissed one of the dark nipples, letting it swell under his tongue. "No," he said as he straightened, "I don't think quite . . ."

Penny licked her lips. She let her body tremble through changes, one after the other, and as she did so her fingers reached under the waistband of Rolls' briefs.

The lift had risen past the servants' quarters, though a spiral staircase circled the shaft. The floors at this height were mostly open rooms whose furnishings were decorated with flounces and lace. Balconies bulged from the outer walls.

"What I would like," Rolls said carefully, "is *you*, Penny."

They glided to a halt at the top of the tower. The dome was several times the diameter of the spire that supported it. Its floor area was divided into four suites, each with its own door off the lift shaft.

"Well, of course!" Penny said, throwing open a door into a huge bedroom furnished mostly in white fur. The outer wall was crystal and brilliant in the sunlight.

She looked at her companion in sudden surmise. "Oh . . . ," she said. "This old thing?"

The woman before Rolls was suddenly a short, slightly overweight nineteen-year-old, with curly blond hair and pale areolae.

Rolls took Penny's left breast in his hand and kissed her hard on the lips. He stepped back and pulled down his briefs.

"You," he said. He smiled broadly. "On the balcony. But you, not the necklace."

Penny's tongue touched her lips again. Her hands rose and paused around the almost invisibly fine filament that supported the jewel that was all she now wore. Then she lifted it off in a convulsive motion and tossed it toward a dresser whose mirror and cosmetics were needless frills here—like most of this palace, like most of their lives, all of them.

The only change in the woman's appearance was that a mole sprouted on the side of her left breast. Its pigmentation was darker than that of the nipple.

"Come and get me, then," Penny giggled.

She turned and scampered toward the circular balcony. The crystalline panels pivoted open as she approached.

Rolls followed. It was necessary that he let her run partway around the dome before he caught her.

But he was as ready to catch her as she was to be caught.

≡ 13 ≡

"I HURT," SAID Hansen, "all over."

He kneaded his thighs viciously as he walked. At least fighting in a battlesuit didn't leave hands cramped the way Hansen's fierce grip on a gun butt invariably did.

Malcolm raised an eyebrow. "You look like you're in shape," he said. "It was a good workout, but . . ."

Hansen checked the double quartet of slaves sullenly carrying the warriors' armor. Malcolm had dragooned the nearest spectators without hesitation when he and Hansen agreed that they didn't feel like walking their own suits back up the half kilometer to the palisade. Furthermore, the train of slaves stumbling along behind them was an excuse for Hansen to walk slowly—and spare his aching legs.

"Yeah, well," Hansen said. "I'm in shape, all right—but I don't have the muscles for this *particular* job. Every piece of equipment you use—and that's as true of a rake as it is of a battlesuit—it takes a little different set of muscles."

A calculated risk.

"But—" said the veteran.

Hansen gripped Malcolm's right hand with his own left. Because of the tan that Annunciation's sun had given Hansen, their skin was almost the same shade.

That wouldn't be true long—if he lived.

"Listen, Malcolm," he said. "Where I come from, we don't fight with battlesuits. We've got other weapons, that's all. It doesn't mean I'm not a warrior."

The two men continued to walk, hand in hand. Malcolm's expression was unreadable. Then he broke into a smile and said, "No, I don't doubt that you're a warrior."

He clapped Hansen on the back. "If Zieborn wasn't enough

proof," he added, "what you did to me this morning surely is. You'll have to teach me some of those tricks."

They'd reached the palisade. The odor of Peace Rock assailed them, though the fact the citadel was on high ground meant there was *some* drainage.

Hansen nodded seriously. "I'll teach you all of them," he said. "There's still a lot to learn about this armor, and everything I learn, you and, you know, the others. They'll have to learn too, Maharg and Shill."

Malcolm sniffed. "Maybe Maharg," he said, concentrating on his feet. There were boardwalks between the huts, but many sections had sunk down into the mud.

"Both of them," Hansen said. "And later, all the rest after we've shown them that it works. We'll start this afternoon."

Malcolm laughed and strode ahead of his companion. "*You* can play with your armor this afternoon, laddie," he called back over his shoulder. "Nancy and I have some other exercises in mind—particularly seeing as I may get my balls whacked off in three days' time!"

There was food being served in the hall. Hansen made do with beer, a slab of cheese, and a wedge—torn rather than cut—from a round loaf of bread. Shill and Maharg had cornered Malcolm, though Malcolm continued to slake his thirst without apparent interest in what his hangers-on were saying.

Hansen decided to leave them all alone for the moment. He made sure that his battlesuit was stowed properly, then walked outdoors, munching on his bread.

There were a number of new warriors in the citadel. Some of the men had traveled with their own retinue of freemen, slaves, and baggage mammoths. The king was going to war, the king was hiring warriors.

Most of the would-be recruits lacked even their own battlesuit. Old men like Shill, youngsters like Maharg, with too little skill, training, and luck to have won their own equipment.

Golsingh would pack them into whatever equipment he had available. One of those hungry-looking fellows would certainly be wearing Villiers' old suit when Taddeusz led the army out in two days' time.

And maybe the hireling would get lucky; but more likely, the new occupant would wind up the same way Villiers had, dead and forgotten almost before his corpse had frozen in the winter night.

Grit from the flour mill scrunched between Hansen's teeth. He liked the flavor of the bread, though. There were a lot of things he liked about Northworld; and a few he was quite sure that he was going to change, whatever else he did here— if he survived.

Hansen stepped into the smithy, now crowded with new arrivals whose battlesuits required repairs. He'd been fortunate in his timing. A few hours later, after these recruits had arrived and been issued units which needed repair, Hansen wouldn't've had the time he needed to practice with the unfamiliar hardware.

One of the apprentices lay on the couch in the center of the shed. Ore was piled on the chest of the armor beside him.

Vasque was arguing with three warriors, each of whom stood beside what Hansen was coming to recognize as a (damaged) battlesuit of reasonable quality. Meanwhile, several lower-status warriors were trying to badger the other apprentice, though the boy was obviously too exhausted even to give coherent answers to the demands being fired at him.

Hansen moved in. "You lot," he snapped. "Get out of the way. You'll be taken care of in good time—better time than you deserve, at any rate."

He sat down beside the apprentice. The hired warriors backed unwillingly, but Hansen's assumption of rank made that rank real among these newcomers—and perhaps generally real in the Peace Rock pecking order.

There were slaves standing against the walls of the single room. Hansen pointed at one and said, "Beer! Something to drink. Now!"

The slave scurried off. People—lower-status people—didn't argue about orders here on Northworld. Of course, Special Units personnel hadn't argued with Commissioner Hansen, either.

As an afterthought, Hansen offered the apprentice a chunk of his bread. The boy took it and began to worry at a corner, not so much out of hunger as in an apparent need to do whatever was put directly in front of him.

"Just how is it that you work on armor?" Hansen asked, pitching his voice reassuringly but glaring at the other warriors to keep them at a distance. "How do you know how to design the circuit architecture, for instance?"

"Uh?" said the apprentice. His eyes were dull with exhaustion. Whatever was involved in fixing battlesuits, it certainly wasn't work that did itself. "Archi . . . ?"

He blinked and focused on Hansen. The warrior's patient interest brought the youth back to the present and the ability to think.

"I go into the Matrix," he said, "and I find the piece I'm supposed to work on. Where it's different from the Matrix, I move things so that it fits. I don't—"

The slave reappeared with a skin of liquid. Hansen took the container and passed it directly to the apprentice. While the youth drank greedily, Hansen asked, "What do you mean by 'the Matrix'?"

It couldn't be whatever Walker had talked about, dimensions and planes of spacetime. . . .

"Well, you know . . . ," the apprentice said. "Though you're not a smith. . . ." His brow furrowed. "It's the way everything's put together, you know, *inside*.

"You're hypnotized, and the first time you need a master to guide you, but it's like—" He gestured with his hands. Beer splashed from the neck of the skin. "—feeling your way through shadows even then."

Hansen nodded gently, to show that he was interested without interrupting the flow of words.

"And it's clearer each time," the young smith said with increasing animation, "but it's still like, you know, kneading mud and ash together into the shape of the armor. Even the master—" he gestured toward Vasque.

His voice lowered conspiratorially. "Even the greatest masters," the apprentice whispered to Hansen, "I don't think *they* see really clear. But the closer you can mold the workpiece into the Matrix—"

"Mold it in your dreams, you mean?"

The youth shook his head.

"It's not a dream," he said firmly. "It's entering the Matrix. And it's real—" he grinned and lifted a section of thigh armor from the table behind his bench. "—as this is."

He handed the piece to Hansen. It was dense and unquestionably real.

Hansen grinned back. *And then again, it might be exactly what Walker had meant; but if it was, it didn't help Hansen a lot.*

"Thanks," he said as he got up. "I figured I ought to know something about the hardware, since my life depends on it now."

And *that* was no more than the truth.

Hansen thought he might find Shill and Maharg in the hall, so he wasn't surprised to see them at the building's entrance.

He *hadn't* expected to see Malcolm stamping toward the pair from one of the huts, tying the sash of his vivid tunic and glowering like a stormcloud. A female slave skipped along the boardwalk behind Malcolm, eyes bright with anticipation.

"I thought I'd take you two out for a little practice," Hansen said to Shill and Maharg while Malcolm was still three strides away. The words were an instinctive game to prove that he was both innocent and ignorant of whatever was going on.

"What in the *hell* is going on?" Malcolm snarled.

"Nothin'," Maharg mumbled. He was rubbing his face. His nose had bled a rusty wedge into his moustache and beard.

"There's a new lot in from the East," Shill said. "'Bout a dozen of 'em all together."

"Seven, yeah," said Malcolm. Hansen noted the way the veteran's anger vanished as though he'd closed a door over it.

Malcolm glanced toward the hall. Sounds of laughter and a snatch of song came through the half-open doors. "Go on."

"Bastards think they're tough," Maharg said. His voice caught.

Because Maharg was so big, it was hard to remember that he was only about sixteen standard years. That didn't make him less dangerous—more dangerous, maybe—but it meant that his emotions were still on the roller-coaster of youth.

Right now, Hansen thought he might be about to cry.

"They are tough," Malcolm said coldly. "Go on."

"They threw bones at him!" Shill said. "He was braggin' about what he'd do in the next fight, and they started throwin' bones at him. And *me*!"

"You bloody damned fools," Hansen said, before Malcolm could speak. The words were so close to those the veteran *would* have spoken that Malcolm blinked to hear them from another mouth.

Hansen pointed at Shill. "You sent for him, didn't you? Grabbed a slave—" the woman who'd followed Malcolm from his ladyfriend's lodging hovered nearby "—and sent her to roust your boss?"

"Well, I thought—"

"If you'd bloody *thought*," Hansen snarled, his arms at his sides and his face leaning close to that of the old warrior, "then you'd've known that the best way to get out of this without a loss of status was to pretend it didn't happen. What d'ye expect? That Malcolm's going in there—"

He pointed at the door with his index and middle fingers together. "—and mop up your dozen tough bastards himself?"

"Wuzzn't that many," Maharg muttered, lifting his nose high, then lowering it again despite the fact that it continued to bleed. "Fuck this. I oughta go to Frekka. They're hiring there."

Malcolm's face hardened. "No true warrior would take service under merchants," he said.

"They got good armor fer *their* people," Shill said. "They know how a warrior oughta be treated."

"Merchants' armor!" Malcolm snapped. "All turned out the same."

"Sure, that's easy for *you* ta say," sniffled Shill. "You got a first-class outfit, you do. But how about somebody like me what never had no luck?"

"You've just had your luck," Hansen said. "You met me. Now, go on in there, one at a time so nobody thinks we're starting anything—which we're not—and get your armor. I'm going to teach you how to use it."

The two hirelings, the old man and the near boy, gave Hansen identical looks of sheeplike defiance. Then Shill spit into the mud, rubbed his lips, and said, "I s'pose practice wouldn't hurt none, with a battle coming up."

He peered through the doorway, then ducked inside.

"You coming with us?" Hansen asked Malcolm.

The veteran shook his head curtly. "No," he said. "No." But ten steps down the walkway toward his girlfriend's dwelling, Malcolm turned and called, "Maybe later. Maybe."

Hansen took a critical look at his two companions on the practice field. He understood Shill's bitter reference to armor now: the hirelings wore junk, little better than the suit in which Villiers had died.

Maharg's suit might originally have been of respectable quality, but that was in the ancient past. Now the plastron was crudely patched, and the legs had sections of varied diameter where stock pieces had been spliced in to repair damage.

Shill's armor didn't even have a distinguished pedigree. It was a collection of bits of flimsy apprentice work, welded together by another apprentice. The join lines were obvious, despite Shill's attempt to hide them with a pattern of horizontal black and yellow stripes.

"How did you guys survive the battle?" Hansen asked in genuine wonder. "Did you stick close to Malcolm?"

"Well, we were . . . ," Shill said, the electronics robbing his voice of the embarrassment Hansen was sure was present. "You know, we watched his back."

"I fought a guy," said Maharg. "He didn't, you know . . . he didn't want to get real close."

And his armor wouldn't've been an improvement over Maharg's present suit if the boy had managed to bring him down. There were a majority of hirelings like these in every army, fodder for the leavening of principal warriors.

That would change.

"Then you were smart," Hansen said harshly, "because if you'd tried to be heroes before, you'd be dead. But now—" he pointed his finger at one man, then the other "—you're going to do things exactly the way I tell you."

"Why?" said Maharg bluntly.

"Because I'm going to make you a baron, boy," Hansen said, glad for the harshness the helmet speaker put into his voice.

He turned his head to the older man. "And you, Shill," he added, "because I'll make you rich. Without me you'll be slopping hogs in a few years, unless you get chopped despite the way you try to dodge around keeping outa trouble.''

The blank face of Hansen's battlesuit couldn't smile. He clapped the men on the shoulders instead and said, "Come on, let's find a quiet corner where I can teach you what these suits can do. Even *your* suits.''

The practice ground was several hectares in size, plenty of room even now when most of the warriors in Peace Rock were involved in either practicing for the coming battle or proving their prowess to Taddeusz and the cluster of high-ranking warriors around him.

Hansen faced a post on the end as far from the warchief as possible.

"All right," he lectured. "Your suits have both identification and designator capacity. Say, 'Mark friendlies blue.' ''

"Huh?''

In Hansen's display, azure crests spiked from the top of the hirelings' helmets. "Just do it!" he snapped. "Do you remember what I said about obeying orders?''

The warriors looked at one another. "Oh . . . ,'' murmured one of them. "I din't know it could do that.''

"Right," said Hansen dryly. "Now, the AI can also designate. The way we're going to win—the way we're going to *survive*, I want you to be very clear on that—is by all three of us striking together. I'm going to mark the target with a flashing white light. When the light changes to red, we all three hit it. Together, that's very important to overload the hostile system.''

"I don' unnerstand," said both the hirelings.

"Bring your arcs up," Hansen said. "Practice, cut . . . ,'' and his right gauntlet quivered with the vibrating power that shimmered in it. It was an insidiously pleasant feeling, the power of life and death in a glittering package. . . .

"Now, watch.''

Hansen centered the post in his helmet display and said, "Mark.''

A pulsing white corona gleamed on the electronic image of the post in his display and that of his two trainees, though the scene wouldn't've changed to naked eyes.

"Strike!" and he slashed his arc weapon forward into the

red glare marking the post, cutting the wood in a blaze of sparks and flying fibers—

While Shill and Maharg stood, with faces that were probably as blankly uncomprehending as the painted fronts of their battlesuits.

Hansen straightened. "Now," he said calmly, "let's try something different. Maharg, I want you to hit the post when I yell 'Strike,' do you understand?"

"Ah . . . All right."

"Mark," said Hansen, lighting the post on their screens. "Strike."

Maharg feinted clumsily. Hansen's arc hit him from behind. The young warrior toppled to the mud.

"Not next year, not next second," Hansen said. "When I give you an order, you do it *now*. Do you understand?"

Maharg started to get up. "You bas—" he growled.

Hansen waited a beat for Maharg to get far enough off the ground that hitting it again would be a useful lesson. Then he slapped Maharg down.

"I am going to make you a real warrior," Hansen said to the youth's prone form. "I'm going to make you a baron, just as I said. But you're not going to argue, you're going to take orders. Do you—"

"You bas—"

Hansen's arc lashed out again.

"Nobody's ever given a shit for you, boy!" he said. He was shouting. "Nobody! But *I* care, and I'm going to make you what you want to be if I have to kill you first! Do you understand? Do you?"

The recumbent suit twitched into life again. "Yessir," Maharg said.

"All right," Hansen said. He was trying to keep the adrenaline shudder out of his voice. He wasn't successful. "Get up and watch how Shill does it."

He turned toward the post. Smoke trembled from a few splinters Hansen had knocked away with his earlier cut. "Mark," he said.

≡ 14 ≡

BY LATE AFTERNOON, Shill and Maharg had gotten surprisingly adept at obeying Hansen's orders. On their own, with the pair of them engaging Hansen, things didn't work as well.

When Maharg was *ad hoc* leader, he tended to strike before he remembered to call the designator to his partner. Shill, on the other hand, dithered. His command to *'Strike!'* was always followed by Maharg's lunge—but usually not by Shill's.

Still, this was only the first day of training. When it came to the real thing against the Thrasey forces, Hansen would be there to give the orders—unless he got his head burned off.

In which case, he couldn't pretend he much cared what happened afterward.

By the time Hansen led his tiny force back across the field, Taddeusz had been joined by Golsingh—in boots, breeches, and a fur cloak. A group of warriors were going through exercises before them.

"That's the lot what made trouble in the hall," Shill grumbled. He angled his steps to pass a little farther to the side of the seven warriors.

"Hold up," said Hansen. A thought struck him.

"Group secure communications," he said, then, "Can you two hear me now?"

"Hey, that's real clear," said Maharg. His own voice was much crisper than it had been on straight audio between the suits.

"Shill?"

"Huh? Yeah, I kin hear."

"When I tell you to report," Hansen said in a controlled voice, "you report. Understood?"

"Whatever," Shill muttered.

"Right," Hansen said. "Now, are you guys up for some serious play? Trying out what we just learned on our friends there?"

"You think we can take *them*?" Maharg demanded.

"Designate hostile forces green," Hansen said and watched spikes of bottle green dance from the helmets of the warriors from the 'East,' wherever that was.

He was getting to like his suit. It would've been useful to have back on Annunciation, where he belonged. . . .

But that was for later. "No," he said aloud. "I think they'll kick our butts, frankly. But it'll give us some practice that we need."

Neither of the juniors spoke for a moment. Then Maharg said, "Hell, I've had my butt kicked before. Once more don' matter."

"Then stick close to me," Hansen said. "Remember your orders. And for god's sake, when it starts, *don't* quit till they're all down or we are!"

"Cut!"

The three warriors stepped forward in line abreast. If Hansen looked to either side he would have seen an underling with a blue spike on his helmet, but for now he was taking that on trust.

"Mark," he said with the seeming leader of the Easterners centered in his display.

The fellow was sparring with two of his own men. His suit was clearly a cut above the one Hansen wore, while two more of the Eastern warriors were almost as well equipped. The other four wore scrapings of the same general quality as Shill and Maharg—but there *were* four of them.

The leader paused. "You see, Lord Golsingh?" he boomed. "I claim the right of prowess to command your left wing!"

"Normal speech," Hansen ordered his AI. His face prickled with sweat, as if this were real, not a game. They were three meters from the Eastern leader.

"I'd always heard that no Easterner had any balls!" he shouted. "I don't think you seven can fight us three *real* men! Wanna try?"

"You—" the Eastern leader gasped in a choking voice. The arc bloomed from his hand.

"Strike!" shouted Hansen, and they struck, by *god* they did, all three together, and the Easterner, off-balance with his pivot, toppled to the mud while Hansen cried, "Mark! Strike!"

Only Shill and Hansen that time, because Hansen had turned a hair to his right and blocked Maharg with his body, but the Easterner dropped, not one of the dangerous pair but he fell in front of one of those, tripping his fellow. Hansen struck into the tangled suits, no time to mark and command.

But his two fellows struck with him anyway, guided by the arc without a designator, as if Maharg could think and Shill could act—but they could, because he'd told them they could or because the gods were good or maybe because men like a leader to follow because it's so much simpler than thinking.

Maharg took the arc of the remaining Eastern champion squarely on the crest of his helmet and dropped. Hansen stepped close and hacked at the man, but the Easterner was both fast and experienced, catching Hansen's arc with his own.

Hansen's right arm shuddered as if he'd grabbed a live AC line. He grabbed the Easterner's wrist with his free hand. As he did so, a sickly arc snaked past his helmet—Shill striking from behind him with a skill born of practice.

The Easterner's weapon dimmed as his AI drained power from it to boost the defenses against the fresh threat.

Hansen struck home and slung his opponent to the side as dead weight.

Two of the remaining Easterners made a convulsive rush at Shill, putting the old man between them and Hansen. Shill screamed momentarily; then his microphone shut down with the rest of his suit's power.

Hansen chopped right, then left. The last Easterner stood like a statue six meters away, too surprised or frightened to take any action.

A kid who froze, or a man as old as Shill who's forgotten this is only play. . . .

Hansen's arc lengthened and took the warrior in the chest. The Easterner turned sluggishly to run. Hansen stepped forward until his weapon was close enough to overwhelm his opponent's armor and drop him.

He stopped, panting heavily.

"You treacherous slimy bastard," rasped the amplified voice of the Eastern leader, rising to his feet.

Now that his suit was reset, mud was coursing off the painted metal with almost the enthusiasm that it had from Krita's armor under similar circumstances. "Now I'm going to kill you."

The dense flux that shot from the leader's right gauntlet wasn't a practice weapon.

"Battle status," Hansen ordered his AI, raising his arc in guard. He'd thought Krita might kill him, but it hadn't crossed his mind that this fellow would take a defeat personally enough to commit murder in front of Golsingh himself.

Because it surely was murder, Hansen going one-on-one with a suit as good as this fellow's. Maybe somebody would—

"Hey!" shouted the king. "Stop that! We need—"

The Easterner cut at Hansen's head. Hansen blocked the blow. His display flickered with the strain, even though the arcs crossed two meters from the attacker's gauntlet.

"Taddeusz! Stop them!" Golsingh ordered.

Hansen backpedaled, praying that he wouldn't trip over a warrior sprawled on the ground behind him. His display would give him a 360° view if he wanted it, but he was afraid the distortion would be more dangerous than the chance of an obstacle.

"Let them play, milord," the warchief replied with the casual certainty of a man who knows that he's wearing a battlesuit and his king is not. "I have doubts about both of them. More than doubts about the—"

"Hey!" boomed an amplified voice.

A warrior strode onto the field behind the Easterner. *Red-blue-silver battlesuit—*

"Watch him, Malcolm!" Hansen shouted. "He's nut—"

The Easterner spun like a dancer, slashing at Malcolm's head. Malcolm got his arc up in time, but the shock of meeting knocked him to his knees.

Hansen stepped forward and cut at the Easterner's live gauntlet. All three armored warriors froze like a group of statuary as sparks roared and dazzled in all directions.

The Eastern leader's suit was of very high quality. The artificial intelligences controlling the other two suits had to drain all power from their servos to prevent the Easterner's arc from finishing Malcolm. A patch of mud beneath the trio began to harden as full-power discharges lashed across it.

Hansen leaned forward and reached out with his left hand, moving against the dead weight and stiffness of his suit.

The Easterner's weapon was slowly driving down Malcolm's guard. Hansen's right gauntlet had grown hot, and his air system reeked with the odor of suede as the lining charred.

Hansen unlatched the Easterner's suit, shutting off the arc and the defensive charges instantly. Malcolm's straining arm slashed upward when the resistance was released, plowing across the Easterner's plastron in a glare of burning metal.

The Easterner fell face down. Steam gouted as mud cooled the glowing mass where his chest had been. Malcolm tried to rise—and failed; then tried to open his own battlesuit. His gauntlet pawed in the general direction of the latch without quite touching it.

Hansen found the latch of his suit by closing his eyes and letting instinct guide his desperate hand. He swung open the front of his clamshell and paused, too exhausted to go further until the pain of his burning right hand goaded him to drag his arms out of their casings.

He stared, dull-eyed, at the steaming ruin of the Eastern leader.

The ruin also of Hansen's hopes for a first-class battlesuit. The steel which sheathed the electronics had a good deal of mechanical strength, but against the full wrath of an arc weapon it might as well have been so much tissue paper. Malcolm had burned the Easterner out of his suit's chest cavity, and in so doing had irreparably ruined the plastron itself.

Oh, the piece could be repaired in time—though certainly not in time for battle against the Lord of Thrasey. But the battlesuit would never be as good as it had been before the damage, not even in the unlikely event that the repairs were done by a smith as skillful as the original builder.

"Well, I said I had my doubts, milord," Taddeusz said. "Lamullo will command the left wing as usual."

Golsingh nodded. "Shall we go back to the hall now?" he said. "I hope there's been a message from Frekka about the suits we ordered."

The king and warchief turned their backs. Hansen swore quietly, trying to gather up enough strength to get out of his armor. Maharg and Shill had stripped and were aiding Malcolm.

Golsingh's blond wife had accompanied her husband to the practice field. Hansen blinked to see her staring at him. Her face didn't change as he met her eyes, then turned and walked on with the other nobles.

≡ 15 ≡

FORTIN WAITED A moment for other members of Rolls' entourage to form around him in an alcove of the entrance hall. When the six big men had done so as planned, Fortin squatted down and reversed his cloak to bring the pink side out.

There was a white beret under his slouch hat. He kicked off his black boots, replaced them with pink sandals, and pulled up white tights to cover his legs as he rose.

The last item of Fortin's disguise was the pink violin, hidden beneath his cloak with the sandals.

At the moment Rolls swept Penny into his arms at the far end of the hall, Fortin stepped through the mirrored door at the back of the alcove. He was an unremarkable flash of pink in the event that any of Penny's servants noticed him at all.

Three women were chattering among themselves in the corridor. They paused when Fortin appeared, then resumed their discussion in marginally lower tones as the newcomer ignored them. Fortin strode down the hall in the opposite direction.

Fortin knew the layout of Penny's palace better than . . . probably better than anyone else, even Penny's servants, because they grew old and died. Penny herself neither knew nor cared about the intricacies of the mansion constructed to her whim. Her focus was narrower—and very different.

A squad from the kitchen staff, looking more than usually silly with their fluffy uniforms grease-spattered, wheeled trolleys of food up one of the side-corridors as Fortin passed. They paid no attention to him.

The food would be served to Rolls' retainers in one of the many refectories on the lower level of the palace. No one would notice that there was one fewer of the men in orange livery than had been admitted to the hall.

A garden of palmettos was planted beneath the staircase at the end of the main corridor. A prismatic slit window high in the wall above provided the plants with sufficient light for growth. Fortin checked over his shoulder to make sure nobody could see him, then tossed his balled cloak behind a screen of the broad, feathery leaves. Penny's upper-level servants didn't wear overgarments.

Fortin skipped briskly up the stairs.

A doorway opened immediately off the spiral staircase; on the other side would be an arbor in the palace rotunda. Fortin reached to open the door, but paused with his hand on the knob.

There were voices from the other side of the panel; male and female servants, several of each. Nothing that would concern Penny, of course, so long as her needs were attended. . . .

Fortin laughed silently and continued up the stairs that now spiraled within one of the flying buttresses. He had more important things in mind than disturbing an orgy—or joining it.

His sandals *whick-whick-whick*ed on the stone treads with the regularity of a metronome.

They all hated Fortin, but they needed him as well. For tasks like this, for the tricks that no other *god* could accomplish. . . .

And that made them hate him all the more; but they had to bear his presence unless they were willing to destroy themselves as well, for the Matrix was balance. If the others slew Fortin, then they let their own lives out in the same stream of blood.

If Diamond were destroyed—

If Fortin were to destroy Diamond—

Then Fortin's fellows, who hated him because he was half android—which they despised—and half North, whom they wisely feared . . . then Fortin's fellows might slay him in their ungoverned rage and bring down all this near perfection which they ruled. Which would be the best trick of all, surely.

The staircase ended in a finial at the top of the buttress. Fortin peeked out. No one was in sight.

A railed walkway circled the top of the rotunda, more to add golden glitter to the appearance than for safety needs. Beyond the railing, Fortin could see fairy-castle turrets, each streaming with bright flags, studding the outer walls of the palace.

Still hidden in the finial, because there were windows in
the spire overlooking the rotunda roof, Fortin stripped down
to his pink jockstrap and sandals. He strode out, wearing an
expression as arrogant as the bulge of his groin.

In the flare of the central spire was an unobtrusive door. It
opened to Fortin's touch. The corridor beyond was decorated
with plaster cherubs, roses, and swags in case Penny herself
chose to use it. In all likelihood, nobody passed through the
hall except the maintenance crews who swept and polished
the roof.

And Fortin. Now.

He ignored the stairs around the elevator shaft. A trio of
servants stepped from a room across the way, carrying bun-
dles of bedclothing. One of them saw Fortin, and they ducked
out of sight again.

Their mistress had the power of life and death, so there
was risk to a servant whom Penny noticed—but not much
risk, because death didn't interest Penny very much.

Their real danger came from the savage whim of a human
promoted to the mistress' bed. Such a one had Penny's ear
and power—until she tired and cast him out. Out, nowhere;
perhaps to menial service, perhaps back to a grubby village
in the Open Lands where he'd been born; perhaps to a void
in the Matrix, for Penny had her notions too, and in bed alone
she could be interested for good or ill.

No sensible servant wanted contact with a doomed man
who might wish to destroy as much as he could before his
own inevitable end.

Fortin walked into the lift shaft and began to rise. Not
because he was one of Penny's favorites, as those who
watched from behind half-opened doors thought; but because
Fortin too was a god.

He wondered if Penny hated and despised herself. Probably not. She wasn't perceptive enough to realize that she
should, that they all should.

Fortin got off the lift at the top level, where the spire swelled
into the huge, gilded egg of Penny's private suite.

Maids were straightening one of the great rooms. They
peered at Fortin through the open door. One giggled. They
were nude except for wisps of white gauze in their hair and
a similar tracery of pink around their hips.

"In no time at all, Hansssen," the snake replied. "I have told you that you musssn't think of duration here, you musssn't. . . ."

Hansen tossed the pry-bar onto his bed. It rang on the planks. "All right," he said. "What do I have to do?"

A ray of sunlight caught the thing Walker was playing with and turned it to a wire of gold. It was a strand of blond hair, long blond hair—

The hair of Golsingh's wife Unn.

≡ 22 ≡

THE DOOR OF Eisner's palace slid open as smoothly as oil moving in water.

Eisner laughed humorlessly from within. "You're alone, Rolls?" she asked. "No troupe of jugglers or dancing girls in attendance?"

Rolls ducked as he stepped into the library. He felt but could not hear the door close behind him.

"I don't need to put on side with you, Eisner," he said. "In fact, I walked instead of riding."

"Should I congratulate you for that?" she asked tartly. "We can do anything we please, can't we? We gods." There was bitterness in the final word.

Eisner sat at the hub of a semi-circular desk whose surface, a gorgeous expanse of burl walnut, was covered with various forms of paper.

Books were interfiled with their open edges together, each marking a place in the other, and in worms of six or eight volumes with each spine thrust into the open edge of the next. Cards and sheets of paper, some of them covered with cryptic notes, marked other places. Swathes of gate-fold hardcopy peeked from the stacks of bound volumes.

There was no dust in the room.

Eisner had a collection of bound sheet music open in front of her. Light fell on it from a hidden source, providing perfect illumination.

"Yes, the problem's always been to decide what to do rather than whether or not it's possible," Rolls agreed.

He held his left hand closed. Eisner glanced at it, then back to his face, but for the moment the big man ignored her interest.

"Did you come for a reason?" Eisner demanded.

"My, what a greeting," Rolls said with a rueful smile.

Eisner rubbed her forehead in self-annoyance. "I'm sorry, Rolls," she said. "With all the time in—" her lips twisted "—in the world, I can certainly talk with a friend. And you've always been as much of a friend as I allowed."

There was a second chair beside the desk, but it too was covered with books and papers. For a moment, Rolls' lips pursed as he considered moving the stacked volumes to the floor. Instead he walked around the end of the desk to look over Eisner's shoulder at the open score.

"What's this, then?" he asked. *" 'I wish that I could,' was the man's sad reply, 'but she's dead, in the coach ahead.' "*

Eisner stiffened momentarily, but she recognized that interest rather than amusement prompted the question. Like her, the big man was a watcher, a searcher. . . .

"It—has to do with the last intruder from the Consensus," she said. "I thought there might be an avenue of approach to locating the threat to Diamond."

Rolls nodded, glancing up at the books whose shelves covered all the walls where low doorways interfered. "Have you thought about what I said, Eisner?" he asked. "About it still being possible for us to be human?"

"We *are* human," she snapped.

Rolls wasn't touching her, but his big form blocked Eisner into her desk alcove. Though he continued to look upward, he shifted to the side as if responding to the nervous anger in the woman behind him.

"I mean," he said gently, still without looking toward her, "that we could resume being fully human. Complete men and women. It's worth taking risks to stay fully human, don't you think?"

"You come closer than most of us, Rolls," Eisner said. The bitterness was back in her voice. "But I . . ."

Rolls turned. When she looked up at his face, she remembered that this big, soft-looking man had led an exploration team, and that he was the one of them who watched against the final day when androids and Lomeri unlocked the pathways of the Matrix and came for long-deferred vengeance.

Risk.

Rolls opened his left hand slowly. His thumb and forefinger held the band that was a shimmer rather than an object, and the jewel below glowed with its own internal fire.

"For one day only," he said as he lowered the necklace over Eisner's head.

"How did you . . . ?" she started. Her voice caught as her mind connected the data it was her life to connect.

And he was right. With Penny's jewel between her breasts—it was worth it.

Eisner stood up. The chair caught the back of her knees. She pushed it away. Her face was changing, and her body filled out as she unsealed the touch-sensitive opening of her coveralls.

Rolls poised, watchful but unwilling to presume even now that Eisner was shrugging out of her single garment.

Nude, she looked at him and then, very deliberately, swept dozens of books onto the floor to clear half of the desk's polished walnut.

"Well, come on, big boy," she said, spreading her arms to Rolls.

Eisner wore the form of a plump, blond woman; a young woman, still in her teens. The necklace dangled brightly across her chest.

There was a noticeable mole on her left breast.

≡ 23 ≡

THE SNAKE RIPPLED down the right arm of the battlesuit and onto the gauntlet, where it shrank and started to vanish. Its single good eye began to glow like a starlit diamond. The tail continued to squirm toward the jewel until all hint of a serpent had disappeared.

"Get into your armor, Hansen," said the mechanical voice of the suit.

Hansen settled himself carefully into his armor. It was awkward to have to back into the suit . . . but thinking of the physical awkwardness took his mind off the real questions.

"Close it, close it," Walker said irritably through the suit.

Hansen was careful to twine the strand of blond hair around his fingers rather than leave it to be found in the cubicle. The cold suede was clammy and smelled of the man who'd died in it.

Hansen's screen lighted with a view of the bedchamber. Across the top crawled the message:

TAKE TWO STEPS FORWARD, THEN TURN RIGHT AND STEP

"The bed's in the way," Hansen protested. Though he supposed he could smash through the frame if he needed to.

OBEY glared huge letters as the rest of the holographic display blanked.

Well, he'd taken orders like that when he was a junior, and he by god expected his own people to take orders when *he* gave them.

Nils Hansen, junior volunteer, took two steps forward. His armored legs didn't strike anything. It was disorienting to walk with no view but that of a command, worse than moving blind. He turned and took another step.

Hansen's display suddenly blazed with cold blue lines,

branching and linking among themselves into faceted patterns. He no longer felt the pull of gravity, though there was something beneath his feet.

"Walker!" he said sharply. He didn't move either his arms or his legs. He felt as though he were standing in the schematic of a crystal lattice—

Or in a spider web.

A tiny red bead began to crawl along one of the blue lines. The pattern went on—forever, in all directions.

Hansen was alone in a universe of crisp, cold invariance, in which one spark moved.

He opened his mouth again to shout for Walker; closed it; and stepped as if the lines in his display were pathways and the red bead was his guide—

As of course they were, and it was.

Hansen stepped onto a wasteland. He faced a horizon silhouetted by the blur of a red sun. The skeleton of something gigantic lay a little distance from him, its ribs reaching toward the light like the fingers of a drowning man.

Hansen stood on a shingle beach, gravel separated out here by the waves in the unimaginably distant past when this planet had seas. Now there wasn't even an atmosphere: what air remained formed a rime on the pebbles.

The louvers on the battlesuit's air system clicked shut. Their sound reminded him that though the armor sealed for river crossings, it didn't have an air pack to supplement whatever was trapped within its volume.

A crystal the size of a house was trundling slowly toward Hansen on jagged spines. The bases of the spines twisted within the mass until the whole—creature—overbalanced forward, onto other tines which twisted in their turn. The effect was a combination of a sea urchin and an avalanche.

The spines and flats of the crystal reflected and diffracted light from the dying sun, but at the heart of the mass burned the spark of Walker's eye, with more life than the glow on the horizon.

"Was that the Matrix, Walker?" Hansen asked as though he were calm. "Is that what the smiths see when they build armor?"

Walker's laughter clicked in Hansen's earphones. "What you saw was a hologram, a pattern of light, nothing more," the voice said. It sounded . . . not human, but no longer mechanical either. "And what the smiths see, that is in their minds. Patterns also, reflections of the absolute."

Walker was staggering still closer. Light danced: on the fracture planes crossing the spines, and from lines of cleavage within the central mass.

Something that winked on the horizon might have been a form like that of Walker.

"There is a price for seeing the Matrix, Commissioner Hansen," Walker said. The spark in the crystal's core fluctuated as he spoke. "And for seeing *through* the Matrix, there is a very high price."

"This suit doesn't have much air, Walker," Hansen said. The great mass had halted just in front of him. Several of the spines, their glitter streaked by milky flaws, waggled slowly above Hansen.

"You're done with this suit," replied Walker, and the crystal toppled forward.

Hansen braced for the impact, but there was none—no contact, just the utter cessation of movement that he'd felt once before, when his intrusion capsule reached the point in space that should have been Northworld.

Was Northworld.

His display blanked. The only sound was the thump of his heart.

Walker's voice, no longer coming from the earphones, said, "You will keep the artificial intelligence and portions of the sensor suite. You will gain for me access to certain information which the androids have on the plane to which North sent them when they came to investigate. And you will gain the battlesuit which I promised you."

Hansen thought he could see glimmers of light, but perhaps they were merely his optic nerves firing in an attempt to save his sanity from the blackness. "I'll need weapons!" he said.

"You have your mind, Kommissar," Walker said dryly.

There was light and warmth and a splash of brown water as Hansen, limbs flailing, plunged feet first into a swamp.

The air was so saturated that the humidity took the edges off the light of the hot sun overhead. Hansen, wearing his coveralls and a dense skullcap sealed in black plastic—all that remained of a battlesuit that could've withstood antitank weapons—was waist deep in mud.

If he wore the entire suit, he'd still be sinking toward whatever passed for bedrock.

The surface was muddy hillocks and ponds—nowhere dry nor deep. Ferns and spike-branched reeds a meter high grew promiscuously across the terrain, but there was no ground cover. Every twenty meters or so sprouted what looked like low trees—but probably weren't, since the branches curling from their tops were lacework similar to the ferns.

Something rose from the squelching mud on the next hillock over. It was a four-legged reptile several meters in length, with a great knobbed sail on its back and a mouthful of fern fronds. There was a collar around its neck.

"And who would *you* be, friend?" muttered Hansen as he stepped out of the pond into which he'd fallen. The creature was obviously an herbivore, but so was a bull.

"It has no personal name," said a crisp voice in his ears, the AI that Walker had said he was leaving; and which Hansen had forgotten, like a damned fool, till the machine intelligence stretched a point and recalled itself to his attention. "It is an edaphosaurus from the herd of the android Strombrand."

The edaphosaurus chewed with a sideways rotary motion of its jaws. The skull looked small in comparison to the bulk of the chest and belly, but the vast cone of greenery disappeared rapidly enough down the throat. The beast cocked its head at an angle and sliced off the next installment of ferns, keeping one eye focused on the intruder as it did so.

Hansen squinted, trying to pierce the thick atmosphere. He could only see a hundred meters or so, and the steamy air washed out colors at half that distance. Hot sun on open water and a vast expanse of transpiring foliage. . . .

Another edaphosaurus plodded from the gloom, continuing through the pond in which Hansen had landed. Its feet and belly sent water in all directions. Halfway up the bank the beast stopped, bellowed, and began to claw at its collar with a forepaw. The webbing between its toes was brilliant scarlet.

After a moment of scratching which rotated the collar a quarter turn without dislodging it, the beast resumed its clumsy amble. Something hooted angrily in the direction from which the edaphosaur had come.

"What are the col—" Hansen started to say when a lizard-headed biped carrying a staff and a radio handset bounded through the mud on the herbivore's trail.

"What's *that*?" he snapped instead.

The biped saw Hansen, halted in a crouch that splashed rippling semicircles in the pond, and bolted back the way it had come. In addition to the artifacts in its hands, the lizard-man wore a short, off-the-shoulder tunic and a collar similar to that of the edaphosaurus.

"That is a Lomeri slave, one of the herdsmen of Strombrand," replied the artificial intelligence. "There are three herdsmen all told."

The shapes in the mist had mentioned the Lomeri, the lizardfolk, when they'd interviewed Hansen for this mission . . . or the mission that led to the mission which led to *this* mission. But those passing references had implied that the Lomeri were a race of the far past who—

"You are thinking of duration again, Commissioner Hansen," said the voice that was as surely Walker's as it was surely answering a thought Hansen hadn't spoken. "Ignore duration, because it no longer applies."

"Are the Lomeri slaves of the androids here?" Hansen asked. He heard a winding note that could have come from either a living animal or a signal horn. He could run, but the Lomeri obviously knew their way about this swamp better than he ever would.

"These Lomeri are slaves," said what was probably the AI, not Walker, "as some androids are slaves of the Lomeri on the plane they rule. There is passage across the Matrix through the Open Lands, and there is raiding from all sides."

Two different horns answered the first. Certainly signals.

"Is North on a plane?" Hansen demanded. "Can he be reached?"

The visible edaphosaur suddenly closed its jaws with a *clop* so abrupt that half-ingested ferns fell in a fan to the mud. The beast turned and ran off into the mist with an exaggerated side-to-side twisting of its heavy body.

Three lizardmen stepped into sight. Their radios were slung

in belt pouches. The staffs they carried were sharpened on both ends.

There was a clicking of electronic laughter in Hansen's ears. "Kommissar, Kommissar," said Walker. "North and Rolls have formed an alliance and merged the planes on which they found themselves. But to visit them through the Matrix requires permission. Which will not be forthcoming if the Lomeri slay you now."

Hansen laughed. He lifted one of the reeds from the mud with a firm pull.

"Oh, they won't kill me, Walker," he said with the comfortable assurance of a man with a short-range task—for a fucking change! "My masters, they sent the best."

Hansen tried twirling the reed. The upward-pointing spikes were each about twenty centimeters long.

The balance changed as mud flew off the root ball. Hansen kept the reed moving as he walked toward the Lomeri by as direct a path as the muddy shore allowed.

"I'm your master now, Commissioner Hansen," Walker said with asperity.

"Translate for me," said Hansen.

"—and if we lose any more of the cattle," said a voice with startling clarity—the helmet excerpted from Hansen's battlesuit contained a first-rate parabolic microphone as well as the artificial intelligence—"then Strombrand'll flay us 'n no mistake."

The lizardmen had halted, chittering among themselves. The skirmish line in which they'd appeared drew together when their quarry started toward them.

"If he gave us decent equipment, they wouldn't fouling stray, would they?" snapped another Lomeri in reply. "So it's his fault."

"It's our hides," the first rejoined.

"Walker," Hansen said. "Can I fix their hardware with the equipment I've got?"

"Yes," said the AI. Its tone was subtly different from Walker's, even though both machine intelligences spoke through the same circuitry.

The Lomeri were slightly taller than Hansen. They were thin and had the dangerous look of figures wound from barbed wire. Patterns of red and orange scales beneath their singlets made them look as though they were on fire.

"Strombrand needs us," said the third lizardman decisively. "He'll let us off with a beating . . . and it's worth *that* to have red meat again!"

He measured the distance to Hansen—five meters and closing—with a grin on his toothy jaws.

. Hansen grinned back. "Oh, but it's not worth trying something that'll get your all four limbs rammed down your throat, is it, boyo?" he said, listening to the speaker in his helmet hiss and clatter with lizardspeak.

He flicked the root end of the reed toward the hungry Lomeri. Water spattered the creature. Instead of blinking, nictitating membranes slid sideways across the large eyeballs.

"Or," continued Hansen, "you could be nice to me and I'll improve your equipment so you won't get a beating ever again."

He darted the reed out, spike-end first, like a Lomeri tongue. The nearest of the creatures flinched back, gripping his staff to his chest.

"Which'll it be, boyos?" Hansen asked.

The Lomeri hunched together, hipshot so that they could all three face the intruder. The AI fed Hansen their whispered words clearly: *How could he . . . Look, he can't be that tough. . . . Did your mother hatch many such fools? He could be anything! Well let's—*

One of the Lomeri—the first one—straightened, took his radio from its holster, and (after a moment's hesitation) tossed it to Hansen.

"Go on, then," the lizardman directed. "Fix it."

Hansen looked at the unit. Its black plastic shell had a dial and a miniature joystick with no other features. A short coil antenna poked from one end.

"Bring it up under your chin," Walker's voice directed. "But continue to watch the Lomeri."

"No fear *that*," Hansen said as he obeyed.

He grinned at the lizardmen. He'd poke the spiky end of his reed in the face of the first to come for him, grab away the creature's staff, and do a quick right and left with the points on the other pair. . . .

Of course, even if the move went precisely as planned, that

left the third lizardman chewing Hansen's throat out with teeth made for nothing else.

Half a dozen narrow, jointed pseudopods grew past Hansen's face from the helmet. They were crystal, and it was easy to guess who—rather than what—had extended them.

The glittering tips prodded at the casing. Harsh light spluttered from a miniature laser cutter; then the faceplate lifted in the grip of one pseudopod while the others probed beneath.

The Lomeri backed another step away.

"Pft!" clicked the voice in Hansen's ears. "Junk, only junk."

Hansen's mind split between two realities. He could still see the lizardmen flicking their tongues in nervous pulses, but they seemed to be projected on a flat screen. The forepart of his vision filled with lines and shadows which Hansen's instinct told him were representations, not forms—but were closer to the concept of a Platonic ideal than anything his own senses could show him.

"Walker," he asked, "how does this unit work?"

The vision sharpened. Blotches of shadow broke into fans of lines or vanished.

"It transmits a signal to the collars of the edaphosaurs," Walker replied. "The dial controls the frequency—badly, but I'll improve that. And the joystick determines the amplitude of the signal which the creature's collar feeds to it as pain induced in the main nerve trunk. A goad of sorts, badly made and underpowered."

Hansen licked his own lips. Funny how dry your mouth could get, even in a saturated atmosphere like this. .

"Walker?" he said. "Can you boost the power and expand the range that the unit covers?"

"I'm tapping it into the Matrix as a powersource," Walker said. "And yes, Kommissar, while I'm at it I'm adjusting the frequencies so that the unit will also control the collars the herdsmen themselves wear."

There was another electronic chuckle. Hansen's vision returned to normal. The pseudopods resealed the unit and withdrew.

Hansen tossed the unit back to its owner. "Try it," he

said. "But watch the power—and if you get to the end of the dial, it'll work on your buddies, too."

The lizardman toyed with the joystick. There was an agonized bellow from deep in the swamp. The Lomeri's finger released the stick.

Distant splashing continued for thirty seconds, then slowed. A second prod was followed by another bellow, much closer. An edaphosaur—the one whose wandering had brought the herdsman to Hansen to begin with—reappeared.

"It *never* worked like that on the cattle," the lizardman muttered in delight.

"Next?" said Hansen.

The Lomeri played with the first sending unit while Hansen worked on the second. Edaphosaurs seemed to have no herd instinct and a tendency to wander. Bleats of pain echoed in all directions as the lizardfolk drove the beasts closer—and, when they were in sight, tortured the sluggish sailbacks for the pleasure of watching them bleat and squirm.

"Now there's only one thing . . . ," Hansen said as he returned the second unit.

Two lizardmen grabbed for it. When one snatched it away, the other jabbed his staff toward his comrade's belly.

Both of the creatures straightened up in screaming pain. The third Lomeri had twitched first the dial, then the joystick of his repaired unit. His laughter had the brittle cruelty of a brick shattering stained glass.

Hansen took the remaining unit as its owner hopped on one leg, trying to raise his head even higher as his clawed hands plucked at the collar which controlled him. The third lizardman threw his joystick back to zero and let both his fellows collapse gasping in the mud.

"The only thing is," Hansen resumed while crystal limbs as angularly misshapen as those of a spider crab reached past his face, "is that in this swamp, the units are going to degrade again. This atmosphere—"

He waved his hand through the miasma of humidity and rotting vegetation. "—is going to crud up what it doesn't eat, so you'll need to find somebody to fix your hardware again."

He tossed the third sending unit back to its owner.

The lizardmen looked at one another. The nearest shifted his grip on his pointed staff.

Hansen smiled at him. "I wasn't lying about feeding you yourself either, boyo," he said.

The lizardman shrank back.

"So I think I better leave this with whichever of you wants it," Hansen said. He lifted the helmet from his head, judged the distance, and lobbed it in a high arc that descended directly in the center of the three Lomeri.

Mud gouted as all three creatures jumped for the prize. One grabbed it with both hands and shrugged off the others with a quick twist of his shoulders. He squawked as one of his fellows stabbed him hard enough in the belly that the staff's modest point tented the scaly hide on the victim's back as it tried to exit.

The killer gripped his weapon an instant too long. His uninjured fellow leaped for his throat and clamped it with the jaws that had so impressed Hansen. Blood, as red as a mammal's, sprayed in all directions.

The killer let go of his staff. He tried to pry apart his fellow's jaw hinge, but the teeth had done their work, and his arms were already losing strength.

The surviving lizardman pitched aside the corpse his jaws had nearly decapitated and straightened. He was laughing.

The hideous glee turned in mid cackle to a shriek that mounted the scale of audibility as the Lomeri struggled with his slave collar. The last sound he made was a clicking grunt, an instant before he toppled face down into the pond. His legs continued to thrash, but no bubbles rose from the water covering his nostrils.

The lizardman with the staff through his guts dropped his sending unit. He bent forward, trying to reach the fallen helmet. His fingers touched it, but he didn't have enough strength remaining to pick it up. His limbs splayed as he fell.

Hansen worked the helmet out from beneath the twitching body. Now that he wasn't wearing it, he could see that there was a single blue diamond where the plastic covered his forehead. "Hello, Walker," he said as he put the helmet on.

An edaphosaur grunted happily. The herd was separating again.

"That was unnecessary," said Walker tartly. "You could have killed them yourself with the first sending unit."

"I've done a lot of unnecessary things," Hansen said. His

eyes had no expression, but his palms went cold with the thoughts that flamed through his mind.

"The only ones I regret," he went on, trying to control the sudden quiver in his voice, "are the people I've killed when I didn't have to."

Hansen looked at the bodies. All of them were still moving. He wondered if they'd squirm till it thundered. "If that lot needed to die," he said, "then they'd die. Their choice."

"Pft," said the voice in his earphones. "But so long as you succeed, I won't object to the technique."

"Can you guide me to Strombrand's place?" Hansen asked.

"Of course."

"Then let's go," Hansen said, rubbing his hands on his coveralls as if trying to burnish the feel of death from his skin. "I think he'll be in the market for somebody to round up his herd for him."

and laevo-rotating twins; and it may be that Strombrand can get us access to what his brother holds.''

The section of wall slid downward. Two sullen humans wearing slave collars stood inside with a double-headed android. The slaves weren't much cleaner than Hansen—who'd swum a ribbon of muddy water when Walker assured him that there was nothing beneath of a size to concern him.

The android lounged against the inner surface of the wall. He held a bell-mouthed mob gun in his arms.

''Welcome traveler to the palace of the great lord Strombrand,'' the slaves singsonged together in Standard.

''Boy, you look a treat,'' said one of the android's mouths. The other laughed. ''C'mon,'' the first head continued. ''I'm s'posed to take you to my father.''

His free arm gestured toward the huge dome. His gun continued to point at Hansen's midsection.

The courtyard was mud-surfaced, but there were arched pens—or houses—built into the surrounding wall. Dozens of humans worked at various tasks in the courtyard, all of them wearing slave collars.

They glanced sidelong at Hansen. Their expressions were not very different from those on the faces of the Lomeri as the lizardmen discussed their next meal.

''Father?'' Hansen whispered as he stamped toward the dome. ''Android batches capable of reproduction are destroyed at once.''

''Androids that can reproduce are destroyed—or are very carefully controlled, Kommissar,'' Walker replied. Hansen thought he heard amusement in the tone. ''The batches that can reproduce have a level of cunning which is missing from their normal fellows . . . and which is very useful for certain purposes. For your Consensus.''

Solbarth. Was Solbarth from the same batch as Strombrand?

''And sometimes very dangerous, when they get loose,'' Hansen muttered. *But I was better than he was.*

Slaves at the entrance to the dome hosed off Hansen without ceremony. ''C'mon, c'mon,'' one of them ordered. ''Turn, won't cha?''

Hansen wasn't in a position to complain about the treat-

ment—and behind him, the android's muddy boots were
cleaned the same way.

The interior of the dome was illuminated by tubes of light
along each junction line of the facets. The colors varied from
one bar to the next—never bright, never saturated; never quite
pleasing. Their mixture threw a muddy ambiance around the
hundred or more figures, slaves and androids, in the center
of the hall.

"G'wan," said the two-headed android as he prodded
Hansen in the back with the mob gun. "Grovel fer the ole
man and let's find something t' eat."

You'll grovel for me if you poke me again with that gun,
Hansen thought; but that was just for his soul's sake. A scene
wouldn't help him get the job done, and doing the job had
always been Hansen's goal. It didn't really matter what the
job was, so long as it was his to do. . . .

Hansen stepped through the loose crowd. Several of the
androids were as perfectly formed as Solbarth had been—
physically. Others were hideously misshapen, with extra limbs
and multiple heads like Hansen's guide.

The androids dressed in layers of flowing garments and
were heavily bedizened with gold and jewels. Some of the
human slaves were able to follow the same fashion. The
plump man speaking to the android seated on the room's only
chair ("Strombrand," Walker said, but that was obvious)
wore a gold torque which almost hid the plastic collar which
controlled him.

"The herdsmen still haven't reported in, sir," the slave
said.

"Well, then raise the amplitude when you ask, Donner!"
Strombrand said. "Do I have to tell you everything?"

Strombrand had the normal complement of head and limbs,
but no one could have mistaken him for a human. He was
brutally massive, literally three times as broad as a normal
man. His bare arms were roped with sinew and as thick as
flowing basalt; the coiled bracelets he wore would have fit
around Hansen's waist.

"But we're already broadcasting at a very high level,"
Donner protested. "I'm concerned that we'll harm the fools
if we raise it again, and you *know* how difficult it is to replace
Lomeri."

"If you're talking about the three Lomeri I saw on my way here," Hansen said, stepping toward the throne, "then they're beyond anybody else hurting. They seem to have gotten into a fight and pretty well finished each other off."

"What?" peeped Donner.

"What?" boomed Strombrand, lurching up from his chair. Hansen couldn't help blinking because the motion was so similar to that of an avalanche rumbling toward him.

"Well, it's like I said," Hansen explained. "They'd done each other with spears and teeth, you know."

He shrugged. "There were a couple sailbacks around, which is why I thought of the bodies when you said herdsmen."

"When was this?" the android chieftain demanded. Despite the bestiality of his form, Strombrand's white skin was so smooth that the bars of light lay on it in distinct patches rather than a general blur.

"Three hours, perhaps?" Hansen said. Even without the artificial intelligence—and Walker—Hansen's internal clock could have given the time to within five minutes; but that wasn't anything Strombrand needed to know.

"And the herd's been wandering?" Strombrand boomed. "Well, don't just stand there, Donner! Round up the house slaves and get off after them!"

Sweat beaded on Donner's bald scalp as he wrung his hands together. "Oh, it'll never work," he moaned. "Those *damned* cattle, they *like* to stray, and by the time we get out there in the *mud* they'll all be gone!"

"Did I ask for an opinion?" demanded the android, balling a fist larger than Hansen's head.

"If all you're concerned with is getting back your cattle," Hansen said, "I can call them home for you."

All eyes in the room focused on him.

"Clever, clever Hansen," Walker whispered in his ears.

"Of course," Hansen continued, "there's something I need that you can help me with, Lord Strombrand. Shall we make a pact, you and I?"

The android seated himself again. His right index finger tapped the arm of his throne. It sounded like a maul striking a chopping block.

"What sort of pact?" he asked.

"There's a question I want to ask your brother's data bank," Hansen said. "Will you help me get the chance to ask it?"

Strombrand's great brows drew down in a scowl. "That?" he said. "It's not Strelbrand's, it's all of ours, from when we came here. He'll never give you permission, no matter what I say."

"That's not the deal," Hansen said. "*I* call your cattle back . . . and you use your best efforts to allow me to ask one question of the data bank. Your oath on that?"

"Oaths have power here on Northworld . . . ," Walker said, repeating one of the first things he'd told Hansen on the snow-covered bluff.

Strombrand knuckled his broad jaw. "All right," he said.

The android stood up, more deliberately than he had before but no less threateningly. "But *I'm* not interested in best efforts, stranger. If you don't bring back my whole herd, you'll provide the main course for my dinner tonight. Do you understand?"

"Oh, yes," Hansen said with a cold grin. "I understand you very well, Lord Strombrand."

See to it that you understand me, he thought; and that was not a boast.

Walker's signals prodded the herd of edaphosaurs home while Hansen stood in the muddy courtyard whistling bars from *In the Baggage Coach Ahead.* Later that afternoon as Hansen climbed into an aircar to be taken to the estate of Strombrand's brother, he noticed the chief slave Donner leaning close to one of the sailbacks.

Donner was whistling earnestly, hoping to see some flicker of interest in the reptilian eyes.

Strelbrand's palace was identical to that of his brother.

Strelbrand himself was Strombrand's mirror image; his wife, as broad as either man with two pairs of arms and legs, was still more hideous.

And Strelbrand's reaction to his brother's request was just as Strombrand had warned.

"What?" the seated android boomed. "Is there madness in our batch, Strombrand, that you'd think of asking me this thing? No! No, of *course* not!"

Strombrand was as defensive as a spider in another spider's web. He hunched his shoulders as if accepting a weight. "I'm oathbound to ask you, brother," he said. He didn't look back at Hansen, who stood at his heel.

"Well, then I'm oathbound to tell you you're crazy, brother," Strelbrand said. "You know how much North and his lot'd like to get into that bank!"

"I was oathbound," Strombrand said; *almost* a repetition of his earlier words.

Strelbrand rose to his pillarlike legs. Because of the dais under his throne, he stood taller than his brother. "Tell your oath-lord, Strombrand," he said, "that I alone can enter the chamber."

Strelbrand's wife whispered something into his ear.

"And my daughter Acca, of course," the android chieftain added. He grinned like the earth cracking open. "But she can't enter it, because she can't leave, can she?"

The laughter of the crowd followed Strombrand and Hansen back into the courtyard.

"I told you so," the android muttered to the human as they got into the open aircar.

"So you did," agreed Hansen. "So we'll come back tonight, to the tunnel beyond the walls that leads to the chamber holding the data bank."

Strombrand paused. "You know about that?" he said in something between threat and wonder.

"Go on, lift off," replied Hansen. He smiled. "And yes, I know a lot of things. I know that you'll keep your oath to me tonight, don't I?"

Strombrand slammed his throttles against their stops to lift in the muggy air. The monstrous android couldn't possibly have been afraid of the expression he saw on Hansen's face.

The night was as warm and humid as midday. A haze of light seemed to cling to the thick atmosphere. Strombrand set his aircar down on the riverbank with a squelch.

Bubbles from the rotting vegetation rose in a series of muted belches.

They'd landed next to a metal plate two and a half meters in diameter. It would have been almost invisible by daylight, but the mud covering the metal had a faint phosphorescence

which emphasized the unnatural circularity. Strelbrand's mansion wasn't far off, but the mist would have hidden it even if the sun were up.

"This is the correct location," Walker whispered approvingly in Hansen's earphones.

"Very good, oath-brother," Hansen said to the huge android. "Now, if you'll just open the tunnel and turn off the protective systems, I'll say we're quits."

Strombrand looked at his passenger. "Who are you?" he growled.

A small lizard in the reed-choked stream raised its head at the sound, then dived beneath the surface with a quick thrust of its broad forelegs.

"I'm the man who whistled your cattle back," said Hansen. "Shall we go?"

Strombrand cursed like thunder and got out. The vehicle slurped from side to side as he moved. He adjusted the sling holding the nozzle of his laser. The powerpack on his back would have required a separate vehicle before a normal man could have moved it.

"If I'd known what you were going to want," the android said, feeling through the muck for the handle, "I'd never have made the oath."

Hansen said nothing.

Insects bumbled into them and buzzed away again: tiny wasps which sipped plant juices for want of nectar in this flowerless world, and biting flies adapted to the cold-blooded sailbacks and their kin, uninterested in the human and android after a preliminary sniff.

Hansen saw iridescent motion against the lights of the instrument panel; he snatched left-handed. Furious wings burred against his palm and closed fingers.

At least he hadn't lost his speed.

The door lifted with a horrible sucking noise. The light from within diffused above the entrance. Strombrand gestured downward. "There you go, then,"

Hansen got out of the vehicle. "After you," he said with a gesture of his own. "You still have to disengage the automatic defenses."

"I didn't promise to die for you!" the android shouted. "If there's a risk, it's yours to take."

"But there isn't any risk for you, Strombrand," Hansen replied mildly, pointing toward the opening with his right index finger. "Because the defenses think you're your brother, so you can turn them off. As you and I both know."

A great-throated carnivore sent a grunting bellow up from deep in the swamp, responding to Strombrand's voice. The big android cursed and plunged into the tunnel.

From outside the entrance, the tunnel appeared to drop straight into the earth. Strombrand was walking as though one edge of the circle were down. With each step, his body rotated another few degrees around the axis of the tunnel.

Golden light from the far end suffused the interior. It winked softly from the android's jewelry and the bright fittings of his laser pack.

Strombrand's broad body shrank faster than distance should have required. Ripples formed between the android and Hansen as though Strombrand were crossing hot sand.

Sparks suddenly enveloped the center of the tunnel. Strombrand paused, lapped in blue fire. He took another step forward and manipulated a switch in the wall. The sparks died away; the curtain which had seemed to fall over the tunnel lifted.

Strombrand continued walking. Hansen slowly released his breath. A second gout of sparks surged over the android so fiercely that the man waiting outside the tunnel felt his own hair lift.

Again Strombrand walked on through. His huge body had shrunk to the size of a marmoset in the center of the golden ambiance.

He reached the end of the tunnel and waved a tiny arm back at Hansen.

"Go," said Walker. "But be careful."

"Go teach your grandmother to suck eggs," Hansen said evenly as he stepped into the tunnel and felt a surge of buoyant energy wrap him.

There was no feeling of vertigo or disorientation as Hansen strode toward Strombrand. Once the human looked over his shoulder to see whether the rotation he'd noticed from the outside was evident from this viewpoint; but there was only mist at the tunnel entrance—and anyway, it was a foolish thing to consider now.

Strombrand grew to his full misshapen enormity. The door behind him was the source of the golden light. He gestured toward it with a hand the size of a power shovel and said, "All right. I've opened the way for you. You and I are quits now."

Hansen opened his left hand. The wasp he held buzzed from him, seeking the light. It touched the surface of the door and disintegrated in a flood of golden radiance.

Hansen smiled. "Open the door for me, oath-brother," he said.

Strombrand's shadowed eyes were pools of black fury. He thrust at the center of the door.

There was a loud click. The glow lighting the tunnel shut off, but the door panel swung slightly ajar and a degree of illumination crept around its circular margin.

"My oath is kept," Strombrand said. "Acca will deal with you—but that's no concern of mine."

He strode back along the darkened tunnel without waiting for Hansen's reply.

"It is safe now," said Walker.

Hansen touched the metal panel gingerly. It was warm and as massive as a vault door—but the android's touch had disengaged its defenses.

Hansen leaned his weight against the doorleaf. For a moment, inertia withstood his thrust; then the circle of light around the panel began to widen.

"Stranger!" Strombrand called from the end of the tunnel. His powerful voice was attenuated by more than distance. "I've opened the way for you. I've kept my oath!"

Hansen looked over his shoulder. The android was sighting down the nozzle of his laser.

"Don't move!" Walker ordered in a tone of absolute command. Hansen froze. His eyes and mouth were open, waiting. . . .

The laser blast was a corkscrew of green light curling down the walls of the tunnel instead of following the straight path along the axis to Hansen's heart. His eyes tracked the bolt's helical progress, though at light speed there should have been no sensory impression except the shock through all his nerves as the center of his chest vaporized. . . .

The blast of coherent light struck and rebounded from the

door between Hansen's chest and right arm. Steam puffed from the sweaty fabric of his sleeve. Because the door was ajar, the bolt caromed a dozen times from the walls of the tunnel as it flashed back to the entrance.

Strombrand's body ignited in a crackling green dazzle. His scream was terrible but very brief.

Hansen blinked and rubbed the bare skin of his cheek which prickled from the actinic glare.

"Walker," he said. "What does she look like? Acca?"

"Does it matter?" the machine voice responded.

Hansen shrugged. "I suppose not."

Walker's laughter clicked. "Go on, Kommissar," he said. "Go on. We've come this far."

≡ 25 ≡

HANSEN STEPPED INTO a sun-dappled woodland. It was late spring, and the tips of the fir branches were bright green with new growth. The squirrel chittered wildly as it peered around a treetrunk at the intruder.

Hansen probed at the ground with his fingertips. He touched a yielding surface—but not the mat of needles his eyes told him to expect. He reached for a fir tree and found nothing, only an illusion of light through whose ghostly ambiance his hand gestured.

A tall nude woman ran barefoot past the false trees. Her braided red hair was long enough to fall to the back of her knees when she was at rest. A male cardinal flew from a pollen-bright bunch of cones as she flickered by.

Then the bird and woman were gone. Even the squirrel was silent—and none of them had existed to begin with.

The door had closed behind Hansen. No sign of its presence remained. He licked his lips and walked in the direction the woman's image had taken.

Hansen stepped into a meadow. The grasses waved high over his head. The stems were studded with tiny pastel flowers; birds fluttered among them.

He couldn't tell which way the woman had gone. His body touched nothing as he brushed through the sunlit display.

The woman was walking toward him. The grasses parted for her. A chickadee hopped from a green milkweed pod to her shoulder and back again, calling its brilliant, cheerful song.

The sun burnished golden highlights from her hair, but her skin was the pure white of an android.

Hansen stepped into her path. "Lady?" he called. "Acca?"

The image stepped through him without contact. He turned and ran after it/her onto a drift-swept volcanic plain. Here and there a patch of gray-green lichen grew where winds had scoured snow from the ropy basalt.

A golden battlesuit strode across the rock toward Hansen.

He halted. His body wanted to run, but there was nowhere to run. . . .

"Acca," Hansen called. "I've come to you."

Hansen could not only hear the sound of the battlesuit's steps, he could feel the impacts through the springy reality of what appeared to be lava.

The figure was within ten meters of Hansen. It raised its right gauntlet and ripped the air with the lethal blue fountain of its arc—higher than the distance still separating guard and intruder.

"I must kill you," the suit said in a woman's melodious voice.

"There's no must, Acca," Hansen said. He spread his open hands. "You make your own fate. I was sent to you."

The arc cut off. The battlesuit continued to advance, step by measured, armored step.

"I have everything here!" Acca said.

The volcanic waste shimmered into the meadow, the forest; a rocky skerry on which elephant seals roared their challenges back to the tossing surf.

"Now you have everything, Acca," Hansen said. "I was sent to you."

The golden armor halted almost close enough for him to touch it. "You can't leave now," Acca said.

Hansen nodded. "I don't want to leave, Acca. I was sent to you."

The battlesuit's right arm reached down to the latch and tripped it. Hansen gripped the edge of the heavy plastron and helped pull it open.

The woman inside was the original of the images which Hansen had followed through the images of places.

The spring forest grew about them again.

Acca accepted his hand as she stepped out of the golden

armor. She looked him in the eyes and asked, "What do you want?"

"You, Acca," Hansen said. "And to ask one question of the knowledge which you guard."

He smiled. "But first you," he said as he put his arms around her naked, perfect form.

They lay on a beach whose sand had the smooth resilience of rubber beneath them. The light of a full moon turned the sheen of the open battlesuit to silver. Hansen didn't recognize the constellations.

He kissed Acca's throat. She smiled and purred, but her eyes did not open.

"Darling?" he said. "Now I need to look at the data bank."

She raised her hands to his neck.

"Why that?" she murmured. Her fingertips traced the flat muscles of Hansen's shoulders and chest.

Moonlight turned her coppery pubic hair to silver. Hansen touched her groin, very carefully because the past hours had surely caused bruising.

Acca closed her eyes firmly again. She began to breathe in a series of gasps at decreasing intervals. He knelt and took one of her nipples between his teeth gently, tonguing it until her shuddering climax had come and passed.

"Now, darling," he whispered. "The data bank. One question."

Acca moaned softly. She made a gesture toward empty air. A terminal formed there, abruptly as solid as Hansen or the battlesuit standing in rigid majesty.

"Place me in front of it," Walker ordered through the earphones, "and get into the battlesuit. It will fit you."

Hansen kissed the woman's lips and got up. *He'd always done whatever the job required.*

He set his helmet on the ground. The air through his perspiring scalp felt cool and pure.

Acca looked up at him with languid eyes. "Don't play with the suit now," she said. "Come to me. Just hold me."

She smiled. Hansen closed the battlesuit over himself.

The display was diamond hard. Acca stared at him in dawning wonder.

The jewel burning in the center of the plastic helmet had extruded crystalline pseudopods into the casing of the terminal.

"What are you doing?" Acca called. She waved at the terminal, but it ignored her by remaining solid. "Please come out. Please, whoever—"

Walker was growing like a time-lapse image of ice forming in a supersaturated atmosphere. Highlights streaked his crystal limbs, but a single blue spark winked at his heart.

The mass grew above Hansen and about him, distorting his vision of the surroundings. The universe started to shift.

Very faintly, Hansen heard Acca calling, "Please, whoever you are. Please don't leave me. . . ."

For a moment, Hansen in his golden suit stood on frozen shingle beneath the huge red sun. The crystal surrounding him began to cloud and crack, like ice in shadow on a warm day. Bits dropped from the outer surface of the mass.

"Walker?" Hansen said, outwardly calm but unable to control the jolt of adrenaline that made his limbs quiver.

Walker's form was crumbling to white sand which dribbled across the gravel of the ancient beach. Hansen could still see the blue glint, but it hovered in airless space before him. He was hearing speech and almost words again. . . .

". . . sen, I sum . . ."

The universe shifted again. Bright sunlight, a red and gold battlesuit; muddy ground—

He saw the practice field below Peace Rock. The whole community was standing around the circle of posts to hear Taddeusz issue his formal challenge.

"Appear or wander an outlaw and coward," shouted the warchief's amplified voice, "destined victim for the hand of any man, slave or free. Hansen, I summon you!"

"Display energy levels," Hansen whispered.

The ground was solid beneath his armored boots. He heard the crowd's gasp.

Taddeusz was twenty meters from him. To the sensors on Hansen's new battlesuit, the power levels of even the warchief's royal armor were varied—and vulnerable.

"Cut," Hansen said. His weapon snarled as it traced a line across the mud at Taddeusz' feet.

"You should have learned, Lord Taddeusz," Hansen

shouted across the field, "not to summon what you lack the strength to send away."

"Dog spawn!" Taddeusz spat. His rippling arc crossed Hansen's at midpoint between the combatants.

The prickling of incipient overcharge unexpectedly lifted the hair on the warchief's arm.

It must have startled him, but Taddeusz was an old campaigner. He snatched his weapon back, let it vanish into his gauntlet, and thrust his left hand.

Hansen saw the charge levels building, but he didn't move to block the stroke. They were still twenty meters apart, and if the armor Hansen had brought from—bought from—Acca couldn't take the impact, he might as well learn it now.

The world roared. Hansen's display lost definition and color, and his every hair—from head to the tiny ones curling on the backs of his big toes—straightened as much as his garments would permit.

Hansen twitched his gauntlet. His arc touched Taddeusz' and cut it, breaking the circuit.

The warchief switched hands. Hansen slashed. Taddeusz' AI shifted power from attack to defense, but his armor's scarlet and gilt burned away in a line from wrist to shoulder.

Hansen let his opponent back a step uncertainly.

"Taddeusz," he said. "You see that I don't need to fear you. Let's stop this now."

Taddeusz lunged forward. The arc fanning from Hansen's gauntlet absorbed the thrust before it touched his golden armor. Hansen twisted his hand and overloaded the weapon close to the warchief's gauntlet.

"Taddeusz!" he shouted. "I haven't touched your daughter. I swear it on my honor!"

He'd've sworn he hadn't touched Unn, Acca, or anybody at all if he'd thought it would prevent an unnecessary killing. But even the truth was useless here. . . .

Taddeusz stepped in, his arc flickering from one gauntlet to the other as the warchief searched for an opening with the skill of long practice and natural talent. Hansen shifted his own broad arc, reading Taddeusz' power shifts to block each threat before it occurred.

Golsingh wore tights and a black velvet doublet as he

watched expressionlessly from the sidelines. Unn and Krita stood to either side of him. Malcolm and Maharg were to Krita's left.

The air was bright and warm, so only a few of the spectators were wrapped in furs.

Taddeusz attempted a furious overhead cut. Hansen caught the stroke and held it, stepping closer while power draining to Taddeusz' weapon froze the warchief's armor.

Hansen's left gauntlet spat a second arc. He thrust surgically, aiming for Taddeusz' ankle. Paint blistered.

The warchief's weapon went dead as his battlesuit overloaded. Hansen stepped back and let Taddeusz fall on his face in the mud.

"Listen to me!" Hansen said. "I don't want to kill you. Stop this nonsense, take your armor off, and let's discuss the good of the kingdom."

Taddeusz rolled to his back. Balled dirt stripped from his red and gold armor as his suit powered up again.

The black scars on the warchief's arm and ankle were a reminder of how badly he was overmatched. Hansen let him rise.

"There'll be no good in this kingdom so long as you live," Taddeusz said. He turned the palm of his right hand toward Hansen.

Hansen brushed his opponent's gauntlet with a low-amplitude arc from his own suit. Taddeusz' bolt was deafening even through the battlesuit, but the touch of Hansen's weapon steered the charge into the ground. Mud, burned to brick and shattered, blew in all directions.

"Taddeusz!" Hansen shouted. He was sweating despite anything his battlesuit's flawless climate control could do. "Don't make me kill—"

The warchief's armor shuddered and gleamed as he reset it again. It was a fine suit, a royal suit. It recovered quickly.

"—you!"

"You're a coward and no man at all!" Taddeusz shouted. "I'm going to kill—"

Hansen's arc slashed at Taddeusz' neck. The red and gold battlesuit resisted in a momentary blaze of blue fire.

Sparks of blazing metal replaced the electrical discharge,

white droplets that pattered onto the ground where they raised puffs of steam.

Taddeusz' helmet fell. For a moment the headless battlesuit remained upright. Then it too fell.

Hansen turned to Golsingh. "M-m . . . ," he said.

His voice caught. Somehow during the fighting he'd bloodied his nose.

"My king," he said. "Lord Golsingh. I regret . . . I regret . . ."

Golsingh nodded. Unn was cold-faced, but the scarf in her hands was twisted into a silken rope.

"I regret the death of your foster father," Hansen continued with sudden assurance. "If you permit me, I'll pay you the blood debt in the best way possible."

He took a deep breath. "Make me your warchief in Taddeusz' place, and I'll lay the kingdom at your feet!"

Golsingh nodded. "Yes, Lord Hansen," he said.

He looked around the circle of spectators with eyes as hard as Hansen's own before adding, "And there will be none, I think, to deny the appointment."

≡ 26 ≡

NORTH WAS THE Matrix. His mind flowed through the shattered pathways like melt-water dancing down the rocks of a cataract. He was all the knowledge in his universe, and it was freezing him.

With the skill of long experience, North's consciousness sifted the rush of chilling, killing data, but there was too much. . . .

A party of Lomeri, riding triceratops and carrying energy weapons, herded long-necked sauropods through a forest of conifers. The trees overtopped even the giant dinosaurs by scores of meters.

Humans in armor powered by energy differentials within the Matrix arrayed themselves outside a port city. There would be a major battle with hundreds of warriors on either side. Hovering over the field, just out of phase with the combatants, was a leash of North's own Searchers. The hard-faced women were ready to transfer the brain patterns of dying warriors into their data banks and bring them back to North.

Crystalline machines stumbled ceaselessly over the barren wastes of a world so old that it forever kept the same face to the huge red sun it circled.

A slave-stealing expedition of androids, as disparate in appearance as a necklace of pearls and broken fragments of oyster shell, poised beside one of the discontinuities between planes. The androids were heavily armed. Across the veil of the discontinuity lay scrub woodland and crumbled rockpiles which once had been chimneys. The raiders would have to go far to find human habitations.

Rao took leave of Ngoya. He looked awkward and dis-

mayed at the concern his wife could not completely hide after
so many repetitions of the event. He was fully armed, and
the vessel in which he would pursue raiders across the Open
Lands was a battleship on the scale of a tank. The one human
servant who would accompany Rao watched his master with
mingled fear of the coming task and impatience to get it over
with.

Eisner in the form of Penny braced herself against her desk.
She had wrapped her legs around Rolls so that her heels forced
him deeper into her.

The people in the common area of a village on Diamond
looked up in horror and surmise. A child began to cry but
shushed as his mother picked him up. The whole crowd stood,
linking hands. Someone began to sing in a quavering voice;
the whole park joined in a hymn to love and growth and the
sun that follows the rain.

The shadow that fell across Diamond was not from a cloud.
There was a subtle shift of energies as molecular vibrations
elsewhere in the Matrix changed phase—and reverted, so that
sun streamed into the park again, while the uniformed populace of Ruby frowned and checked weapons and tensely
watched a sky boiling with auroral discharges.

Ruby snapped fully into vibrational phase with Diamond.
The common area went red, then black. Ruby soldiers
pounded one another on the back and shouted in triumph,
but as black blurred to nothingness, there was no sound except the fading memory of a hymn to life. . . .

North rose from the Matrix in the usual gasping terror of
a man bobbing to the surface through icy waters.

"Dead," he whispered. "Killed." His face was terrible.

His last vision from the Matrix was the sight of a tank
curvetting in the cloud of red dust its fans raised. It was
painting the sky with blasts from its weapons.

≡ 27 ≡

A KILOMETER FROM the outskirts of Frekka, ages of plodding caravans and grazing had turned the mammoth prairie into a barren waste: dusty now at high summer; muddy in season; and less depressing only in the depths of snow-swept winter because the whole continent was too bleak to contrast.

Part of the dust raised by the hooves of Hansen's pony had settled over him like a yellow drapery; much of the rest seemed to have clogged his throat. Messengers had run ahead when Hansen reached the bridge over the ditch protecting Golsingh's encampment. He was pleased to see that among the friends waiting for him at the flap of the king's tent was Malcolm—holding up a skin of beer.

Golsingh would have traveled in royal state, but Malcolm and Maharg must have had equally hard, dusty rides as they marshaled the other contingents from distant holdings. With luck, though, they'd've had less difficulty than Hansen had, ᵥₙcing lordlings to provide the warriors that their oath to king required.

ɔlsingh helped Hansen from his pony and tried to embrace him while Hansen slurped beer from the spout of Malcolm's flask.

"Any trouble?" Malcolm asked, as though the warchief would have been two days late—and ridden in alone—if there *hadn't* been trouble.

"The messenger arrived warning you'd been delayed, of course," Golsingh said. While the Lord of Thrasey pretended nonchalance, the king feigned reasoned coolness.

Hansen looked at the lowering sun. "The rest're two hours behind me," he said. "They'll be in before sunset."

He'd swallowed the first swig of beer. He rinsed his mouth

with the second and spat it on the ground. Better late than never.

"Glockner held us up," he said.

"Said he wouldn't give you the men?" asked Maharg.

"Nothing that straight," Hansen explained. "You know Glockner. Took a day to round up enough baggage mammoths, and then some of them showed up lame. Third day, Glockner and about half the men I'd picked for his share of the muster, they came down with flu or something."

Malcolm shook his head angrily. "Well, we're probably as well off without that tricky bastard," he said. "But after we're done here, I'll go—"

"Oh, he's coming," Hansen said as he drank again. "He's back with the rest. Everybody got healthy faster 'n you'd believe when I put my suit on and burned down Glockner's hall."

Maharg and Malcolm laughed. Golsingh's face blanked for a moment, and when he opened his mouth it was to say, "Rough work, Lord Hansen."

"Not as rough as hanging Glockner on a rope of his own guts," Hansen said flatly. "Which was the next step."

He met the king's eyes. "Peace is the desired end, milord . . . but for the moment, I'm your warchief."

Golsingh said nothing, then clasped Hansen's shoulder again. "Yes, I see that. It's a matter of knowing what to do. And you've proven already that you know better than—" he smiled his hard smile "—I did before our association."

"Figgered you had something like that in mind when y took Glockner fer yerself," Maharg said. "Hell, I could handled him."

Hansen grinned. "Yeah," he said, "but you would've made sure they all stayed inside when you burned the hall. This time I wanted his troops more 'n I wanted a lesson for the other barons. Matter of emphasis is all."

"They aren't proper warriors," Golsingh said suddenly. "Frekka's aren't."

He nodded westward, though the walls of Frekka were the better part of a kilometer away, out of sight beyond broken ground. "They wouldn't meet us mid-way for battle."

"They had scuts in armor shootin' bolts at us from the walls, too," Maharg put in. "Won't call 'em warriors."

Hansen's face stiffened. "That sort of game could get real expensive," he said.

"We need Frekka," Golsingh responded sharply, then tried to soften the words with a smile. "You convinced me of that, after all, Lord Hansen. Blasting the city to the ground won't do any good. . . . And after all, we could simply move back out of range until you arrived."

He cleared his throat and smiled again. "Until we'd consolidated our forces."

"We've got warriors on guard at night," Malcolm said. "But I also thought maybe any freeman or slave kills a Frekka scout, then he should get a battlesuit and eat at the bench."

"They show they done it," added Maharg, "by bringin' us the ears."

Golsingh nodded. "That was Marshal Maharg's idea," he said. "And I approved both."

Hansen handed the beer to Malcolm. He kneaded first his buttocks, then his thighs, with his fingers. Hard to tell which parts hurt the most after he'd been in the saddle for most of three weeks, but at least a pony beat walking. A howdah on a mammoth, now . . . But that wasn't done; and anyway, he didn't feel comfortable around the huge beasts even when he was safe in his battlesuit.

"No reason not to go inside," the king said. "I'll have a meal prepared?"

"Sounds good to me," Hansen replied, taking Golsingh's gesture as a directive and ducking under the tent flap.

It bothered him sometimes that he'd knocked his fellows—his friends—so off-balance that they became indecisive as soon as he was around. They—all three of these men, the marshals and the king; and a number of the others he'd trained at Peace Rock and Thrasey over the past six months—could handle the new style of war without difficulty.

They had *done* so; this camp was proof of the fact. But as soon as Hansen appeared. they all stood around with their fingers up their collective ass.

Hansen sat cautiously on a camp chair while slaves bustled with a meal of cold boiled chicken and vegetables.

There was no delaying the real question, because all the royal forces were mustered now. All the help Golsingh was going to get was camped around him at this moment.

"What sort of numbers are we looking at?" Hansen asked.

The king licked his lips. "Many," he said. "I think— perhaps a thousand."

"Shit," said Hansen quietly.

He held a chicken drumstick while he hacked at the thigh joint with his belt knife. The knife didn't hold an edge worth a damn. "Where'd they all come from?"

"There's ships in the harbor," said Maharg. "Pirates."

"They've allied with three or four sea-kings," Malcolm agreed. "The Syndics have equipped the pirates with better armor in exchange for helping defend Frekka."

"Then they're bughouse crazy," Hansen said as he took a mouthful of meat. "People with money always think they can buy people with—" he started to say 'guns' "—weapons. What they buy is masters, if they're not damn careful to pick folks with honor."

None of the other three were touching the food. Either they'd already eaten or something had spoiled their appetite.

The enemy numbers had sure-god spoiled *Hansen's* appetite, though he couldn't let it show. With luck, the royal forces amounted to two and a half, maybe three, hundred warriors.

"They have a number of, I suppose, sailors and craftsmen wearing partial armor," Golsingh said. "The suits cover only the torso and one arm, so they don't really provide any protection; but they still have arc weapons, and they can be turned out much faster than complete suits of even poor quality."

Hansen shrugged. "We didn't expect it'd be easy," he said. "They're crazy to arm the pirates who've been bleedin' *them*, and the poor working scuts *they've* been bleeding, or I miss my bet."

He tossed the chicken bones toward the tent flap. "Anyhow," he added, "crazy or not, they're going to lose."

Hansen said the words because he thought it would cheer up his friends. He found, to his surprise, that he meant them.

"Sir?" called a messenger from beyond the flap of the tent in which Hansen slept alone. "Marshal Malcolm says there's troops coming from the city."

Hansen rolled to his feet, dropping the pry-bar back on his cot. "Got it," he mumbled as he climbed into the golden

battlesuit. His muscles ached, his mouth felt like a wiping rag, and his sinuses were packed with yellow dust and mucus.

And all of that started to clear again with the familiar surge of adrenaline through his body. There'd be plenty of time to hurt later, if he survived.

Hansen's armor latched over him; the world sharpened. He'd set the brightness default to display 100% of normal daylight. The night's waxing moon provided enough light to kill by, but the amplified images were better by several orders of magnitude.

He wondered if the Syndics of Frekka had realized the full potential of their battlesuits. There hadn't been any sign of that in previous clashes with Frekka's hirelings.

The merchants *were* willing to ignore the traditional disdain for fighting at night, but that didn't require so much intelligence as it did a willingness to change the rules when the rules didn't suit them.

The Syndics didn't operate under the morality of shopkeepers, who know their customers and know they have to do business with them tomorrow as well. The leaders of Frekka had graduated to an attitude that had always been common among the higher reaches of business and finance, when merchants saw a path to heaven through monopoly.

But Golsingh was in the way of that apotheosis; Golsingh, and Golsingh's new warchief. . . .

"Upper quadrant, map display," Hansen ordered his artificial intelligence. "All powered suits."

At the scale of the map, the attackers were a worm of red dots creeping from the blur of the city. The royal camp was a blue sea which brightened as additional warriors scrambled into their armor.

"Camp, secure commo," Hansen said. "All royal elements, do not, I repeat *do not*, leave your positions. Camp Marshals, enforce my command by whatever means necessary."

Half a year hadn't been enough time to turn all the warriors of Golsingh's army into disciplined soldiers. Malcolm might have qualms about striking down over-eager types who threatened to get in the way of the warchief's planned response, but he'd do it.

Maharg wouldn't hesitate an instant before using his new rank and battlesuit on warriors who'd scorned him six months earlier.

"Suit, rank and number of attackers," Hansen asked.

Red holographic figures overlay the map, rating the attackers' armor from Class 3 down to Class 12—a startlingly low quality, presumably indicating the partial suits to which the king had referred. There were fifty-seven all told in the attacking party, with a majority of their equipment in Class 12.

Cold meat for troops who knew what they were doing.

Which most of the royal army didn't—but Hansen didn't need most of the army.

He'd thought of calling the twenty-man command he'd organized under Maharg 'The Guards,' 'the Special Unit,' or the like. . . . But that would have made it a prestige appointment and made it difficult for him to keep out the sort of headstrong champions who had neither aptitude nor interest in learning how to *use* the suits they wore. So instead—

"All elements," Hansen said. "Marshal Maharg and Unit Four will deal with the raid. I'll accompany them. Marshal Malcolm—ah, Malcolm under the guidance of the king—commands the camp until I return."

"Hansen, you're not leaving me here!" Malcolm snapped, identified by his voice, by the tiny purple number on Hansen's display, and by the fact he was speaking on the command channel to which only the king, the marshals, and Hansen himself had access.

"Right!" said Maharg brightly, a usage he'd picked up from Hansen.

"Lord Hansen," said Golsingh, "I must forbid you to go out there. It's quite unnecessary, and you shouldn't be hazarding yourself in the darkness."

"Malcolm," Hansen said, "*shut up* and do your job! Lord Golsingh, with all respect—shut up and let *me* do my job!"

Hansen was panting and his legs quivered. He hadn't moved his body since he closed his armor and got on with the business of organizing the defense.

If he survived, maybe he'd apologize to the friends he'd just insulted. More likely, he'd figure he'd done what needed to be done at the time; which was never grounds for an apology.

"Maharg," Hansen called as he stepped into the open, "have the men ready. I'm on the way."

He forgot to allow for the helmet's bulk when he ducked through the flap. His head pulled the tent down behind him. Hansen's servants scuttled about the wreckage, squealing in concern.

The twenty-man team and their leader knelt just outside the north gate of the encampment. "Suit, tag Unit Four white on all unit displays," Maharg said as Hansen crossed the ditch.

Good, the boy was learning.

"Unit, secure commo," Hansen said as he clasped Maharg's shoulder in recognition.

The map quadrant of Hansen's display showed the attackers several hundred meters to the west of Golsingh's camp, stumbling in single file over the broken terrain. *Definitely* not using their suits' light amplifiers.

"Right," said Hansen. "We're going to take them in the middle. That's where their top people are. Maharg, you take Red Team and push the leaders into the ditch around the camp. I'll chivvy the rear ranks back to Frekka with Blue Team. Everybody clear?"

The response was jumbled, but Hansen's AI threw a gratifying eighteen of twenty-one possible up in the corner of his display.

"And everybody on 100% normal daylight?"

Sixteen *rogers*, followed by five more in mumbled embarrassment.

"Remember, it's just like training," Hansen added. "Except these guys aren't fit to wipe the asses of the people you trained against. Right?"

Rogerrogerroger.

"Let's move!"

Unit Four moved fast in the night, but they had a considerable distance to cover in order to attack perpendicularly to the enemy's line of advance. The Frekka forces halted in a grove of birches two hundred meters from the royal camp. They were bunching up as troops farther back in line reached the leaders.

They really didn't see Death arriving on their left flank until Hansen, twenty meters from a pair of stragglers, said,

"Cut!" and the bright snarl of his arc sent Unit Four in at a run.

The first two targets required no more skill than a bandsaw needs for boards. Only the chests of these Frekka personnel were armored. Their legs burned like torches when the surge of Hansen's arc boiled all the water out of them.

There was an incandescent crackling along Unit Four's line of advance. The least of the men in Hansen's unit wore armor as good as the best suit among the Frekka troops, and trained teamwork would finish what shock had begun.

The trees to the left were aflame. Because of the way the Frekka forces had bunched, Maharg's Red Team had more than a fair share of targets—but Hansen was on the far right of the line, and he wasn't about to screw up an attack plan himself because he got greedy.

A dozen Frekka warriors hesitated on either side of the gully they'd been crossing when Unit Four slaughtered the men marching ahead of them. They turned and ran when Hansen faced them.

"Blue Team," Hansen shouted as he strode after them— *the golden suit had enough power to jump the gully rather than struggle down one side and up the other—*

"Follow m—"

There were two Frekka warriors in the gully as Hansen started to leap it. Their suits were in a class with the first one Golsingh issued to Hansen. An arc slashed across Hansen's crotch as he rose for the jump.

Instead of clearing the obstacle, he crashed into the far bank like a turtle who'd tried to fly.

Hansen's ears rang. The unexpected pain of his nose was as stunning as being struck by a thunderbolt. All around him was a roaring that fused clay into bubbling glass in a blue glare. Over the sound of the arc weapons he could hear men shouting.

Hansen's display turned fuzzy. The upper right quadrant still showed the red dots running toward his own white marker like flies headed for fresh carrion.

The pain of almost-blocked electrical discharges stopped abruptly. Hansen could smell the hair crisped over most of his body, but now the blazing arcs surrounded him at a slight

distance. It was as though he rode a bottle through the heart of a tornado.

The red dots vanished. Hansen's display sharpened, but his eyes were too blurred with pain to focus on anything.

"Sir?" called one of the pair of his own men who were trying to lift Hansen upright. "Are you all right? Are you all right?"

Hansen managed to pat one of the men on the back; but it was almost a minute before he felt able to speak again.

Hansen assumed it was another slave entering the tent. He continued sponging at his face, treasuring the sting of cold water, until he heard Golsingh's voice say, "You all may leave. I'll take care of any needs the warchief may have."

Hansen opened his eyes. The slaves scurried out, setting the flames of the oil lamps dancing.

The king wore a sequin-patterned shawl over a pair of light coveralls. His face was serious.

Hansen dabbed at his face again. His nose hurt like Hell itself, but he didn't think it was broken.

"I'm all right," he said. It struck him that the king's coveralls were modeled on Hansen's own pair.

Golsingh dipped a finger in the basin of water. "Wouldn't you like it heated?" he asked.

"It's okay."

Hansen wrung out the rag and met the king's eyes as well as his swollen nose would permit. "Lord Golsingh," he said, "I fucked up. I'm sorry."

Golsingh nodded. "Yes," he said, "you did."

The king sat down on the cot, blinked, and moved the pry-bar out from under him.

"Peace is very important to me, Lord Hansen," he said. Hansen went back to mopping his bruised face so that he wouldn't have to meet Golsingh's eyes. "The most important thing in my life."

Golsingh cleared his throat. "The—dream, if you will, that one day the men of this whole continent will be free of the necessity of fighting these interminable, useless wars.

"I suppose," he went on with a rising inflection which indicated he supposed no such thing, "you as a fighting man find that as—unpleasant as Taddeusz did?"

Hansen looked at the king out of the corner of his eye. "No," he said, "I don't. If I can work myself out of a job here, then . . . then I'll have accomplished something. *Something*."

He shrugged, then barked a laugh. "Anyway," he said, wondering if Golsingh would understand just what he was admitting, "the job I'm doing at the moment's always been the only important thing to me. That hasn't changed since I wound up here."

"Yes, well . . . ," Golsingh said to his warchief's back. "In a duel, skill and the quality of one's armor are the important factors; but in a battle, a melee . . . often the better man falls to the lesser."

"I said I fucked up," Hansen said. "That doesn't mean I shouldn't've been out there tonight, it just means that I don't know everything. Yet."

"You've trained the men very well," Golsingh said. "And the Thrasey contingent, of course. We miss your company when you're in Thrasey, you know."

He cleared his throat again. "Unn often asks when you'll be returning. When you're at Thrasey or . . . just away from Peace Rock."

Hansen looked at the king. "Krita's still missing?" he asked.

Golsingh nodded. "Yes," he said. "Nobody . . . we know no more than we did last month. Nothing."

He toyed with his moustache before resuming, "Unn—we—would be very upset if something happened because you'd put yourself in a position that someone else could have handled just as well."

Hansen held the rag over his face and eyes. He wondered if the hot, prickling flush he felt crawling over his skin was visible to the man sitting behind him.

"You see," Golsingh continued softly, "I need you if my—dream of peace is to succeed. And that's more important to me than anything."

"You don't need me," Hansen replied in a thick voice.

He dropped the cloth into the basin and faced the king. "You've learned the important part," he said. "Strike for the head and never mind the little shit, that'll come when the head falls."

Golsingh opened his mouth to speak, but Hansen chopped him off with an abrupt motion of his hand.

"Tactics?" Hansen continued. "Malcolm and Maharg can handle that now. Maybe there's still some tricks they haven't got yet, but they've learned how to *learn*, and that's the important thing.

"You don't *need* me anymore."

The king stood up. His face wore a quiet smile. "Be careful tomorrow," he said. "That's all I ask. We ask."

He walked to the flap, then looked over his shoulder again at Hansen. "After all," he said, "you're also my friend."

Hansen continued to stare at the tent flap long after it had closed behind Golsingh.

≡ 28 ≡

"WE HAVE TO destroy them!" Rao snarled, more to himself than to his peers gathered with him in North's hall. "Ruby destroyed Diamond, so we have to destroy Ruby."

"We mustn't let anger rule us," said Miyoko. She stared at her tented fingers, and her words—like Rao's—were a personal litany.

"We'll destroy Ruby," North said from the high seat. If Rao's anger was volcanic, then North's face was a thundercloud and his words clipped flashes of lightning.

From behind a veil of light Penny snapped pettishly, "We can't do that, we're *linked*. And anyway, it's just one of those things that happen, and I don't think we ought to let ourselves get so upset."

Dowson pointedly dropped the shield of light behind which he usually sheltered to save the sensibilities of his peers. He floated before them, a brain in a tank of oxygenated fluid.

The outer surface sublimed from the cone of colored ice beside him. His words washed across the assemblage: "Our oaths and our selves guarantee the existence of Ruby."

"Forget that!" said Rao as his wife clutched his forearm with tears of concern in her eyes. They all knew the degree of single-mindedness of which Rao was capable, but Ngoya knew her husband best of all. "We guaranteed Diamond, didn't we? And they destroyed it. Ruby *killed* Diamond, so Ruby has to die!"

He started to get up. North's right eye focused on him like the single sharp point of a spear. "Sit," North said.

Rao met North's glare without fear; but he let Ngoya guide him back into his seat.

"Eisner," said North, "do you have any suggestions?"

Eisner, pinch-faced and cold, continued to look straight ahead of her. "Dowson is correct," she said without affect. "The Matrix has its own logic. If we destroy Ruby, we destroy ourselves."

She stopped speaking. Her fingers formed a perfect flat pattern in her lap and her eyes did not blink. No one else said anything.

"Rolls, then?" resumed North with the playful lethality of a cat pawing prey too frightened even to run. "Do you have something to add?"

Rolls looked at him. "I'm not afraid of you, North," he said.

North smiled. "You'd be a fool if that were true, Rolls," he said. "But you're not a fool."

Rolls swallowed. "All right," he said. "The others are of course correct. But yes, we have to avenge Diamond."

"Ruby isn't responsible for anything!" Penny whined. "They just—it's what they do. It's what we *created* them to do, to be. So why are we getting so upset?"

"We aren't talking about justice, Penny," North said in the silky, terrifying voice he'd used from the start of the council. "Merely cause and effect, what was done and what therefore must be done. Isn't that right—"

His head turned like a gun mount rotating. "—Fortin?"

The white android face deliberately turned away. "Whatever you say, dear father," Fortin remarked in the direction of the doorway.

There was a tremor of fear and anticipation in his voice. "You told us that Ruby had to be destroyed, so no doubt you're going to destroy Ruby."

Rao got up again. "Sure," he said. "I'll do it. That murder was the work of Chaos, and we can't compromise with Chaos."

"You idiot!" Saburo cried, the insult bubbling out behind the rush of his own fear. "*You're* Chaos with that attitude. You'll doom yourself and maybe *all* of us if you do that!"

"There's no need of that, Rao," North said without apparent anger. He rose in his seat, craggy and gray and as lethal as a murderer's worn knife. "Fortin is quite right. I'll take care of the matter."

He raised his hand. Black wings began to whisper toward the hall.

The others rose also, walking toward the door in emotions as various as there were individuals.

Rolls looked over his shoulder and called to the terrible man standing before the high seat, "You can't send your Searchers, you know. They can't *enter* Ruby. Only we can do that. Only a god!"

North smiled. His face was as bleak as a frozen gully.

"And if you think to open a path for your machine warriors," Rolls added from the doorway as the others stepped past him, "you can't without disturbing the balance of the whole Matrix. Not even you can do that!"

"Go on, Rolls," North said. "This is mine to deal with now."

"Ruby could defeat your machines!" Rolls cried. "Any number of them! The Matrix—"

North pointed his index finger. "Go now, Rolls," he said.

Rolls plunged out of the crystalline brilliance of the hall. Sunlight on the meadow was warm and gorgeous, but the ice in his marrow didn't want to melt.

The animals on which they'd ridden to the council were excited by their masters' return. Penny looked at the hourglass muscularity of the human who guided the deer pulling her chariot and said, "If you want to know what's *really* bad, I can't find my necklace."

Ngoya turned on her suddenly. "I can't believe even *you* could be so shallow that you'd think your necklace was equivalent to, to the *horror* that passed to a whole world!" the dark woman snapped.

"Easy for you to say," Penny retorted, her face hardening into something unexpectedly shrewd. "If your precious Rao came home in two pieces, would you say that was nothing—" her voice became whiny "—to a whole world?"

Ngoya flushed.

Rao heard his name and turned. "Huh?" he said. "Ngoya, what're you waiting for, anyway?"

"I'm good at finding things, Penny," said Fortin. He sauntered toward her. "Would you like me to try?"

"Good at losing things too," Penny said with a sniff of doubt.

The android formed the thumbs and forefingers of his hands into a square. Within their pale frame, an image began to take shape: ermine fur, a mirrored dresser—behind the dresser, something red and glowing.

Where he'd returned it.

"Look familiar?" Fortin asked nonchalantly.

"It can't be there," Penny breathed. "That was the first place I looked."

Fortin shrugged and pressed his hands together to snuff out the image. "Look again, then," he said. "Or don't. It's all one with me."

Penny leaped into her chariot and shouted orders to her driver.

Fortin caught Rolls' eye and smiled. "Everybody gets what they look for," the half android said. "Don't they—partner?"

Rolls mounted his restive elk. His face was stony, but Fortin's laughter behind him boiled through his mind like the memory of Diamond dying.

North watched as the light began to scatter and refract in the center of his hall. Black planes, like stress fractures in clear ice, formed and vanished and reappeared in sudden solidity.

A machine and the woman riding it came into phase.

The physical reality had no wings. The machine's slender body stood on oversized, jointed legs like those of a katydid or a cave cricket. The trunk of metal and crystal was slender, barely large enough to form a comfortable saddle for the hard-faced woman who sat astride it.

She dismounted and bowed to North, standing before his high seat. "Master," she said, "you summoned me specially. There is—"

She raised her face; her features were without expression. "—someone in the Open Lands you want killed. Shall I get my armor?"

North smiled at his Searcher. "You're very eager, little one," he said approvingly. "But no, not 'killed' this time but a killer."

She nodded again and set her left hand on the saddle pommel, ready to remount.

"Do you believe in god, my dear?" North asked archly, toyingly.

The Searcher blinked. "You are god, Master," she said.

He shook his head. "The only real god *here* is balance," he said, no longer playful. "There is a man needed to preserve balance, throughout the Matrix."

The woman nodded, but without particular interest. Her eyes reflexively examined the structure of her machine, the dragonfly of matter which took her in a bubble of spacetime between the planes of the world, at North's will and by his dispensation.

"Yes, Master," she said. "I'll fetch you his soul."

A beam of light through the ceiling struck her hair. It raised auburn highlights from a tight coil that had seemed black as the heartwood of ebony before the rays pierced it.

North shook his head, smiling. "Not this time," he said. "Not his soul alone."

The Searcher's eyes widened with surprise.

"Mind and body," North continued. "Mind and body and soul, I suppose, if men have souls."

For a moment North's visage was as terrible as the advancing edge of a glacier. The cold fury was not directed at the woman, but she felt herself shrink inside for all her courage.

Then the silent storm passed, and he, smiling again, said, "I chose you in particular, Krita, because he's someone you used to know. . . ."

≡ 29 ≡

GOLSINGH RARELY SOUNDED impatient. Because the words were so clipped and precise, Hansen couldn't be sure whether he was hearing an exception when the king said over the command frequency, "If they don't come out soon, we're going in. And I'll build a new port over the ashes of Frekka."

"They're coming out," Malcolm reported from the right flank.

The mid-morning sun fell squarely on the gray stone walls of Frekka, half a kilometer from where Hansen had marshaled the royal army. The ground between the two dipped slightly, no more than one meter in twenty—a swale of no military significance but some interest psychologically.

Painted, polished metal winked from seven gateways as the Syndics' army shambled out of Frekka.

Hansen instinctively used his map display instead of looking to either side to check his forces. Pitiful forces, considered as an army of men: 309 warriors and a thousand or so armed freemen and slaves. As a unit of tanks, it would have been very large, though, and his warriors would be a match for tanks in close terrain. . . .

"Hell *take* 'em," Maharg muttered from the left flank. "There's really a shitload of the bastards."

Golsingh, separated from Hansen in the center of the line by only a score of expectant warriors, said, "Most of them wearing half-suits. Walking corpses, as we know from last night."

Hansen checked the digital readout in his display. His mouth pursed, not that the numbers were news to him.

"Still," he said judiciously, "there's more of them in decent armor than we've got all told."

"Yeah, laddie," said Malcolm. "But they don't have a soul, that lot."

Malcolm was right.

Hansen suddenly realized that he'd spent all his time on Northworld trying to teach fighting men the difference between soldiers and mere warriors. Warriors were the undisciplined rabble that was good for nothing but dying when it met trained troops. That was an important distinction, but—

There was a difference between a soldier and a merchant, too. You can't simply bean-count your way to victory. Some of the most ruthlessly efficient armies in history had been composed of ex-clerks and shopkeepers . . . but that took training.

Golsingh had Nils Hansen. The Syndics of Frekka had no one but themselves—and no chance.

Still, there surely was a mother-huge lot of the bastards the Syndics had hired.

The wings of the Frekka army began streaming down the gentle slope. A few score of the warriors wore wildly-decorated armor—pirates, brutal and well-accustomed to sudden death, but untrained in the business of attacking enemies who were both prepared and equipped.

The remainder of the flanking units was of half-suited levies, each man staggering under the weight of the plastron and carapace which couldn't protect him against an arc. They were threats only in the way gadflies threatened cavalry, biting from behind and throwing the lines into a confusion more dangerous than the sips of blood they drank.

The advancing forces kept a cautious distance between themselves and either flank of the royal army. The Frekka main body, containing most of the fully-equipped warriors, held their places under the walls of the city.

Merchant logic.

"They think it's going to hurt us to walk all the way to them," Hansen said. "The damned fools. Their men'll shit their pants watching us come at 'em like Juggernaut."

"We await your order, Lord Hansen," Golsingh reminded with the same touch of almost impatience. .

"Secure, general commo," Hansen told his AI. "Right. Everybody remember your training. Your job is to keep step with the other guys in your team and kill whoever the team

leader designates. Don't worry about your rear, there's people to cover you. Walking pace, don't get hasty. There'll be plenty time.''

Hansen's mouth was dry. There ought to be something inspiring to say, but he couldn't think what it was. His knees were shaking, and all he knew was that he wanted to stop talking and go kill something.

"Move out, guys," he said. "Let's kill 'em all."

The royal army bellowed as its hundreds of armored legs crashed forward. If the sound didn't scare the Syndics, then the poor bastards were stupid as well as ignorant of war.

As his forces advanced, Hansen switched to a 360° field and suppressed the map display. He wouldn't need sharp vision for several minutes, so for the moment the compressed panorama of the whole field was more important.

A party of warriors charged out of the Frekka line, following their instincts instead of orders. When they saw their fellows were standing fast, they paused—a score against oncoming hundreds—and scurried back into line, just as thirty or forty more warriors decided to join their charge. The Syndics' formation was disintegrating while the royal army was still five minutes from slaughter.

The flanks were Hansen's real concern. Those hundreds of half-armed troops could sweep around the royal army like light cavalry, like Hannibal's Numidian horse which plugged the last Roman chance at Cannae. . . .

Hansen's fear was the Syndics' hope, and both proved illusory. Men wearing half-suits were slower and clumsier than warriors whose armor carried its weight with power from the Matrix.

The royal advance slipped past the encircling jaws at two steps a second. Half-armed clerks and artisans staggered after them under the burden of their equipment, concentrating on keeping up—

Until they met the sudden arc-light scything from the royal troops detailed to meet the expected danger. Unit Four on the left, twenty warriors from Malcolm's brutally-trained Thrasey contingent on the right; picked men whose battlesuits could saw a tree—or a bare leg—at thirty meters.

And did.

Better-equipped pirates charged from either flank with the

instinctive reaction of men—even the worst of men—to do *something* when they see their fellows being slaughtered. Some of the pirates wore excellent armor; all of them were experienced killers.

The royal troops butchered them anyway.

One of Maharg's warriors went down in a blaze of sparks when a sea-king with great bronze wings welded onto his helmet struck off his feet. His conqueror died an instant later. Three arcs hacked him simultaneously and continued cutting after the pirate's vivid armor lay in bits on the smoking ground.

That was the only casualty on the left flank. A couple men were down on the right, but so were scores of pirates and nearly a hundred half-armored artisans.

The remainder fled. Golsingh's freemen were sniping at them with crossbows. Hansen could see several clots of slaves, some holding a victim down while others probed his vitals with their knives.

The screams of the dying accompanied the royal army's triumphant rush up the hill toward Frekka.

Hansen switched back to standard display and lit his arc weapon.

Hansen had arrayed the left and central divisions of his army with about two meters between one man and the next to either side. The Frekka warriors covered the same front but at nearly twice the density. Training couldn't change the fact that when the forces closed, many of the royal troops would face the arcs of two or three opponents—and would therefore be killed.

Black wings hovered, though there was nothing in the sky except a shimmer as of heated air.

Directly before Hansen was a figure whose armor was gold like his own, but carved and decorated like a temple frieze; a Syndic rather than a champion. The warriors to either side of the Syndic were veterans wearing battlesuits scarred by the combats they'd won. They braced for the contact, while the man in carved armor hesitated as if to dart back through the gate behind him.

When the lines were twenty meters apart, Hansen ordered, "Left and central divisions, hold in place! Remember your orders! Hold in place. Malcolm, hit 'em!"

The right wing, led by the Thrasey contingent and heavy with the army's better-equipped warriors, formed a dense ball and smashed its way into the Frekka forces. The warriors to their immediate front, trapped between stone and a wall of ripping arcs, could neither fight nor run. A few escaped through the nearest gates. The rest died.

Malcolm turned his unit left and marched it down the twenty-meter corridor between the city and the remainder of the royal army, taking the Frekka line in the flank. The warriors in the rear of Malcolm's division faced around and, merely by threat, scattered the survivors of the Syndics' light forces.

It was like watching a bowling ball roll through chaff.

The execution of Hansen's plan wasn't perfect, though he got a better degree of obedience than he'd expected from warriors he considered half-trained.

Men nerved to kill or die can lock their focus on the target before them, forgetting their training, their orders—their names. Parts of the royal army charged home in a blaze of sparks. Elsewhere, Frekka warriors broke ranks to meet the royal onslaught. In either case, snarling combat drew more troops in from either side.

But the plan worked well enough, because there still was an unshaken royal line at the moment the Syndics realized they no longer had a left flank and their center was beginning to disappear into the same flaming meat-grinder.

The gold-armored Syndic facing Hansen turned and bolted through the gate behind him. All along the line, men wearing richly-decorated battlesuits broke and ran.

"Get em!" Hansen bellowed on the general push, but there wouldn't have been any way to hold the warriors of his army longer anyway.

The veterans who'd been guarding the vanished Syndic closed a half-step reflexively. Hansen cut at the first. The warrior's arc caught Hansen's and blocked it, but the overload threw a nimbus of blue haze around the figure and began to blister the paint on his right forearm.

The second bodyguard stepped closer and chopped at Hansen's waist. Hansen was prepared for the stroke and parried it by switching his arc to his left gauntlet.

The first warrior took his release as a gift from providence

and lumbered toward the gate. Hansen sheared through the second man's suit at mid-thigh, then caught the first from behind while he was still between the gate towers.

The man's battlesuit was very nearly of royal quality. It lost motive power but held until Hansen swiped his victim to the side with his gauntlet almost in contact with its target.

"Through the walls!" Hansen shouted as he led the nearest of the royal forces through the gate. "Don't spare anybody with a weapon!"

Which wasn't, part of his mind told him with amusement, a very necessary order.

Even this major entryway curved abruptly just inside the gate, and the houses of Frekka leaned over the cobblestoned street. Most of the dwellings had been built at two stories, but they'd been raised by third-floor lofts as expanding business increased the need to house drovers and artisans within the walls.

Thinking of walls. . . .

The Syndics' army had broken, even the right wing which hadn't really been engaged. Frekka warriors massed at the gates the royal army hadn't yet captured. Many of them were trying to climb over the three-meter walls.

Now that their leashes had been slipped, Golsingh's men weren't waiting to go in turn through the gates either.

There were snarls behind Hansen as arcs gnawed the base of the heavy stonework. Quartz popped, mortar blazed as limelight, and fracture lines forced by differential heating shattered the biggest blocks in moments.

Sections of the wall crashed down. Undamaged ashlars from the higher courses bounced crazily, knocking over warriors who weren't quick enough to dodge them.

A roofing tile broke on Hansen's helmet.

He looked up. An old woman wearing a shawl over a dress embroidered with pearls stood on the roof coping. She was lifting a second tile to hurl down at him.

The woman dropped the useless missile and began to scream as the faceless gold helmet turned toward her.

Hansen lowered his gauntlet and smashed through the doorway into the house. The lintel was a 6x6 timber. His helmet struck it squarely. The timber didn't break, but it tore away in a shower of plaster and broken wainscoting.

The stairway was to the left off the front hall. Hansen took the steps one at a time, placing his armored boots directly over the stringers. He still wasn't sure the treads would take the weight of his battlesuit, but they did. . . .

The entrance to the loft was a ladder at the far end of the second-floor hall. The old woman was halfway down it. She saw Hansen coming up the stairs and screamed, trying to scramble back the way she'd come.

Hansen reached the base of the ladder while she was at the top of it. He jerked the heavy frame out of the wall to which it was pegged.

The old woman dangled from the loft opening, bleating like a trapped rabbit. She'd lost her shoes and her thin legs threshed like a drowning swimmer's. She wore black stockings held up by incongruous flowered garters.

Hansen started to laugh. He tossed the ladder aside and caught the woman easily when her arms let go.

"Listen to me," he said, using the amplification of his suit's speakers to overwhelm her terrified cries. "You know where the—the city hall, the headquarters is."

The woman's eyes and mouth clopped shut as the words hammered her. She opened them. "The Palace of Trade?" she asked.

"Right," said Hansen, walking back to the staircase with his prisoner cradled in his left arm. "You're going to guide me there."

He didn't figure he needed to voice a threat. Besides, his heart wouldn't've been in it. This old lady seemed to be the only person in Frekka with any balls.

The street to which Hansen returned was chaos. Royal troops thronged it, some of them coming from the opposite direction in their confusion. A number of the warriors were clumsily draped with loot. Several houses were already burning, sending flakes of dingy white ash down across the street and men.

"Suit," Hansen said to save his AI the trouble of guessing whether it should take the next words as a direction to it. "All elements in line of sight."

Then, "Listen up, you dickheads!"

Every warrior in sight of Hansen stiffened at the radioed command.

"This is your warchief," Hansen continued. "Follow me to the headquarters and we'll take their surrender."

He paused. "And *any* bastard I see with loot after the next thirty seconds, he spends an hour in the latrine pit when I get things sorted out!"

Hansen looked down at the old woman in his arms. She was actually clinging to him.

"Now, madame," he said as quietly as he could and still be heard over the sounds of battle, "let's go to the Palace of Trade. And the quicker we get there, the safer everybody's going to be."

Hansen's armored worm squirmed toward the center of Frekka, directed by the old woman's pointing arm. He started with about twenty warriors and a handful of slaves and freemen, but their numbers increased at every intersection. There were a number of abandoned battlesuits which unarmored members of Hansen's entourage appropriated.

The civilian populace had mostly hidden. Occasionally someone scampered like a rat back into an alley at the warriors' clashing approach. There was no resistance, though several times a Frekka hireling stumbled into Hansen's group and was cut down as he tried to run.

Hansen's passenger spat in the direction of each smoking corpse. "Cowards!" she snarled. "If they'd been men, they'd've met you in the field!"

"Lord Hansen," Golsingh said on the command push. "I'm in a gate tower as you suggested—" 'ordered' would've been a more accurate description of Hansen's tone when they laid their plans before the battle, but Hansen's temper was always short when it was about to hit the fan "—and I can see warriors boarding ships in the harbor."

"Right," said Hansen. The maze of close-built houses and curving streets had left him without a clue as to his location. Was the Palace of Trade near the harbor? Was—

"Right," he repeated. "Broadcast over a general frequency that no warrior will be harmed if he takes off his suit. And—d'ye have a couple other people with you in the tower?"

"Roger, Lord Hansen."

"Right. If any of the ships put out from the dock, have one of your guys fire a bolt at it."

"We can't possibly harm armored warriors at this distance,

Lord Hansen,'' the king protested. "Even my suit doesn't have that much power."

"*Not* you!" Hansen snapped. "I don't want *you* a sitting duck for some slow-learner."

He took a breath. His mouth was dry, while his throat and nasal passages had been scoured by ozone from the omni-present arc weapons.

"Milord," he said more calmly. It looked like there was a square at the end of the current street. "You can't hurt the armor, but the ships'll burn like tinder . . . and one thing a battlesuit *won't* do is swim. Trust me."

It was a square. Across it was a stone building of four high stories whose corners were raised further by twenty-meter spires. The leaves of the arched central doorway were ajar. Darting through the gap stood the gold-armored Syndic who'd faced Hansen—briefly—outside the walls.

He disappeared inside. The bronze-clad doorleaves closed.

"Come on!" Hansen bellowed as he broke into a run. "Don't kill anybody inside until I do!"

Hansen's arc licked the doors from across the courtyard. The bronze blazed green at the first touch. The wood under-neath was a better insulator. It flamed up instantly, but the panels might have held until Hansen struck them with his suit's full mass—had not at least twenty more of his men ripped their arcs into the same point as they charged.

The doorleaves blew open in splinters. Hansen, the old woman still in his arms—too terrified to scream, forgotten in the greater need—was the first of the men through their flam-ing tatters.

Oil lamps hung in brackets from the high ceiling, but their glow was insignificant compared with the hard blue-white arclights quivering from the gauntlets of the battlesuits.

The man Hansen had chased into the hall was climbing out of his armor. He was a fat old fellow, blinking in wide-eyed terror at the killers who'd burst through the doorway behind him.

"Don't!" he whimpered. "Don't! Don't!" He screwed his eyes closed.

He was dressed in silk and cloth-of-gold. So were most of the thirty or forty others, men and women alike, who'd gath-ered in the building before the enemy arrived. More battle-

suits, generally of good quality but covered with rococo decorations, winked in the royal army's weapons. All the suits were open, empty.

The Syndics and their hangers-on had surged for the back door when Hansen's arc blew open the front. They rushed back as abruptly. Hansen raised his weapon, his mouth open in amazement to think that they were about to attack him barehanded when they wouldn't face him with armor.

Another party of warriors burst in through the back door. Maharg's all-crimson suit was in the lead.

"All right!" Maharg thundered. "Who's the boss here?"

"*I* am, Marshal," Hansen boomed back.

"Oh, sorry, sir," his abashed junior said on the command channel. "I didn't know—Malcolm, you made it too?"

Malcolm touched the warchief's shoulder. "I've got my Thraseys ringing the building," he said. "That gives us an organized reserve if we need one—which I doubt."

"Right," said Hansen.

He pointed his index finger at the Syndic quivering in his armor like a clam half-drawn from its shell by a crow.

"You," Hansen said. "Are you the Chief Syndic or whatever?"

The fat man opened his eyes, closed them again, and said, "There's no chief. I'm, I'm Bennet."

Something shook in the air. Hansen thought it must be the shock of buildings falling, but no one else seemed to notice the vibration.

"Do you have authority to surrender the city?" Hansen demanded. "Does anyone here have the authority?"

A man from the group Maharg herded back into the room threw himself at Hansen's feet. He was young but already fat and as bald as Shill the day he died.

"We do, we surrender, Lord Golsingh!" he babbled. "We're a quorum! We surrender! O gracious king—"

Hansen had an urge to kick the scut away. He repressed it to a shake of his armored boot—which had the desired effect of making the fellow scuttle back with a squeal.

"The king's not here," Hansen said, raising his voice to be heard over the increasingly loud clatter from all around him, even the stone floor. . . . "As the Warchief of Peace Rock, I accept your surrender on behalf—"

"The king's here!" a man shouted from the doorway. "He's here!"

Hansen turned. Golsingh's splendid blue armor was silhouetted in the arched opening. *Underlings, no matter how respected, do not give commands to monarchs.*

"Your Excellence—" Hansen said, but the sound of the black pinions enveloping him was too loud even for his own ears.

The old woman in the arms of his battlesuit began to scream and point upward. Hansen's viewpoint hung suspended among the chandeliers and quivering stone vaulting.

He could see the empty interior of his armor—and the crypts beneath the building where a score of servants hid among the stored regalia and wine casks for public banquets. The white heart of the planet blazed up at him—

And was gone in weltering images of ice and beasts and huge red sun, which ended in a view of a light-struck hall infinitely greater than the one from which he'd been plucked a timeless moment before.

Hansen's feet were on a black floor as smooth and flawless as polished diamond. Twenty-odd curtains of light ringed the walls.

"Welcome, Hansen, once Commissioner," said the blur at the farther end of the hall. "We have a task for you."

≡ 30 ≡

IT REMINDED HANSEN of the place, the plane, where the lords of the Consensus briefed him.

The resemblance wasn't physical. He stood in a hall of such purity that the walls and roofbeams bent the light without dimming it. The floor beneath him was black but so smooth that Hansen felt he was standing on the soul of nothingness, the ancient ether which science had long denied even as an ideal.

The Palace of Trade had vanished. The Syndics, the conquering warriors in their battlesuits . . . everything except Hansen himself was gone.

The lords of the Consensus had been vast bulks, hinting of whale shapes but vaster even than fluid oceans could support. Here there were dazzles of light along the sides of the hall's empyrean perfection . . . and Hansen knew at an instinctive level that it was the same.

"Fortin," said a voice from the veil of splendor at the end of the room, "you will explain to Hansen his task. As for the others of you—you've seen that I have the situation in hand. Leave it with me, then."

Hansen had heard that voice—that *sort* of voice, he meant, but it went beyond that—before. The fellow outlining the mission, with all the weight of power and certainty behind him, telling others what they *would* do and what they *would not*.

Hansen always thought he'd be that sort of man when he had the rank, but he'd been wrong. *Commissioner* Hansen, and people jumping when he spoke—but he'd never been certain of anything except himself, and he couldn't give a man an order and make it sound like he expected to be obeyed.

Obeyed *or else*, if it came to that; but it was the *or else*

Nils Hansen believed in, and that wasn't the same thing at
all. . . .

The iridescent curtains were moving, shifting toward the
doorway; moving faster than a man could move over the distance . . . if the distance were as great as it seemed, which
instinct suggested it was not.

"Penny?" said the voice of insouciant command. "You've
recovered your necklace, I believe?"

"What if I have?" whined a girl's voice, almost close
enough for Hansen to touch the speaker though the nearest
of the auroral veils was/seemed a hundred meters away.
Then the same voice, sulky, "Yeah, Fortin found it for me.
Why . . . ?"

"To borrow, as you know. Because of Diamond. Because
it's necessary to achieve balance."

For all the assurance with which the male officer spoke,
Hansen could read the slightest doubt underlying the words.
This I ask, the doubt admitted, *and though I would like to
command it, I cannot.* . . .

The tone of a man who knows he *must* depend on others,
but hopes they won't realize the fact.

Hansen began to smile.

The rainbow veils swept out of the hall like sun-struck sea
mist scattered by a breeze. From the mass of them came a
male figure, huge, walking toward Hansen with something
winking from the fingers of his right hand. As he came closer,
he shrank until he stood before the ex-Commissioner as a
person no taller than Hansen himself. . . .

But that was not the surprise.

"Solbarth," Hansen said. "What are *you* doing here?"

The pigmentless, beautiful android lost his look of superior
disdain for an instant. He glanced toward the single shield of
light remaining, the one at the end of the hall from which the
commanding voice rang.

"What?" the android said. "I'm not Solbarth. Any Solbarth."

"You're Solbarth," Hansen said. His assurance was suddenly no more than a ploy, a tool luck had offered him to get
more information. "You're a criminal, and I captured you on
Annunciation."

He grinned. "You haven't forgotten *me*."

The android blinked. "My name is Fortin," he said. "As for being a criminal—I'm a god."

Fortin's laugh barked harshly, falsely. "It may be that you knew a batch sibling of my mother," he said with empty dismissal. "I'm half android, you see."

Laughter boomed from behind the veil of light.

Fortin shook his head to clear away discomfort and settled the mantle of disdain about his visage again.

"No matter," he said. "We've brought you here to restore balance in—"

"*I* brought him here," interrupted the commanding voice.

Fortin smiled. Enunciating as clearly as the notes of a jade bell, he resumed, "My father brought you here to restore balance in the Matrix. You will be inserted into Ruby, a portion of phased spacetime. You'll be disguised—"

Fortin hefted the necklace in his left hand. Hansen had a sudden vision of himself in drag, dripping with jewelry and his hair done up with ruby-studded combs.

"—but they'll be awaiting you. And they'll probably have warning of an impending attack."

The hidden speaker said, "Their threat warning system is very good. On Ruby, everything to do with war is almost ideally good. Wouldn't you say so, Fortin?"

The minuscule fluttering of the android's—half android's—nostrils was the only sign he'd heard the interjection.

"Your task," Fortin continued, "will be to penetrate Ruby's Battle Center. The main computer there has already been programmed to carry out a particular phase shift. You must—"

"No," said Hansen.

Fortin's face froze. "Don't think to cross me, human," he said.

His malevolence would have surprised some listeners; but not Commissioner Hansen, who'd spent three years tracking down one Solbarth, a criminal of almost incredible savagery. . . .

"No," said Hansen. "There's no 'must' from you for me. *You*—"

He tapped out with a fingertip that stopped just short of the android's chest "—can't order me to piss on your boots. Though that I might do for fun."

Laughter rocked and boomed from the end of the hall.
Hansen whirled on the sound.

"D'ye think I'm a gun you can point?" he shouted. "Do you? Well, you're fucking wrong!"

"Do you remember Diamond, Hansen?" the voice asked. "Where you first entered our continuum . . . not at our request."

It occurred to Nils Hansen that this pair was going to threaten harm to the gentle folk of Diamond unless Hansen did their bidding. An extortionist's trick, a hostage-taker's strategy.

And Hansen would have to react in the only way his soul would permit—kill Fortin, kill the voice behind the curtain of light; kill and keep killing until they killed *him*.

And perhaps the survivors would be less quick to use that gambit again with a man who was every bit as ruthless as they.

Fortin saw the look in Hansen's eyes; something close to an expression of sexual climax suffused the perfect android features. It froze Hansen and sickened him, as if he'd entered a room with murder in mind and found his intended victim eating a plateful of feces.

"This is what happened to Diamond," said the hidden man. "This is what you must avenge, Commissioner Hansen."

The hall vanished. Hansen hung in nothingness surrounded by the common area of the city-building where his capsule had landed. The room was full of standing, singing people, but he saw them as photographic negatives while something else printed through in their place.

Then he was truly among them, seeing Lea and remembering how her body had touched his with a warmth that was no flirtation. There was the little boy who'd waved and called Hansen's name, and—

He saw their flushed faces and the tears streaming down their cheeks as they sang of joy and sunlight.

The sun was a black pit out of which thundered a platoon of tanks rolling *through* the singing innocents rather than over them, grinding away the substance of their universe and not merely their bodies.

In place of the open park was a canyon walled by black

houses as massive as coastal forts. Citizens in uniform danced in the street, firing slugs and streaks of ravening light into the air. Through all the celebration, the tanks roared triumphantly.

"You remember Diamond," said the commanding voice. "This is Ruby, which destroyed Diamond. I brought you here, Commissioner Hansen, to destroy Ruby and preserve balance."

The vision was gone, the hymn that was worse than the screams that should have accompanied the descent to some spicule of nothingness and death. . . .

Hansen shuddered uncontrollably. He worked his hands, watching the fingers bend and the skin mottle with strain over the knuckles. "Go on with the briefing," he said.

Fortin laughed. "We thought this was a job you'd be willing to do for us," he said smirkingly.

Hansen looked up. The android stepped away reflexively.

"I won't do anything for you," Hansen said. He spoke very distinctly. "I'll do the job—*this* job. But not for you."

"Which is all we ask . . . Kommissar," said the voice from behind the veil.

≡ 31 ≡

THE FIGURES SURROUNDING him in Fortin's hall of ice weren't hidden by their curtains of light, but Hansen's mind was focused on the insertion ahead.

Gods, humans, or diffracted shimmers, it was all one with him. He barely heard the swarthy, densely muscular man say, "Just how often *do* you visit Ruby, Fortin?"; and that penetrated Hansen's concentration only because of the threat beneath the words.

Fortin's finger tapped the bemedaled breast of the jacket Hansen wore, checking for the slight bulge of Penny's necklace. "All right," he said. "Here's the ring."

Hansen slid the large diamond in a gold band onto the middle finger of his left hand. His finger joints were barely larger than the shafts of the phalanges. The ring fit easily, then clamped with a tiny prickling.

"Seconds to insertion," Hansen thought.

"Forty-seven," the ring's AI responded, using the nerve pathways of Hansen's body.

"It's connected?" Fortin said nervously.

"It's all fine," Hansen replied. "Look, I'm briefed and ready. Just step back."

"I don't like to see my necklace—on somebody else," murmured one of the spectators.

"And *Fortin*!" another chuckled. "That's a look *you* haven't tried—or have you, dearest?"

"That's not your gunhand, is it?" Fortin fussed. "It won't interfere?"

Hansen glowered at the android face of which his own was for the moment a perfect copy.

"My gunhand," he said distinctly, "is the hand I've got a gun in at the moment."

He flexed his left fist. The artificial intelligence flashed harder echoes of light across the ice and the fawn-gray uniform Hansen was wearing.

"It won't interfere. Trust me." Hansen's face formed a sort of smile. "Nothing interferes with that."

"Five seconds to insertion," said the machine voice in Hansen's mind.

"Here we go," Hansen said aloud, stepping toward the discontinuity as though his briefing officer were not in his way—and Fortin wasn't; he'd jumped aside as his double strode through the space.

Hansen began to giggle. He was wondering if the necklace would hide the stains if he pissed the pants of this beautiful dress uniform. The thought wasn't the worst way to release tension at the start of an operation.

He stepped into the faceted blur in the center of the hall and—

His polished shoe ground down on the gritty red soil of a drill field. An officer stood in front of a platoon of infantry. They were drawn up at attention but armed to the teeth. Dust, blowing across the field from the fans of eight APCs, aided the excellent camouflage pattern of the troops' fatigues.

The field was scooped from the side of a mesa. On the rim above, a tank company aimed its weapons toward Hansen. Each of the two-squad armored personnel carriers mounted a light cannon in its forward cupola; the guns were centered on Hansen's chest also, though some of the weapons would have to blast through the bodies of the infantrymen at attention.

Hansen didn't assume *those* gunners would be any slower to shoot than the others.

The waiting officer threw Hansen a sharp salute. "Sir!" she said. "I'm Major Atwater, in charge of your escort. We're very glad to have you with us again, but I have to warn you that we're on heightened alert. It's been raised to Threat Level 3."

Hansen returned the salute crisply but brought his arm down to point at the pair of APCs waiting with their hatches open. "Then let's get the hell out of an obvious target zone like this, Major," he snapped.

Major Atwater spun on her heel. She bawled, "First Pla-

toon, saddle up!'' though the formation had disintegrated with troopers running for their vehicles almost before the first syllable was out of her mouth.

"The other vehicle is commanded by Lieutenant Filerly," Hansen's AI informed him.

The infantry poured aboard the armored personnel carriers with the grace of belted ammo cycling through a machine-gun. The APCs lifted to hover half a meter off the ground.

Atwater leaped aboard behind her troops. The hatch of the other vehicle clanged shut. Hansen reached for the equipment belt beneath his coat and followed the major. Within the APC, the crew chief's finger was on the hatch switch.

Hansen threw toward the rear of the troop compartment the contact grenade he'd snatched from his belt. Wearing the uniform and appearance of Major Atwater, he dropped backward out of the closing hatch.

The grenade belched orange from the hatch and the firing ports. Ammo went off in a crashing secondary explosion.

The armored personnel carrier staggered in the air. Hansen rolled to his feet and ran. The blast-ruptured fuel cells burst in a cataclysmic fireball, hurling bodies and other debris in a wide circle.

"Filerly!" Hansen shouted as he ran toward the APC which had taken aboard the other two squads. "Pick me up! The Inspector General's been assassinated!"

The armored personnel carrier, already several meters in the air, did a touch-and-go grounding whose violence proved the driver was nervous. The platoon leader, Lieutenant Filerly, hung out of the reopened hatch and jerked Hansen aboard.

Hansen grabbed the microphone flexed to the vehicle's radio.

"This is Rainbow Six," he lied, aware of the nervous intensity with which Filerly stared at his CO's scorched fatigues. "Blue, Green, and Yellow elements, land and secure the area. I'm taking Red Two to headquarters immediately to report."

The APC's driver was listening on the general push, because the big vehicle surged forward before Hansen gave him a direct order.

The holographic periscope in the cupola showed the other six vehicles of the escort landing and dropping their side pan-

els to spew troops. Wind scattered black smoke from the puddle of fuel and wreckage.

Hansen rested his fist against the vehicle's computer/communications console. He felt a faint crunching as his ring chopped a micropathway through the console's casing. The unit began to hum and buzz without Hansen's direct input.

"The officer commanding the headquarters guard detachment is Colonel al-Kabir," said the artificial intelligence in Hansen's ring. *"He's off duty and asleep at the moment, but he will shortly be roused because of the raised threat level."*

"Have the security police confine al-Kabir to quarters on orders of—of the High Council," Hansen thought. "You can do that?"

"It is done," the AI responded with what Hansen suspected was an electronic sneer.

"You've got his appearance?" Hansen added.

"Full physical details are in the central files," the AI said. *"Of course."*

"All units!" squawked the console unexpectedly. "Threat Level 2 is in effect. Repeat, Threat Level 2 is in effect."

"Ah, Major Atwater?" Filerly said. "We don't have clearance for even the outer HQ Zone when the threat level's above 5."

"I've received the handshake from the headquarters identification unit," the artificial intelligence said. *"It will recognize us as Colonel al-Kabir."*

"Proceed to the main entrance, driver," Hansen ordered coldly. "The High Council has cleared us through because of the information I'm bringing."

Lieutenant Filerly looked at him doubtfully, but it wasn't the business of a Ruby officer to question a direct order.

They were overflying wind-carved badlands at less than ten meters' altitude. The tops of the richly-layered plateaus loomed above the vehicle. Occasionally Hansen caught sight of antennas or a dug-in missile array flashing by beneath them.

"I hope you're—" the platoon leader started to say, and the APC howled out of the ring of miniature buttes into a vast area of ocher dirt, pocked and studded with armaments.

Guns and missile batteries tracked the vehicle, but none of them fired. Hansen glanced sardonically at the lieutenant,

wondering what the expression looked like on his present female features.

"Be ready as soon as I'm out of the vehicle," Hansen thought.

"I am ready to act as soon as we are out of the vehicle," the artificial intelligence corrected coldly.

A concrete elevator head that looked like a pillbox stood in the midst of four tanks with their bows facing outward.

"In the middle of the tanks?" the car's driver asked.

"Land in front of the two nearest tanks," Hansen ordered.

Each tank's main armament was a 20-cm laser, augmented by a coaxial automatic cannon and blisters holding a variety of other guns. All the weapons that could bear did so as the APC grounded in a spray of dirt and grit. Hansen reached past the crew chief and pressed the door switch.

The hatch cycled open. Hansen stepped out into the shimmer of dust and heat haze in the guise of a fifty-year-old man with a shaven scalp and a colonel's star-in-square lapel insignia.

"Hey!" cried Lieutenant Filerly, reaching for his holstered pistol as he watched the transformed figure stride toward the elevator door opening in obedience to the command of Hansen's ring.

The AI snapped out a second prepared command to the defense array. Both tank lasers ripped the armored personnel carrier at point-blank range, hurling bits away in the blast and sparkle of the automatic weapons joining the chorus of destruction.

Hansen dived into the elevator cage. The back of his neck and ears stung with the awful radiance bathing Lieutenant Filerly and his vehicle. As the elevator door slammed shut, Hansen saw one of the tanks sliding forward to crush anything remaining in the blaze of slag and fire.

"The entrance guards are under Captain Alsen," the artificial intelligence said.

The cage dropped two levels and stopped at the first support area. A company of shock troops were drawn up behind portable barriers across the corridor in both directions. Their guns tracked Hansen as he got out of the entrance elevator and stepped toward the red-painted door of the shaft beside it.

"Captain Alsen," he ordered crisply, "interdict *all* further entry to HQ region."

"But sir . . . ," the black-helmeted guard officer said. "We've been alerted to expect Field Marshal Yazov soonest."

Hansen set his ring against the keyslot controlling the elevator.

"That message was false, Captain," he said. "The enemy has penetrated our communications system. Any vehicle entering the outer HQ Zone must be destroyed at once."

He felt a minuscule *click* through his ring finger. "I'm reporting to the Citadel at once, as ordered."

"Aye aye—" Alsen was saying before the door slammed shut on the remainder of his words.

The interior of the elevator cage was polished steel. As it plunged downward, Hansen saw that he now looked like a moustached wrestler going to fat. Though he still wore fatigues, they had epaulets and his insignia were the wreathed stars of a field marshal.

"Thank you, ring," he thought.

"There is no need to thank me."

"Does this shaft go all the way to the Citadel?"

"We will drop beneath the Citadel level," the artificial intelligence informed its wearer. *"I've keyed us down to Computation Control."*

Hansen didn't realize how fast the cage was dropping till it slowed and the inertia bent his knees as though he'd jumped off the roof of a building. The door opened.

The walls and ceiling of the corridor were covered by mirrors, seamless except for emergency doors every hundred meters. There was a low-frequency vibration in the air.

"Left," directed Hansen's AI.

There were a number of people already striding up or down the corridor. They wore white smocks, the first citizens of Ruby Hansen had seen without uniforms . . . though the smocks were, now that he thought about it, uniforms also.

The technicians glanced at him as he passed and, though no one challenged him, he could feel them continuing to stare at his mirrored figure as he walked onward.

"How far?" he thought.

"Turn right at the cross-corridor," the ring said instead of answering.

Hansen wasn't as frightened as he should have been. It was like a house-clearing operation. He was moving so fast that

he had no time to think about anything except the step he was taking *now*. Move and shoot—and keep it up until there's nothing else moving in the target area. . . .

The mirrors suddenly lost their opacity and opened vistas of Ruby's surface: missile batteries rising, searching for targets; children too small to bear arms marching in lock-step toward shelters; adults all over the planet grabbing weapons and reporting to battle stations.

Hansen turned the corner. Another figure marched in the mirrored walls to his left and right: Colonel al-Kabir. Smock-garbed technicians stopped and stared.

"How *far*?" Hansen's mind demanded of the artificial intelligence.

"To the left at the next corridor," the machine responded grudgingly. *"And a hundred meters."*

The reflections of al-Kabir quivered suddenly into Major Atwater, keeping pace with Hansen. If Hansen turned his head, the reflections turned also. . . .

"Sir?" called a technician. "Sir."

Hansen took the corner with a crisp military pivot. He was sweating. Alongside him strode the Inspector General with Fortin's cold, pale features.

Hansen could see the outline of the door he wanted in the wall ahead, but the mirrored reflections beside him shook. The real Nils Hansen flanked the false Field Marshal Yazov.

"Threat Level 1!" screamed a public address system. "Intruder! Intruder!"

Technicians were reaching under their smocks for weapons, but now Hansen was in his element. His left hand hurled a grenade behind him as he screamed, "Shut the crash door!" hoping his AI could react before the grenade did.

The pistol he drew was standard issue for Ruby. Its recoil was heavier than Hansen was used to, but it pointed like an eleventh finger and its bullets were explosive.

The skull of the first technician exploded in a red flash that blew her blond hair in all directions like chair stuffing. Hansen aimed for the center of mass of the second and third techs, dropping them both before they'd cleared their own pistols.

The emergency door clanged shut behind Hansen, then started to reopen as the PA system screamed, "The intruder

is operating the electronic controls! Close and lock all doors
manu—''

The grenade blast knocked Hansen down, but the part-open
door protected him from the fragments that shattered the walls
and the humans on the other side of it. He scrambled to his
feet, pulling a spool charge from his equipment belt.

The door of the Computation Control room slid halfway
open and stopped. Hansen leaped through, unreeling the
spool charge behind him. His pistol centered on the forehead
of the technician straining against the door's manual control
wheel. Only as the door slammed shut again did Hansen fire.

The ballooning horror of the man's face was echoed by the
strip of spool charge which detonated under the door's pressure. The multi-dogged valve torqued in the explosion, locking itself inextricably closed.

Technicians holding unfamiliar weapons started from their
seats. A line of explosive bullets rang on the back of the
wedged door and the floor where Hansen had been an instant
earlier.

Hansen's form became that of the headless female technician he'd killed in the hallway. His left hand hurled the last
piece of equipment from his belt—a spoofing bomb. It
popped, deploying half a dozen miniature projectors.

Black-suited holographic gunmen capered about CompCon,
some of them upside down. Technicians gaped and fired.
Their bursts destroyed equipment in arcs and implosions, but
the blazing gunfire didn't—couldn't—affect the holograms.

There were five technicians within the sealed room. As
sickly layers of powder and explosive residues quivered at
further muzzle blasts, Hansen moved his body only as much
as he needed to get an angle on the next target.

He killed each technician with a single shot. The last of
them, screaming in disbelief, pointed her machinepistol at
the center of Hansen's chest and continued to squeeze the
trigger even as the headless corpse aimed its gun at her left
eye. The technician had emptied her weapon before the dancing holograms sputtered and vanished.

''Quickly,'' said the voice in Hansen's brain as the last
technician fell, all but the splash on the wall behind her.
''They're starting to drill through the door.''

Hansen was holding his breath in a subconscious attempt

to keep from vomiting the acid that was the only thing in his stomach. The renewed threat focused him. He looked for an undamaged terminal.

"In the left corner!" snapped the artificial intelligence.

Rather than reload, Hansen snatched an unfired pistol from the holster of the man he'd killed at the door controls and ran to the indicated console. He could hear tools cutting. They were very fast, very organized, the folk of Ruby; very skilled in the arts of war.

He put his ring against the terminal's control board.

Ruby wasn't facing a world of pacifists this time.

Almost simultaneously with the *click* from Hansen's finger, the lights in CompCon dimmed and the sound of electronic whispering hushed. He had his gun out, looking for a target.

"I'm shutting down other functions in order to bring up the matching program again," the AI explained. *"It's no longer in the active memory."*

The sound of computers working resumed at a higher, more insistent, note.

Something appeared in the center of the room—not a tank but the memory of a tank like the one which had ground through the crowd on Diamond while Hansen waited with a chair.

This time he had a better weapon—not the pistol, but the artificial intelligence on his finger which was turning Ruby against itself.

Hansen began to laugh. The electronic ghost disappeared, replaced by a scene from the field where Hansen arrived. Nervous troops were forming a perimeter while officers and non-coms checked the bodies scattered when the APC exploded. A lieutenant had turned over the corpse of Major Atwater. The escort commander had been stripped by the blast, but her features were still recognizable.

"Yes . . . ," the AI whispered to Hansen's mind in satisfaction.

The leaf of the heavy door was beginning to glow a soft rose that brightened into golden radiance.

Hansen began to shudder. He thought at first it was reaction, but then he noticed that the wounds of the dead technicians were beginning to steam in the frigid air.

"What's—" he said and stopped, unable to frame the question lucidly.

"We are repeating the cycle," explained the AI. *"We are putting Ruby in phase with Diamond."*

With where Diamond was *now*.

In the center of the room, the ghost image of a Ruby family huddled in its bunker. The youngest of them was a boy of ten. Their fingers were poised on the controls of the weapon systems poised around and on top of their bunker. They had no target, and their faces were growing pale. . . .

A hollow drill pierced the door to CompCon. Its snout quivered and twisted, seeking Hansen.

Hansen fired first. The charge of his explosive bullet was an orange flash against the yellow-white blaze of the door. He fired twice more, smashing the drill point before it could loose its own lethal greeting.

There was a *bang!* from within the panel itself and the glow dulled to red.

"The door has a self-sealing core," said the AI. *"All the defenses here are redundant. It will hold long enough, I estimate."*

The room was colder than the surface of a dead planet. A second drill began to gnaw at the door.

Another ghost, holding out her hand to him. Lea, surrounded by icy darkness; her hair unbound, her voice—surely her voice, not a memory.

Her voice calling, "No, Hansen, not this. Not for. *us*."

But yes, for them. For all the folk whose souls wouldn't let them fight for themselves, who'd rather die than kill—

That was Diamond's decision, and it did Diamond honor. But the folk of Diamond already knew that Hansen didn't belong with them. . . .

"There . . . ," said the artificial intelligence.

The door to CompCon collapsed in blazing fragments. Hansen fired into the opening, but Ruby was fading and merging with Diamond, spiraling down an icy black helix with nothing at all at the bottom. . . .

≡ 32 ≡

HANSEN'S BOOTS CLASHED on the floor of the light-struck hall. A wisp of smoke trailed from the muzzle of his pistol, but he'd emptied the magazine back in another universe.

The figures seated along the sides of the room were no longer veiled in light. They shouted a mixture of triumph and greeting as they rose and tramped across the adamant to Hansen, their forms shrinking with every step.

"Well done!" boomed the stocky, swarthy man as he clapped Hansen on the back. "Couldn't've done better myself."

"You couldn't have done as well, Rao," said a woman with an oriental face. "Brute force would have failed."

"Rao," Hansen repeated. "From North's team?"

"Once I was," Rao admitted. "Once I was."

Rao's powerful hand closed over the pistol Hansen still held.

"But let me take this, boy," Rao added. "Not the rules, here, you know. Makes some of 'em a little nervous, you see."

Hansen recognized other faces from his briefing on Annunciation. The big man was Rolls, who'd led the initial exploration unit, and—

A plump young woman squeezed through the crowd, using her elbows expertly, and slid her hand beneath Hansen's jacket.

"My necklace?" she demanded. "You have my necklace safe?"

"Uh?" said Hansen. "Sure."

He lifted the gossamer strap; the woman snatched it away as soon as it was clear.

"You're Penny, aren't you?" Hansen asked. "From—"

"Yes," she responded, a regal and statuesque redhead from the moment the jewel dropped over her head. "And you and I *must* see a lot of one another."

The figure seated at the end of the hall had not joined the general throng. He was fully in shadow until the sun moved above the crystal ceiling. A prismatically scattered beam fell across the craggy face in a rainbow.

His right eye blinked. His left did not.

"Walker!" Hansen shouted.

The tall figure stood.

"North," he said, laughing. "But sometimes Walker."

The others backed a few steps away when North spoke. Hansen looked at them, then toward their leader again. "Where is this place?" he asked. "Where are we?"

"North found the path through the Matrix," said a decisively plain woman. Eisner, Hansen thought; one of the exploration unit. "We travel all eight planes of the Matrix now; and the Matrix itself is the ninth."

"We're gods," said Rolls. "You can think of us that way, Hansen."

There was more in his tone than satisfaction, but Hansen didn't have enough information to guess what the other emotions were.

But the real question—

"What's going to happen to me, then?" Hansen asked.

North began to laugh. Others of the self-proclaimed gods smiled or blinked in surprise.

"You don't understand, do you?" said Fortin with the air of detached amusement that was the attitude Hansen knew to expect of the android.

"Then tell me," Hansen said. He didn't need a gun in his hand to make the words a threat.

Fortin's face chilled. "It's very simple," he said. "Only one of *us* could enter Ruby from the—inside of the Matrix. So we had to make you one of us before we sent you in."

"Welcome to godhead, Kommissar," North said.

His terrible, thunderous laughter echoed through the hall.

≡ AUTHOR'S NOTE ≡

THE POEMS OF the Poetic Edda (sometimes called the Elder Edda) cover various aspects of Norse myth, mythic history, and folklore. They aren't in any sense a structured belief system, though their odds and ends comprise almost everything known about ancient Norse beliefs. They were written over a period of centuries and across the sweep of the Norse world (including Greenland). Though the subjects are pagan, most of the verses were put in their final form by Christians.

The disparate pieces were then hammered to fit by an anonymous Icelandic redactor who was not only Christian but also remarkably limited both as an editor and as a poet. In addition, the redactor was missing pieces of some of his poems, and there is also a large gap in the sole text of his compilation.

Put in short terms, the Poetic Edda is a confusing hodgepodge which hadn't particularly interested me when I read it twenty years ago. Anyway, my training was in classical languages and history, not those of the Norse/Germanic world.

Then in 1986 I took my family to Iceland for a three-week vacation. While I was there, I picked up a copy of Hollander's excellent translation of the Poetic Edda and read the verses among the geography in which they had been compiled and (in part) written. I found them stunningly evocative.

Iceland's contrasts would probably have had a considerable effect on me anyway. For example, one day I stood on the largest glacier in Europe; the next day I was on an active volcano. Similar stark dichotomies pervade all the physical features of the country.

Iceland was the right place—the right places—to appreciate the Edda.

I returned with the certainty that I was going to use the

Edda as the basis for my own fiction, though I was damned if I knew just *how* I was going to do that. I read some secondary materials (particularly Dumezil and H. R. Ellis Davidson) regarding the structure and themes of the Norse myths, but that course wasn't productive; not because the authors were wrong, but because their truth wasn't my truth.

So I did what I'd been taught to do by the best teacher I've ever had, Professor Jonathan Goldstein, when I was an undergraduate at Iowa: I went back to the primary sources. I paraphrased the complete Poetic Edda, and took notes on the Prose Edda (or Snorri Edda, written by Snorri Sturluson, Iceland's greatest literary figure, in the thirteenth century) and the Volsung Saga (which covers the material in the missing portion of the Poetic Edda).

Finally, I went over the resulting 15,000 words of notes and chose elements which I thought would work in a science fiction novel. Initially I tried to include too much for a single volume, but I kept whittling away at the material until the length seemed satisfactory.

The myths which became major facets of *Northworld* are:
a) the Death and Avenging of Baldr;
b) the Peace of Frothi;
c) the Theft of the Mead of Skaldship; and
d) the relations of Gefjon and Heimdall referred to in the *Lokasenna*.

The above themes are not part of a single episode or cycle within the Eddas. For the sake of my classically-trained soul, I've woven them together in a logical progression; but that progression doesn't exist in the original.

In the present context, I'm a storyteller, not a scholar writing an exegesis on Norse myth; but I *have* tried to reflect the worldview I briefly shared while staring across the smoking basalt wastes of Iceland.

The world of the Eddas was harsh and unforgiving; but it wasn't without nobility. I hope both aspects come through in *Northworld* and the later novels I've planned for the setting.

Dave Drake
Chapel Hill, N.C.

HANSEN EXPECTED A rough palisade around a squalid village, and a sanitation problem worse than that of Peace Rock.

Instead, the high black wall which loomed from the mud and mist was seamless. It had the smooth glint of plastic or surface-sealed concrete. Beyond the wall was a geodesic dome, also black and bulging nearly a hundred meters into the air. The low towers at intervals along the outer wall were too small for living guards—

But just about right for the sensors and weapons of an automatic defense array.

Hansen stopped.

"Go up to the gate and claim admittance as a lone traveler," Walker ordered. "Strombrand should feed and house you for three days."

"Right," said Hansen, keeping his arms at his sides and his hands open toward the sensors. Walker didn't want him dead; that was one of the few things that Hansen *did* know with confidence.

Of course, that didn't mean that his crystal master couldn't misjudge the odds. . . .

"I claim shelter as a traveler!" Hansen shouted to the blank patch of wall that he'd identified as a gate without asking Walker. Though there was no difference in the sheer plastic surface, the mud had been trampled into a trough leading to this point.

The mini-towers to either side buzzed internally.

"Strombrand has the information you want, then?" Hansen asked as they waited.

"Strelbrand controls the data bank," Walker replied. "They are batch brothers, Strelbrand and Strombrand, dextro-